THE KITCHEN WITCH

WITCHES OF PALMETTO POINT BOOK 11

WENDY WANG

CHAPTER 1

J en Holloway walked the perimeter of her father's property looking for broken protection jars. Her sister Lisa, walking a few feet ahead of her pointed to one of the small orange flags Jen used to locate the buried jars.

"I've got another one here." Lisa took the shovel in her hands and gently circled the flag, as if determining the best way to approach the buried treasure. The tip of the shovel pushed through the loamy soil with ease and she carefully scooped away the five inches of dirt to reveal the grimy, rusty, metal top of the Mason jar. She kneeled and gently scraped away enough dirt so she could lift the ward from the hole.

Jen hurried her pace as much as she could within the brush growing thick between the trees of the woods behind her father's house. Jen approached the hole with a little trepidation.

Lisa lifted the top of the pint jar with her gloved hand. An irritated scowl twisted her lips. "Sorry Jen, but this one's broken too."

Jen kneeled next to her sister and peered into the hole at the various protection items used to ward off danger and keep her and her young daughter Ruby safe.

"I don't understand," Jen said, dismayed at the muck and broken glass, all that remained of her careful efforts to set boundaries with the jars, lines anyone intending harm couldn't cross.

"This is the second month in a row I've lost jars like this. It's almost like they all exploded."

"How many does this make?" Lisa asked.

"Thirteen." Jen rose to her feet and scrubbed her nails through her short hair. "That's not even counting the broken sigils on the house." She folded her arms and let out a heavy sigh.

Lisa put the remnants of the jar back into the ground and covered it, then retrieved the flag. She tossed it into a canvas bag Jen had carried with her to collect the jars, so she could refresh the contents and reinforce the protections in place. Dirt loosened from her gloves and scattered across her feet when she brushed her hands together.

"It's almost like somebody came and dug them up and broke them purposefully and then covered them back up.

Is there any chance that somebody knows what these flags mean?"

Jen shook her head thoughtfully. "I don't think so. I bought them online from a pet store. They're for marking underground electric dog fences. Why would somebody think they were anything different?"

"You're right, I just had to ask, that's all." Lisa put her hands on her hips and glanced around the woods. Birdsong filled the surrounding trees and a sultry summer breeze rustled through the canopy. "What do you want to do next?" She brushed a gnat from her face and left a slash of grime on her cheek.

"Well, since screaming at the sky won't help, I suppose I'll just have to make new jars and repair the sigils where I can. I just wish we could figure out what's going on."

"Maybe we should talk to Ben. See if he has any suggestions for something less breakable." Lisa toed the freshly dug earth at her feet.

"If I talk to Ben, I'll have to tell him why I have so many layers of protection on this property, beyond what any normal witch would have," Jen said.

"And that's a bad thing... why?"

"He'll want to get the Defenders of Light involved. And then I'll have to come clean to him about Mark."

"Don't you think you should come clean about Mark, anyway?"

"Says the girl who didn't tell her boyfriend about her two dead fiancés." Jen rolled her eyes.

"Ouch. Those claws are sharp, girl."

"I'm sorry," Jen said. "I know I should tell Ben. It's just"

"You're scared. I know. I've been there." Lisa took off her glove, touched Jen's shoulder and gave it a gentle squeeze. "But if there's anything I've learned in the last couple of months, it's that sometimes things seem bigger in your head than they really are, and secrets in a relationship are like termites—they eat away at it."

"I know this is ridiculous, but what if he doesn't like me anymore?" Jen tried for confidence in her voice, but her vulnerability came through despite her efforts to put up a front for her sister.

"Ben is in love with you, Jen. And trust me, he would die for you."

"Yes, but would he forgive me?" she said, searching the surrounding woods as if they held an answer, but really avoiding Lisa's penetrating gaze.

"There's only one way to know for sure," Lisa said.

Jen looked around the clearing before meeting Lisa head on. "I'll think about it." Lisa was usually her rock, but this subject touched her most sensitive nerves, too delicate for any kind of criticism. Of which Lisa often had a few well-chosen barbs handy.

"In the meantime, we should replace all these jars and repair the sigils on the house."

"I'll do some research to see if there's another layer of protection spells I can add. Something unbreakable."

That sounded good.

"Sure. But let's be careful with unbreakable spells. They can backfire," Lisa said.

"I know. That's why I don't use them lightly."

"How many more of these do we need to check?"

Jen sighed. "Two more. It's a good thing I bought jars recently."

"Yes, it is." Lisa nodded before she started toward the next orange flag.

CHAPTER 2

"Mr. Stonehill, you have a visitor." Brenda Pascal's nasal voice resonated through the intercom on his phone, invading Mark Stonehill's quiet corner office. He scowled and looked away from the spreadsheet on his computer. Why did she always interrupt him like this when she knew he was up to his ears in work? He pressed a button on the phone and snapped, "How many times have we talked about this, Brenda? Unless it's life or death—"

"I'm sorry, sir," she said. "I'll let Mr. Bridges know you don't have time for him now."

"Wait. Who did you say?"

"Mr. Bridges?" The intercom crackled in his ear, and her voice dropped to a harsh whisper. "He said you knew what this was about, and I told him you're booked this afternoon, but he insisted." More static filled his ears. Brenda was shuffling papers by the sound of it.

"You can send him in," he said without apologies for his abrupt tone. With a few deft keystrokes, Mark saved and closed the spreadsheet on his computer screen.

"Yes, sir." The intercom went dead, and a few seconds later the door buzzed. Mark came out from behind the desk, preparing to greet Bridges.

His enormous office looked out over one of the best views in the city. From his desk he could see San Francisco Bay and part of the Golden Gate Bridge. Today, though, he wasn't drawn to the sailboats tilting in the wind or the hills of Berkeley and Oakland in the distance.

It was the news he hoped Bridges would have for him. The man had come highly recommended from one of his mother's dearest allies, but if he wasn't able to bring him more information than any of the other private investigators, he'd hired he'd send him packing, too. The door opened and Brenda ushered Paul Bridges into the spacious modern office.

Mark extended his hand. "Bridges, it's good to see you. What's it been? Six months?"

Paul Bridges shook it. "About that," he said without emotion and dropped his hand to his side. He stood about five foot seven and only weighed a hundred and fifty pounds soaking wet. He wore his black hair slicked back with gel and his dark brown eyes darted around the room, taking it all in before he visibly relaxed and let go of the rigidness in his well-muscled upper body.

"I'm assuming, because you're here, that you have some news for me. Let's sit." Mark gestured to the sleek white leather couch that dominated one end of his office.

He'd told the designer he liked modern and the color scheme should be subdued. Black and white with shades of gray. Bright color made his eyes hurt and rattled his nerves. He had selected the white couch from pictures, and the designer had suggested the two black leather and chrome chairs that rounded out the conversation area.

"I do have news." Bridges took a seat on one end of the couch and Mark settled on the other end, his body tense. "I found them."

Mark sucked in a breath. "That's fantastic. Where is she? Did you get pictures?"

"Yep." Bridges reached into the inner pocket of his jacket and pulled out a slim kraft envelope. He tossed it onto the couch between them. Mark stared at it for nearly a full minute before he reached for it. His stomach fluttered. It had been nearly nine years since he'd seen her. Part of him wanted to savor this moment. Finally, he took the envelope and pulled a dozen 4 x 6 photos from inside. Most were taken on the street outside a restaurant, but there were two more intimate photos taken from inside her house. The first captured her and her daughter snuggled on the couch, a book open on Jen's lap.

Mark stared at the child's face, trying to see something of himself in her. "How did you get this?"

"I won't lie. It took quite a bit of magic. She is very thorough with the protections around her house. Almost like she's trying to stay hidden. But I finally broke through and planted two cameras inside. This is a still from a video feed," Bridges said, a smug look on his face.

The next picture made Mark's stomach roil. Even after all these years her energy drew him in, her smile, her fairy-like beauty. He hadn't expected to feel something for her, other than curiosity and it made him shift uncomfortably. The photo was just as up close and personal as the first one—Jen sitting on the lap of a man with sandy brown hair and a round, babyish face. She had her arm draped casually around his shoulders and his hand rested on her lap with a familiarity he found annoying.

"Who is this?" Mark kept his voice cool, despite the throbbing in his ears.

"That is Ben Sutton. He's the deputy director of the Witches Investigation Unit at Defenders of Light."

"DOL? Really?" Mark said. Blood rushed to his neck and face, heating his skin. "I wonder if he knows about her past?" What he really meant was I wonder if he knows about me. For now, he kept his thoughts to himself.

"That I couldn't say, sir," Bridges said. "How would you like to proceed? I'm sure we could make it look like an accident, although... it appears her sister is dating a local deputy."

"I don't want you to kill her," Mark said offhandedly as though he were listing instructions for caring for the family dog. He collected all the photos, stacked them together and slid them back into the envelope.

"Yes, sir," Bridges said.

"But I am going down there, and you can come with me, since you know the lay of the land." Mark rose from the couch and pressed the intercom button on his phone.

"Brenda, I need you to make travel arrangements for Mr. Bridges and myself. He'll give you all the details of where we'll be going. Can you take care of that for me, please?"

"Of course, Mr. Stonehill," Brenda said. "I'll get started right away."

"Wonderful. Thank you, Brenda." Mark turned to Bridges still sitting on the couch. "If you'll excuse me, I have a very busy afternoon. You can give Brenda the details on your way out."

"You're the boss." Bridges sprung to his feet and left the office. Mark walked to the nearly floor-to-ceiling window and gazed out over the city.

"Jen Holloway," he whispered. "I can't wait to see you."

CHAPTER 3

Evan Payne stretched out on his bed, hanging his legs over the side. With one hand, he tossed a baseball into the air, focused his energy like he'd been practicing with his aunt Evangeline, and whispered the incantation, "Slow ball, float then fall." He held his breath. The baseball stopped midair and hung there. His heart fluttered in his chest and the grin spread across his face. It worked.

Cora, his father's housekeeper, rummaged through his dresser picking out clothes.

"I have to remember to ask Mr. Carver what the weather will be like in the mountains this weekend."

Her question broke his concentration, and the magic ended. The baseball fell hard, landing on his face. For a second, stars filled his vision. Sharp pain raced across his cheekbones, and he groaned. Cora kept her back to him.

Tears squeezed from the corners of his eyes, and he sat up on the edge of the bed. Gently, he probed the place where the ball had struck him. It didn't feel crunchy like he thought a broken nose might feel. The baseball rolled off the bed and across the floor, stopped only by the edge of his bedroom door.

"I'm sorry, Cora, what did you say?" Evan said.

She pivoted with a stack of t-shirts in one hand. "I said, I wonder what the weather will be like this weekend. I need to figure out what clothes to pack for you."

"Right. Let me check." He took his phone from the nightstand and quickly found the weather app. After a brief search for the location–Asher Falls–he found what he needed. "It'll be in the high eighties during the day and low seventies at night."

"You sure?" She raised an eyebrow.

"Yes, ma'am." Cora had taken care of him for a long-time, and he knew better than to sass her. He handed her the phone.

Cora took the phone in hand and squinted. Her short silver hair glinted in the overhead light, and the wrinkles around her eyes deepened. After a moment, she handed the phone back to him.

"This is too small for me. I'll just have to take your word for it."

"Yes ma'am," he said.

A soft knock on his door drew his attention and his mother poked her head inside the room.

"Knock, knock." His mother poked her head inside his room. She wore her long blonde hair in a braid over one shoulder. Her blue-and-white striped top had fluttery sleeves and stretched past her hips over a pair of khaki Bermuda shorts.

"Hey, Mom," Evan said. "What are you doing here?"

"Well, if I know your dad, y'all will be on the road before the crack of dawn tomorrow morning, so I wanted to stop by and give you a big hug and tell you to have a wonderful time on your trip."

"Okay," Evan hopped to his feet and wrapped his arms around his mother. She held him close, and it surprised him a little when he let go first, and she kept holding on.

"Mom." He squirmed in her arms. Wasn't he getting too old for this stuff?

"Sorry, honey. You used to love to be cuddled." She chuckled and squeezed him tighter before dropping her arms. Her gaze shifted to his face. "What happened to your nose?"

His hand flew to the place the ball had struck him. "Nothing." The sentimental look on her face made him squirm. "Mom. What?"

"Nothing, honey." She swiped a thumb across his cheek. "You're just growing up too fast for me, that's all. You and your dad will be hiking the big falls this year. You feel ready for that?"

"Oh, yeah." He nodded. "I'm totally ready."

"Good." She dug into the bag hanging across her body and pulled out two boxes. "I brought these for you."

The long thin box looked like every jewelry gift box he'd ever seen. The other box intrigued him more. The worn corners and yellowing paper on the outside of the perfect square made him want to run his fingers over it to see if he could surmise the contents with his newfound abilities. He took the square box from her hands first and felt the little thrill go through him. It surprised him when the box seemed to vibrate against his palm. He wrapped his fingers around it and tried to figure out what was inside, but his mother's expectant face made it difficult to concentrate. He focused on opening it instead. The top took some coaxing and when he finally got it off, he gaped at the contents.

"What is this?" He dug out the round watch-like thing. The dingy, well-used brass felt cold against his palm, and he detected a slight vibration, as if asking to be held.

"That is your great-grandfather's compass. Your dad loaned it to me a couple years ago when I went on that trip with Jen, Lisa, and Daphne. You remember?"

Evan shrugged. "Yeah, I guess."

"It helped me out on that trip, and I've been meaning to give it back to your dad for a while, so I thought I would give it to you instead. Then when you're done with it, you can give it back to him."

"Do you think he'll give it to me for good?"

"Probably. You just need to ask. And be responsible for it. It's very old and precious to him."

"Cool. Is the other box for me too?"

"Of course." She handed it to him. The top on this box slid off with no resistance, and inside on a piece of cotton batting he found a chrome-plated multi-tool. He grabbed the tool and threw the box on the bed behind him.

"Wow. This is very cool." He explored the different tools, sliding them out one by one. A screwdriver, bottle opener, even a tiny pair of scissors. "I will definitely use this one."

"Well, it's yours. And if your dad asks where you got it from, let him know."

Maybe it was something in her voice or her face. Or maybe it was just some feeling rolling off her onto him. But he sensed his mother wasn't overly fond of the tool. Was it because his dad gave it to her? Or because she just didn't need a knife to carry around? A pocketknife came in handy and he carried one with him almost everywhere, except school because knives and weapons weren't allowed.

"And promise you'll be careful with it. Okay? Several of those blades are very sharp."

"Yes ma'am. I can handle it."

A smile spread across his mother's face. "I know you can." His mother shifted her attention to the woman standing at the dresser with a couple pieces of folded clothing in her hands.

"Hi Cora. You're so quiet, I almost didn't notice you there."

"Hi, Mrs. Carver, I mean—Miss Payne." Cora smiled. "You're looking well."

"Thank you, I was just about to say the same about you."

Cora hugged the t-shirts to her chest.

"I see you're packing for Evan," his mother said.

"Yes ma'am. You know how that goes."

"I do." His mother turned to Evan and cocked her head. "You know, if you're old enough to handle that knife you should be old enough to pack for yourself."

"Right," Evan said dubiously.

"Well, since you're packing, Cora, you may as well add some rain gear in there."

"Mom, the weather's not calling for rain."

"Maybe not, but it never hurts to prepare. Right, Cora?" She looked him in the eye and for a second, he could hear her thoughts whispering at the edges of his mind. *It's going to rain.*

"Yes, ma'am," Cora eyed the shiny tool in Evan's hand. "That's an interesting gift for a thirteen-year-old."

Evan sensed his mother bristle at the comment. "It's a great gift. I have a pocketknife that my grandma gave me, so this tool isn't really that different from mine. This one just has more stuff on it, that's all. Could come in handy in the woods."

He didn't know why he felt the need to defend his

mother. But sometimes that's all he did, especially whenever his dad or his dad's family was around. He couldn't believe he had to do this with Cora.

"I trust Evan. He's usually careful with sharp things. He's been working with his great aunt on different" Her voice trailed off.

"Craft projects. My aunt likes to do crafts, and I sometimes help her out," Evan interjected. "She's the one who taught me how to sharpen my pocketknife."

Evan exchanged glances with his mother. She gave him a grateful smile.

"Yes, she did. And you have done a great job handling it and taking care of it. Which is why I'm giving you this tool."

"Of course." Cora's lips curled with disapproval for a split second. "It's really none of my business, I guess."

"Why don't you walk me out, Evan?" his mother said.

"Sure thing," Evan said. He tucked the multi-tool into his front pocket and put the compass down on his nightstand.

Then he followed his mother out to her car.

"You know, I'm really proud of you." His mother opened the driver's door to her Honda.

"For what?" Evan asked.

"For growing into a smart, thoughtful young man."

"I don't know how thoughtful I am." His cheeks filled with heat.

"You're more thoughtful than some thirty-year-olds I

know." She cupped his face and kissed him on the forehead. "You be good. Make sure you listen to your dad. Y'all will be in some backcountry. It'll be important to stick together, okay? And keep your rain gear handy."

"Yes, ma'am. I will," he said.

"I love you, kid." She grinned and climbed into her car. The window rolled down with a mechanical hum.

"Love you too, Mom," he said.

She put the car in reverse, stuck her arm out the window and gave him a brief wave before she backed out and drove away.

CHAPTER 4

Bells tinkled through the restaurant, signaling a new patron had just walked through the door. Jen Holloway looked up from the clipboard in her hands to see if Dottie, the server on the floor, had seen the customer come in. It took a minute to understand what she was looking at. Once it registered that the tall lanky man with mahogany hair and jade green eyes was not an apparition, her clipboard clattered to the floor. Her breath caught in her throat and the urge to run nearly overwhelmed her. This could not be happening.

Mark Stonehill sauntered up to the counter and took a seat in front of her.

"Hi Jen. It's been a while."

Mark laced his fingers together. A cocky grin played at the corners of his lips. That grin. It had drawn her in nine years ago. It had elicited giggles and brought a blush to her cheeks. The casualness he used when he addressed her made her skin prickle. How could he act like no time had passed?

Jen scooped up her clipboard and hugged it to her chest. Her mouth opened, ready to spew, *"Get out!"* but she barely managed a strangled, "Hello." She swallowed hard and cleared her throat. "This is a surprise."

It was the understatement of the century. She thought she had protected herself from this very thing. And more importantly, protected her daughter from him. Her heart beat so hard in her chest she thought for sure she would pass out. When the floor didn't rise to meet her, she leaned against the counter behind her hoping to ground her to this place and haven of community that she'd built with the help of her aunt.

"It looks like you're getting ready for something," he said. "You always dragged out the clipboard any time you needed to make a list. It's good to see some things never change."

"What are you doing here?" She licked her lips, surprised at how dry her mouth felt.

"Any chance I could get some coffee?" He pointed to the stack of clean cups on the counter behind her.

Jen glanced around. No one seemed to notice the biggest threat of her life sitting casually at the lunch counter. Why would they? He looked like any other person, albeit a little too handsome for his own good, and for hers.

"Sure." She laid the clipboard next to the napkin dispenser, grabbed a cup, paired it with a saucer, and filled it to the brim with steaming hot coffee. A little liquid spilled over the side when she placed the cup in front of him. She jumped back, out of arm's reach, as if he might pounce and sink his teeth into her like a lion.

His grin softened. "Any chance I could get some cream?"

"Of course," she muttered and reached into the mini fridge below the coffee maker. Rows of petite china pitchers filled with half-and-half took up the entire top shelf. After she placed one on the counter, she nudged it toward him and kept her distance.

He spun the pitcher around and grabbed it by the handle before he dosed his coffee. The nearly black liquid turned a pale mocha color, and he stirred in three sugars.

"You act like you're afraid of me." He glanced up at her from beneath his thick eyelashes. "When really it should be the other way around."

"I don't think so." She straightened her back. What was she doing? This was her restaurant. Her community. She jutted her chin and narrowed her eyes. "You didn't answer my question. What are you doing here, Mark?"

"My daughter's birthday is next week, right? She turns eight."

"You mean *my* daughter. You told me yourself you didn't want her." A high-pitched screech filled her head as if a cicada with a bullhorn had suddenly lodged itself in her ears.

"I know what I said. And I know now what it's cost me. So, I've changed my mind."

"No." The word came so easily it frightened her a little. She never said no. She was the amiable one. The peacemaker. The nurturer. It was why everyone loved her. No was not in her vocabulary.

"That quick, huh?" He brought the cup to his lips and took a sip. He moaned quietly. "You always made the best coffee. Why is that?"

Jen's entire body thrummed. "You came a long way for nothing."

"I don't think I did. I missed you." He took another sip, closed his eyes, and inhaled deeply. His expression reminded her too much of his sex face and she squirmed. Knowing Mark, that's probably what he wanted. To make her uncomfortable—keep her off kilter.

"I don't believe you," she said.

"I know what my brother told you. I wish you had come to me first instead of disappearing."

His gaze settled on her, and for a second, she felt a familiar tug. Charm oozed from him like honey, and like a bee, she couldn't resist him. But what else would she expect from a sorcerer of his magnitude? Everything and everyone he enticed into his life came from the spells he cast on himself and those around him. For all she knew, he was casting a spell on her now. She broke her gaze and stepped sideways. She loved Ben. She needed to focus.

"Devon didn't tell me anything," she lied. "Your reaction to the news that I was pregnant was the only reason I needed to disappear. Now, when you're done with your coffee, I'd like you to leave."

Mark carefully placed the coffee cup on the saucer. The sound of china clinking skittered across her nerves. "I'm not going anywhere." His gaze slowly moved around the busy café. "Do you think they know why they love your food so much?"

"I'm not kidding, Mark. You need to leave, or I will call the police."

A smug grin spread across his face. "Still afraid of your own power I see."

"I'm not afraid of anything. But you are not welcome here."

Mark reached into his front pocket and pulled out a money clip. He removed the bill on top and threw it on the counter next to the cup. Jen scowled at the hundred-dollar bill.

"Please don't make me get a lawyer so I can see my daughter. You know very well how messy I can make things."

The bell over the door rang again with his departure. Jen's stomach lurched, and she bolted for the bathroom in the back, praying to get there before she lost her breakfast.

CHAPTER 5

E van walked behind his dad, listening to the sounds of the forest surrounding him. Birdsong filled in the spaces between the puffs of his breathing. The incline steepened gradually on the well-worn trail. Despite all the sports and running he did regularly, his thighs burned a little, and it took effort to keep up with his dad. Sweat gathered at the nape of his neck, wetting the collar of his t-shirt.

He'd hiked the lower part of the trail plenty of times, even when his parents were still together, but today, he and his dad kept going once they met the marker where they usually turned back. Finally, he was old enough to do the harder hike, the backcountry camping his father loved so much. A thrill went through him when they started up the trail that morning, but now the only thing going through him was a bit of hunger, and the desire to rest. If he complained too much, his dad wouldn't hesitate to turn around. To go back to the "kiddie" trails.

"There's no shame in a less strenuous hike, Evan," he could almost hear his dad say. "There are grown men who struggle on the trails we're doing this week."

No, he wouldn't be the reason they turned back. His father trusted him enough to do this. Maybe his dad even believed in him.

He'd stood outside the closed door to the kitchen and eavesdropped on his parents talking in the kitchen when his mother had dropped him off Saturday morning.

"I want y'all to have a good time," she'd said. Through the louvered door of the kitchen, she'd just been a shadow leaning against the island. "But you might have a better time if you're mindful of your words. Sometimes, I swear you don't understand how much you affect him."

"Why? Because he's so sensitive?" his father had mocked.

"Because you know exactly how your father's words affected you. I know you still want to hang the moon for him. But you've got to change your approach. He's not a little kid anymore. Show him you believe in him."

"I really don't need your parenting advice, Charlie."

Evan's chest tightened, and he took a shallow breath, then waited for the argument to erupt.

"Scott, you're the one that wants a deeper relationship with him. You're the one that's going to have to do the work to get it. I refuse to argue with you. I just hope you'll think about it."

"Fine. I'll think about it. Are you traveling this week for work?"

"I don't know at this point. Probably not, why?"

"We probably won't have much cell reception, but just in case he needs to call you for something. Bad dream or whatever."

"I'll keep my phone with me, but just in case, you should prepare to deal with it." Evan knew the tone she used. The no-nonsense, you need to be more responsible tone.

"Great." His father deflected.

Evan let out his breath, thankful there'd been no yelling.

"How're you doing back there?" His father stopped and spun around to face him. "Do we need to take a break? It's getting pretty hot out here."

"I could use some water."

"There's a pretty view at a lookout up ahead. Are you okay until then?"

"Sure." Evan nodded and pushed to catch up to his father before the two of them started up the trail again.

"We're making good time," his dad said. Gravel and dry red dust crunched beneath their feet. "I remember when you were little. By the time we'd gotten to the halfway mark on the lower trail, you were asking to be carried."

Evan shrugged. "I'm not so little anymore."

"No, you're not." His dad glanced at him and met his gaze. He'd grown so much in the last year that the pains in his legs and arms were almost worth the ability to look straight into his dad's eyes. Another inch and he would be taller than his father. Almost the same height as his mother. His mom always said that her father, Evan's grandpa and namesake, was the tall one in the family. Evan Payne had been six-foot-four. Evan hoped he'd grow that tall someday. How cool would it be to look over the heads of everyone?

"Here we go." His dad pointed to an opening in the trees and an outcropping of enormous granite boulders that looked over a steep drop off and the valley below. As much as he loved the ocean and beach, something about seeing the gentle slopes of the Blue Ridge Mountains soothed his soul. He'd told his mom that one day he was going to walk the Appalachian trail its entire length, just so he could say he did it.

His dad dropped the heavy pack he carried to the ground and stretched his back. Most of their equipment, including the small tent and propane stove they would use to cook their dinner, was inside.

Evan dropped his pack too and unzipped the top. Inside, two stainless steel bottles full of water clanked together. He handed the one to his dad and opened the top of the other one. The water rushed over his lips and down his parched throat. Once he'd drunk enough, he returned the top of the bottle and pressed the cool metal to his sweltering face.

When he camped with his dad, they roughed it. There were no cushy beds. They fished for their supper or ate MREs his dad made if they weren't lucky. They drank water from the falls, or a stream cleansed with a little tablet his dad said, "killed all the bad bugs that could make them sick."

Evan put the bottle back in his pack. He untied the kerchief around his neck and mopped his brow and the back of his head with it.

"We should get a picture together." His dad closed his bottle and handed it back to Evan.

"Sure." Evan nodded and dug his phone out of his backpack. His dad struck a pose with a grin on his face and his hands in the air, gesturing to the beauty behind him.

"Good one, Dad." Evan took several photos in quick succession. It made him feel so much lighter when his dad relaxed and grinned this way. He wished it didn't take a hike into nature to get his dad to loosen up.

"We should take a selfie together." His father waved him forward. Evan forced a smile. He hated taking selfies. They never came out right.

"Sure." He handed the phone to his dad, since for now, he still had longer arms than Evan. His dad draped one arm around his shoulders and held the phone up to encompass the majestic landscape behind them. His dad clicked the button twice then tapped on the icon, opening his pictures to look them over.

"That's weird," his dad said. "There seems to be some sort of glare just over your face. Let's do it again."

"Can I see?"

His father handed the phone to him. Evan scowled. Just as he suspected. A strange vaporous orb hovered over his face in the pictures.

"What's wrong?" his dad asked. "You look like I just shot your dog."

"I don't have a dog."

"I know son, it's just an expression. It means you look upset. What's going on?"

"Nothing. It's just this always happens whenever I take selfies." He zoomed in on the photo to get a better look at the light. Some shadows showed up looking almost like a face. "Do you think people have died on this trail?"

"Jesus, Evan, that's a very morbid thing to ask." Then his dad muttered, "Sounds like something your mother might say."

"Do you?"

"I don't know. I guess it's possible. Why?"

"It's just a question, I guess." Evan tucked his phone back into his backpack.

"You don't want to try it again? Let's try with my phone." His father had pulled his phone from his back pocket before Evan could argue.

"Fine, but it's just going to come out the same."

"You don't know that. Come on, let's take another picture." His dad put his arm around him again and took several pictures this time. Evan peered over his dad's shoulder, watching him thumb through all the photos. Only one came out with no light over his face. "I'm not sure what's going on with this."

"Looks like whoever it was got bored and moved on," Evan muttered.

His father glared at him. "What?"

"What?" Evan answered.

"Are you saying you think this is a dead person?" His father looked at him with the same incredulous expression he often used with Evan's mother.

"Just forget it, Dad. You got a good shot." Evan donned his pack and fastened it to his back. "We should get going if we're going to set up the campsite by this afternoon."

His dad stared at him a moment, with his lips in a tight pucker. Finally, he cleared his throat. "Evan, I'm just trying to understand. That's all."

"It's no big deal. I get orbs and lights like that anytime I try to take selfies. Mom told me once it's probably a spirit."

"Do *you* think it's a spirit?" His dad's gaze darted around the surrounding forest. "Do you see any spirits here?"

Evan turned in a circle, giving each viewpoint a good long look. Sometimes he saw spirits the same way his mom did. Sometimes he just felt them. Sometimes he heard them. And sometimes he dreamed about them. He shook his head. "Not right now."

"Maybe we should call your mother. This is really more her area of expertise." His dad peered down at the phone in his hands. He cursed under his breath. "No signal."

"I thought that was the point. Coming all the way out here. No screens except to take pictures."

"It is. We're here to connect with nature and each other." Scott shoved his phone into the side pocket of his khaki cargo shorts. "Listen, if you see a spirit, I want you to tell me, all right?"

"Really?" Evan studied his father's wary tan face. "You sure about that?"

His father's eyes wrinkled at the corners, and the lines of his forehead grew deep.

"It's okay if you don't want to," Evan said. "I know it's kinda creepy."

"No, it's not that. I just don't know how I would help you."

"Just knowing you're there and that you want to help is enough."

"I'm always here, son." His dad reached for his shoulder and gave it a gentle squeeze.

"That's pretty much all it takes. You ready to get back on the trail?"

His dad nodded. "Sure," he said and lifted his heavy pack with ease.

CHAPTER 6

J en sat at the back corner booth resting her head
in her hands.

"Drink this." Evangeline put a fizzing glass of
ginger ale in front of her and slid into the booth
across from her. Jen could feel her aunt's wise stare fix
on her.

"You know, if you're not feeling well, you could go
home. I can handle things here."

"It'll pass," Jen said. "I just need a minute."

"Honey, what happened?" Evangeline asked.

Jen clenched her teeth together. What was there to
say? *The father of my child showed up. The man I told you
wanted nothing to do with his daughter is suddenly issuing
threats so he can see her. Oh, and by the way, he's from the
oldest sorcerer family on the West Coast. In terms of magic, he*

was out of my league then, and he's certainly out of my league now.

"Nothing. I just got dizzy, that's all." She couldn't keep the secret forever, but she would keep it for now. At least until she figured out exactly what to do.

"Are you... pregnant?" Evangeline lowered her voice. Jen looked up and met her aunt's gaze. "No, of course not. It's nothing like that."

"Well, it's something. Maybe you should go to a doctor. You look awfully pale."

"I'm fine. Really," Jen reassured her. "You know, if you're okay with taking over this afternoon, I think I will go home."

"Of course."

"Thank you." Jen took a sip of the ginger ale. The last time she'd had ginger ale she'd been twelve and home with stomach flu. As soon as she took a sip, whatever spell her aunt had cast spread through her, working its magic. By the time she finished the glass, the flutter in her stomach, the feeling she might vomit again, had disappeared.

"There." Evangeline smiled. "You have some color back in your cheeks."

"Thank you," Jen said.

"What kind of healer would I be if I couldn't cure an upset stomach?"

Jen rose from the table, and Evangeline followed. "Whatever it is, honey, you don't have to carry it alone."

"I know." Jen smiled at her aunt. "I'll get my bag and head home now."

"Good. Get some rest."

"I will," Jen said.

But first she had one stop to make.

CHAPTER 7

"Hey, come on in." Lisa waved Jen into her office.
"Take a seat. You look—" Lisa paused and
looked her sister up and down. "Why are you
all shadowy and gray?"

Jen flopped down in the modern leather chair and
examined her arms. "What do you mean?"

"Not your skin, silly. Your energy."

"Oh. I didn't know I was."

"What happened?"

Jen glanced over her shoulder at the open door
leading to Lisa's office. "Can anyone hear us?"

"Just a sec." Lisa rose from her chair to close the door.
"Bustle and business stay outside this door. No one can
disturb us till I give the word. So mote it be."

Lisa positioned the second chair in front of her desk to
face Jen and sat down. "Now, tell me what happened."

Jen opened her mouth to speak, and the words gushed out like a dam had burst. Her sister's face changed from sympathetic to horrified and finally settled on pissed off. Lisa hopped up from her chair and paced back and forth.

"Who the hell does he think he is? Coming here threatening you like that. He has no right to her. His name isn't even on the birth certificate."

"I know, but could he push it? Legally, I mean?"

Lisa stopped in her tracks and gritted her teeth. "He could. It would require you agreeing to a paternity test. He would have to present a compelling reason to get a judge to sign off on one though. But we can fight it. Tooth and nail if that's what it takes—and maybe some magic thrown in."

Jens stomach gurgled again, and she could taste bile rising in the back of her throat. "There's something else I have to tell you."

"Oh, my goddess, you've gone gray around the gills. What's going on?" Lisa kneeled next to her sister and took her hand. A grimace crossed her face. "Your hands are like ice."

"Sit down, please." Jen gestured to the chair across from her and Lisa took a seat. She opened her mouth to speak, but nothing came out.

"Honey, you're scaring me."

Jen took a deep breath. "I never told anybody this. Not even Ben. Mark... Mark and his family" She chewed on her bottom lip, wishing she didn't have to say the words out loud. Her sister's concerned gaze bore into her. "They're sorcerers. In fact, they're the oldest family of sorcerers on the West Coast."

Lisa's eyebrows raised halfway up her forehead and she covered her gaping mouth with her hand. "Oh. My. Goddess."

"That's why Ruby's magic came in so early," Jen said.

"So, when you came home from San Francisco to stay, and you told us Mark was a powerful witch, what you really meant was sorcerer?"

"Yes. I know. I'm sorry. I didn't want y'all to be disappointed in me. I never saw it coming. By the time I realized what he was, what they all were, I was in love with him."

"I'm surprised he didn't want the baby. Having a half sorceress child out there with all that power must have made him wonder about her," Lisa mused.

"Well, he wants her now. I'm terrified that all he has to do is wave his hand to make that happen."

"I don't believe so."

"What do you mean?" Jen said. She could almost see the gears of her sister's mind whirring and it didn't surprise her when Lisa countered her question, with a question.

"Do you remember the first time you found broken protection jars around Daddy's property?"

"I always find a broken jar or two. That's why I check

41

on them regularly. But I guess it's been about two months since I started finding three or more."

"When were the sigil's broken?" Lisa said.

"I noticed it this month. That's why I wanted to make sure we repaired them all the other day."

"Mark's rich, right? I remember you telling me that."

"Yeah, his entire family is. Why?"

"He must have had an investigator looking for you. My question is, why did it take eight years for him to come looking?"

"I" Jen stared into her sister's green eyes. Mark's brother Devon had sworn to protect her and to keep her shielded. She remembered that night so clearly, she could still taste the tears she'd shed when she'd overheard Mark talking to his mother about her and the baby, and how he didn't need a kid right now.

When his mother had suggested that keeping Jen and the baby around might be useful, her blood had run cold. She knew then she had to get out of San Francisco and protect her baby no matter what it took. Sorcerers were known for their blood sacrifices, and there was no way she could expose her child to that, much less let the baby become the sacrifice.

The memory came to life with the same feeling of dread. Devon Stonehill had caught her eavesdropping on that conversation. "Whatcha doing, Jen?" he'd said in that creepy voice that made her skin crawl.

He'd slunk out of the shadows of the Stonehill

mansion like a demon looking for trouble, his hazel-green eyes trained on her like a panther. Why did she always feel like a rabbit caught in a trap when he was around? She had swiped at her cheeks and backed away from her listening spot at the door to Mark's study.

"Nothing," she lied. The grin baring his shiny white teeth and the mischievous twinkle in his eyes told her everything she needed to know. He didn't believe her. And he wanted something.

"I'm tired, Devon. So, if you'll excuse me—"

"Is this about the baby?" The confidence on his face made her recoil.

"I don't know what you're talking about." She sniffed and pushed past him.

"I know what they want to do, Jen," he whispered harshly. "I can help you, if you let me."

Jen stopped in the middle of the hall leading to the grand foyer. She turned and faced him. "What do you want, Devon?"

"Come on, it hurts me you think I'm not doing this out of the kindness of my heart."

"Well, in the time I've known you, I've never seen you do a single kind thing, so it's kind of a given. Now, what do you want?"

His gaze shifted from her face to her chest. Jen instinctively crossed her arms. "No." She gave him the sternest expression she could muster. "And I can't believe that even you are slimy enough to want sex with your brother's girlfriend."

He chuckled, and a wolfish grin spread across his face.

"Pretty full of yourself, fairy girl. It's not you I want. It's that amulet you're wearing around your neck."

Jen wrapped her hand around the convex silver pendant with the triskelion on it. When Mark had given it to her after six months of dating, she'd thought it sweet, but the hungry look in Devon's eyes told a different story.

"Why? It's just a protection amulet. I'm sure they're a dime a dozen."

"You don't even know what you have. It's a lot more than just a protection amulet, sweetheart," Devon said. "You give me that pendant of your own free will, and I'll get you out of here and make it nearly impossible for him to find you."

"Nearly impossible?" Jen said.

"Well, he is my older brother, and he is powerful."

Jen's mouth turned dry as ash. "How powerful?"

"Powerful enough you don't want to stick around here. Trust me."

Trust me. She had trusted him, and now eight years later her daughter might have to pay for that trust.

"Jen. Jen? Are you listening to me?" Lisa snapped her fingers in front of Jen's face.

"I'm sorry. I got lost in my thoughts there for a minute. What did you say?"

"I said whoever he hired to find you can't be a regular

private investigator. He must be a sorcerer too. Otherwise, how would he even know to look for protection jars and sigils?"

"Oh, my goddess, you're right." Jen leaned forward and put her head in her hands.

"Has anything at the house been disturbed?"

"I... I don't know." Jen's mouth gaped like a fish thrown on shore, gasping for air. Her mind blanked and pressure squeezed her chest. "What should I do? I don't... I don't know what to do."

"We need to tell Ben," Lisa said.

"No." The crescendo of her voice startled her.

"Why not? He has access to resources we don't and we need to protect you and Ruby."

"What if he doesn't like me anymore because of some stupid decision I made when I was twenty-five?"

"Honey, as I said a few minutes ago, Ben loves you. He won't judge you for this."

"You can't know that for sure."

"Trust me, I know. Every time you walk into a room, Ben's aura changes."

"It does?"

"Absolutely. It becomes a dreamy shade of periwinkle blue. Like your eyes," Lisa said.

"You said before that you thought Mark had an agenda. Why do you think that?"

"Because somebody's broken the protection spells around the house and the property. For all we know, they've been inside the house. And if all Mark wanted is Ruby, he would've just kidnapped her. Or worse, taken her and somehow made us forget about her so we wouldn't even know to go looking."

Jen shook her head. "I would never forget my daughter."

"Ordinarily, I'd agree with you. However, if Mark is as powerful as you say, then he'd have no problem casting that spell and wiping Ruby from our memories."

Bitter bile filled her mouth. This time, she couldn't stop her stomach from lurching. She covered her mouth as Lisa scrambled for the wastebasket underneath her desk and got it to her just in time.

"Stay here," Lisa said. She disappeared into the hall and returned a moment later with a paper cup full of water and a clean dish towel. When Jen had finished being sick, Lisa nudged the water toward her. Jen took a sip, swished it around her mouth and spit it out into the trashcan. Then she dried her lips with the towel.

"Thank you. I'm sorry about the mess."

"Don't worry about it, honey. But you have to admit we are in over our heads here."

"I know. What if we just told Charlie? I mean, she's Defenders of Light. She'd have the same resources, right?"

"Jen, why are you resisting this so much? Did Ben say something?"

"Not exactly. But I know how he feels about sorcerers. He hates them."

"Why?"

"Sorcerers killed his parents. His folks worked for the DOL, and while working a case, they ended up dead. That's why the Defenders of Light took him in and raised him."

"Are you afraid that he'll hurt Mark? Do you still have feelings for him?" Lisa asked.

"No, I don't have feelings for him. But he is incredibly" She tried to find the right word. "Charming."

"Do you mean in a smooth operator kind of way or is he using a charm spell to draw people in?"

"Both. The man gets everything he wants from everybody," Jen said. "If he can't charm you, he won't hesitate to use magic."

"Ben won't fall for that. And neither will you. We should talk to Daphne. Glamours and charms are similar magic. She might know a way to repel it."

"If we tell Daphne, everybody will know. You know she can't keep her mouth shut," Jen protested.

"She's an expert and we need an expert."

"I know." Jen hung her head again. "I wish we didn't. I wish all this would just go away."

"We should call everybody together tonight. Let them know what's happening and figure out how to keep Ruby safe. She's the priority here, right?"

"Absolutely," Jen said. "You're right. It's not about me. It's about her."

"We'll put our heads together and figure this thing out.

In the meantime, before you go home, I want you to wear this." Lisa reached for the clasp of the twenty-two-inch yellow gold chain she always wore and unhooked it. A petite gold talisman made from wrapped wires dangled on the chain.

"Your Brigid's cross?" Jen stared at the symbol of her sister's favorite goddess.

"She'll protect you." Lisa wrapped the chain around Jen's neck and fastened it in place. It hung low on top of her white eyelet blouse.

"Thank you." Jen touched her finger to the pendant and managed a weak smile. But the sick feeling in her gut burrowed in deeper while one question bounced through her head. What if it wouldn't be enough?

CHAPTER 8

Dappled light filtered through the overhead canopy and the gravel trail crunched beneath Evan's boots. He hitched up his backpack for the tenth time since they'd started their trek to Guilford's Peak, Evan leading, his father behind him.

"Evan, if you adjust your straps, you won't have to pull up your pack so much," his father said.

"Yeah, sure," Evan said without adjusting his pack.

"We're going to be on open trail soon," his father reminded him a few minutes later. "Just beyond this ridge. You should put on your hat now. You don't want to get sunburned."

Evan kept walking. "I put on sunscreen earlier," he said over his shoulder.

"It's not enough, son. You need a hat, too."

Evan rolled his eyes and stopped in his tracks.

"Fine," he said, releasing his frustration in a huff. He dropped his pack and fished out the wide-brimmed hat that his father had made him pack at the last minute. Even though it was cool with camo colors and an orange headband, he didn't like how much of his peripheral vision it obscured. Since they'd left their first campsite that morning, he couldn't shake the feeling he was being watched. How was he going to figure out what it was if the stupid hat blinded him? He slapped the hat on his head and shot his father a look. "Happy?"

"Hey," his father said, shooting him a dark look. "Why all the attitude? You liked that hat when I bought it."

"It's too big," Evan said.

"It fits you fine," Scott argued.

"I mean too wide," Evan gestured to the brim of the hat.

"Fine," his father removed his hat and held it out. "Switch with me."

Evan eyed the pale khaki hat with vents on the side and brass snaps for holding up the brim.

"Cool. Thanks." Evan put it on, snapping the brim out of his eyes. If something was spying on them, he wanted to be ready. His father walked on, letting go of the budding tension.

Not long after they emerged from the trees onto a steeper part of the trail, the sun beat down on Evan without mercy. The sweet morning air had given way to the heat, but he could still smell water, teasing them as they got closer to the first waterfall on their list of stops. Somewhere at the bottom of the steep drop off, a stream snaked through the trees, just one of hundreds of springs and streams feeding into a larger river system. Evan took off his hat, drew the bright orange handkerchief from his front pocket and mopped his forehead.

"Evan, are you all right?" His father's voice sounded firm. "Do you need a break? We've been at this for almost an hour now."

"I'm fine. It's just hot," Evan said. The last thing he wanted his father to think was that he couldn't hack it. They had only passed adults so far. He liked that feeling of being grown-up. This wasn't a trail for kids.

"Evan, it's okay to take a break."

"We're not that far from the falls, right?"

"Probably another half hour. Why don't we take a rest over there?" His father pointed to an outcropping of large granite boulders up ahead. "I could use some water."

Evan shrugged. "Fine, but we're not stopping because of me."

His father chuckled. "Noted."

The two of them took a seat on the rocks. The warmth of the stone radiated through Evan's shorts, and he pressed his hand flat against the rough stone. What would happen if the rocks got really hot? Could they burn him? Could they cook an egg? He took the bottle from his bag, took a long swallow of cool, purified water. When he was little, he used to hate the purified water, even though he really couldn't tell any difference. Maybe his father would see it as a sign that his son was really growing up if he didn't complain about such things. Sometimes it was hard to tell what his dad was thinking or feeling—unless he was mad. That emotion came through loud and clear.

"How much longer do you think until we get to Guilford's Peak?" Evan asked. "I promised Mom I'd send her pictures."

"Probably another hour past the falls. Not sure we'll have a signal that far up." His father retrieved his water bottle and took a long swallow.

A shadow moved into Evan's peripheral vision, and he froze. He moved his eyes to get a sense of what it might be, but he kept his head straight. The form of a girl not much older than him came into view. His breath quickened, and a chill raced down his back. Blood trickled down her face from the side of her misshapen head. Something (or someone?) had hit her so hard, the blow had formed an indentation in her skull.

Evan squeezed his eyes shut to block her out. He automatically reached for the string of rough-cut stones on his shorts he'd made with his mother's help. He'd clipped it to a carabiner and attached it to a loop on his waistband to keep it at close reach. His thumb found the black tourmaline first. He traced every groove of the stone before moving to the clear quartz next. Finally, he pinched the small pentacle charm between his thumb and forefinger and whispered, "Mother goddess, protect me from all spirits who wish me harm," three times then ended with, "So mote it be."

"Evan? Are you all right?"

Evan opened his eyes and forced himself to look in the direction he'd seen the spirit. He breathed a little easier. She'd disappeared.

"I'm fine."

"You sure? If this trail is too much, we can always go back and take one of the easier trails."

"I'm fine, Dad. And it's not too much. Pffft. I'm in better shape than you."

"Oh, yeah?" His father's lips fought against a grin. "We'll just see about that, punk."

Evan squared his shoulders and issued a challenge. "I bet we can reach the peak in less than an hour, if you can keep up." Without cracking a smile, Evan tightened his pack's straps higher on his shoulders and clipped the chest strap in place.

"Oh, you're on, kid." His father slung his pack onto his back and pushed past Evan. He called over his shoulder, his tone playful. "See if *you* can keep up."

Evan laughed now, mirroring his dad's lack of tension, and picked up his pace.

Nearly an hour later, Evan approached the huge outcropping of blue granite known as Guilford's Peak. He glanced over his shoulder. The sight of his father catching up spurred him forward. A few other hikers edged close to the boundary of the large flat rock wall to get selfies of the grand vista of the Blue Ridge mountains. A thrill went through him as he drew closer to the peak. His mom would be so impressed with the pictures.

When the hikers finished taking photos, they moved from the peak to the trail again. But as Evan stepped forward to take up the trail, he spotted a sight that knocked the breath out of him. The dead girl. Stunned at seeing her standing in front of him, he lost his balance. His foot connected with a rock on the trail, and he landed hard on his knees. Gravel and gritty, dry dust dug into his palms. Sharp pain traveled from his hands into his forearms.

"Evan!" His father's running foot falls sounded heavy on the dirt trail behind him. Evan couldn't take his eyes off her. Blood splattered in an uneven pattern across the white t-shirt she wore. She looked over her shoulder as if someone were following her. His gaze connected with hers for only a moment, then she looked over her shoulder again. A scream echoed through Evan's head. He sucked in a breath across his teeth. Instinctively, he knew this was some scene playing itself out. By her clothes and hair, it didn't seem like it had happened all that long ago. By the time the screaming stopped, his father was kneeling beside him.

"Evan, are you okay?"

He couldn't look away from the girl or move his lips to answer his father. When she sprinted for the edge of the rock and leaped into the air, plummeting out of sight, Evan found his footing and leaped to his feet again.

"She jumped. Oh, my goddess, she jumped."

He sprang into motion and took off after her.

"Evan, wait!" his father called after him.

Somewhere in the dim recesses of his brain, Evan heard his father running behind him again. His shoes got traction on the smoother surface of the rock, and he rushed to the edge of the boulder.

The weight of his father's hands on his pack slowed him down, and his feet almost went out from under him when his father jerked him backward by his shoulders.

"Let me go!" Evan choked out the words. "She jumped."

His father's arms went around him, holding him tight in a bear hug. "Shh... shh. No one jumped, Evan."

Evan fought against his father for a moment. "Let me go."

"You're okay. Just breathe through it. There's no one there. It was just... just a spirit. Breathe, Evan." His father took in a deep breath. "In two... three... four. Out... two... three... four... five... six."

After several rounds of counting, Evan mimicked his father's breathing and his heart slowed to a normal pace. The tension in his body relaxed some.

"You can let me go now. I'm okay," Evan said.

"You sure?" The wariness in his father's voice stung more than he wanted to admit.

"Yeah."

His father released him but stayed close behind him as if to make sure Evan could stand on his own.

"You didn't see her, did you?" Evan asked. "Or hear her scream?"

"No, son, I didn't." His father rested one hand on his shoulder. "Do you want to call your mother?"

Evan shook his head. "No. I want to make sure she's not real. I need to see."

"Where did you see her?"

Evan pointed to a long flat rock. For the first time, he noticed thin metal guard rails jutting around the edge of the rock.

"There's quite a drop off, and we're not the only people here. If she were real, you wouldn't be the only one that saw her."

His father gestured to the hikers lingering near the peak. Two of them stared in his direction with concern on their faces.

"Can I at least look? I promise I won't do anything stupid."

"Let me get your hands and knees cleaned up first. You're bleeding."

Evan looked down at his bloody palms. Rocks, dirt, and leaves stuck to his skin. He assessed his knees and noticed the long streaks of blood from the gashes on his knees.

"Fine."

Scott dropped his pack at his feet and unzipped the pocket with the first-aid kit. Once he had cleaned Evan's wounds and bandaged them, the two of them approached the long flat rock jutting out over the valley.

Evan's inched as far out on the edge of the boulder as he could. Heights never bothered him much. He and his father had scaled many rock walls together at his father's gym. But this time, looking into the distance of the tree-tops below, dizziness swirled through him and his stomach flip-flopped. A whisper shimmied across his skin, sending a shiver through him despite the afternoon heat. His skin broke into goosebumps.

Help me. Please. Help me.

Tears threatened to fall, but he fought them. His father could be mean when he cried. *Only babies cry.* How many times had his father said that to him? He swayed a little until firm hands on his shoulder stopped him.

"Evan, do you see her?" His father pitched his voice low. Evan shook his head.

"Okay." His father let out a heavy sigh as if it relieved him there was no dead girl at the bottom of the drop off.

"We should find a place to sit and have our wraps."

"Sure." Evan scanned the trees one last time before he followed his father back to the trail. A small picnic area with a few weathered tables and benches. His father claimed one of the two tables and the two of them ate in silence. The tension stretched between like an over-tightened guitar string. His father's stare weighed on him. He couldn't believe he'd almost let himself go over the edge after her. What was he thinking?

Evan finished the last bite of his tuna salad wrap and finally broke their silence. "I'm not crazy."

His father flipped the cap on his water bottle and gave him a measured look. "No one said you were crazy. All I said was that I didn't see her. It doesn't mean that I don't believe you saw her."

Evan took a swig of water and considered his father's words. "Thank you."

"We can climb down and look for her, if you think it would make you feel better to know for sure."

Evan shifted his gaze. "Really? You'd do that for me?"

"Sure, but if she's a... um... ah..."

"Ghost. It's okay, Dad. You can say it out loud."

"Right." His father wiped his mouth with a clean bandana. "If she is... you know, you may want to let her be."

"Maybe she needs my help. She showed herself to me for a reason."

"It's not your job to help errant..." His father looked around at the other hikers as if he were trying to determine how much they could hear.

"Ghosts," Evan completed his father's sentence again.

"And I know it's not my job, but if I can help, I should. You didn't see her face or hear her scream." Evan shuddered at the memory.

"Right," his father muttered. He folded his paper towel and shoved it back into his pack. "We should get those pictures you wanted to take for your mother and hike to the bottom of the ridge. We'll set up camp down there."

"Really?"

"Really."

"Cool." Evan grinned.

CHAPTER 9

J en fluttered around the kitchen, preparing for the impromptu coven meeting. She filled iced tea glasses and plated the chocolate chip cookies she'd baked after dinner. The words of a strength incantation crossed her lips in silent prayer to the mother goddess. No one asked why she needed to see them tonight. No one argued or said they couldn't come.

Charlie entered the house first and after giving Jen a good long look, she threw her arms open and hugged Jen tight. There was no doubt in Jen's mind her cousin had read her emotions and maybe even her thoughts. But that didn't matter as she relaxed into Charlie's embrace.

"Whatever it is, Jen, it's going to be all right. We're going to make it all right."

"Thank you," Jen whispered. "That means a lot."

"Oooh, hugging," Daphne said from the back door. "Can I get one too? It's been one of those days."

Jen laughed and switched to hugging Daphne.

"You baked cookies?" Charlie eyed the large plate on the table.

"Yes, help yourself. There's fresh tea, too." Jen gestured to the glasses filled with ice and dark amber libation on the counter.

Charlie grabbed a paper napkin from the holder and put a large cookie full of chocolate chips on it. She picked off one of the baked pieces of chocolate and popped it into her mouth.

"Is there anything I can help with?" Daphne grabbed a tea glass and took a sip.

"That's sort of a loaded question, isn't it?" Lisa walked into the kitchen and hung her purse on the back of a chair.

Daphne plopped down at the table and reached for a cookie. Lisa leaned over and smacked Daphne's hand. "Can't you wait, please?"

"Hey! Charlie already took a cookie." Daphne scowled and grabbed the top cookie. Lisa cast a glance in Charlie's direction and Charlie popped the last bite of cookie into her mouth and shrugged. Lisa rolled her eyes and reached for a glass of tea. Lisa took a seat next to Daphne and glanced around the table.

"Where's Daddy?" Lisa helped herself to a cookie.

"He and Ruby are in the living room watching a video." Jen sat in the chair at the end of the table and Charlie sat next to her across from Lisa.

"Is my mom coming?" Daphne traced a finger over her sweaty tea glass.

"I'm here." The screen door shut with a snap behind Evangeline. "Is there tea? It's still eighty-five degrees out there. I'm parched."

"I'll get it." Lisa began to rise from her chair.

"No, no. I can help myself." Evangeline patted Lisa's shoulder, gently coaxing her niece back into her chair. "Y'all go ahead and start."

Jen waited until her aunt took a seat across from Daphne.

"Now what's this all about?" Evangeline asked and took a long sip of tea. She put the glass down in front of her and squared up her gaze with her niece's. "You sounded spooked on the phone."

Panic fluttered in Jen's chest like caged birds. She blew out a heavy breath. "Mark Stonehill showed up at the café today."

"Wait. *The* Mark?" Daphne's brows rose on her forehead and a smirk played at her lips. "Do we get to meet him? Ow," Daphne yelped and leaned down to rub her shin. "Why d'you kick me?"

"Because you're being you." Lisa rolled her eyes.

"I don't know." Jen bit her lip.

"Why are you so scared?" Charlie leaned forward with her elbows on the table. The weight of her cousin's gaze made Jen want to run and hide. Why was this so hard?

"He threatened her," Lisa said flatly.

"Threatened you? Did you call Jason?" Charlie asked.

"Not that kind of threat." Jen let out a heavy sigh. "He wants to see Ruby, and I don't want him to. I told him no, and he threatened to take me to court."

"Well, good luck with that, Mr. Stonehill," Charlie scoffed. "He's not even on her birth certificate, right?"

"No, he's not. But he could push for a paternity test." Lisa glanced at her sister. "And there's more to it."

"More? Sounds intriguing." Daphne reached for another cookie, broke it into small pieces on her napkin, and devoured each delicious bite.

Jen's gaze rounded the table before finally landing on Evangeline. The worry lines on her aunt's face deepened, forming hills and valleys, a map of her years and experience.

Evangeline asked, her voice a soothing balm of calm. "Whatever it is, honey, you can tell us. We're here for you."

The first tears slid down Jen's face. "I'm so sorry, Evangeline."

"Sorry for what?"

Jen shook her head. Her mouth drew into a tight little twist. The words trapped behind her lips. She sniffled. Lisa reached for Jen's hand and gave it a gentle squeeze and an encouraging nod. Jen met her sister's gaze, grateful for the unwavering strength in Lisa's eyes. Jen took a deep breath and blew it out.

"I lied. I'm so sorry." Jen's lower lip quivered.

"Lied about what?" Evangeline asked.

"I lied about Mark. Who he is... what he is."

"Who is he?" Daphne perked up, excitement in her blue eyes.

"He's the oldest son of the Stonehills of San Francisco and he is not a witch like I told you he was."

"What is he?" Charlie asked warily.

"He's a sorcerer from a long, long line of sorcerers. I didn't know that when I got involved with him though."

"That's why Ruby's magic came in so" Daphne leaned on her elbows and the words died on her lips.

Evangeline rose from her seat and she pulled Jen into her arms before she could protest. A dam burst inside Jen —a dam she didn't even know she'd built until now. All the fear and guilt and grief gushed out of her, and she leaned into her aunt's body the way she had when she was a little girl. When the world had overwhelmed her after her mother died. Lisa had just plowed through—pragmatic, even as a child. But Jen had felt every emotion big or small, and thankfully Evangeline had been there then, as she was now. Ready with open arms and wisdom.

They all gathered around her, placing their hands on her, shoring her up. Willing to sit in silence if that's what she needed. Willing to go to war for her. When the tears subsided, Jen pulled out of her aunt's embrace.

"Thank you." Jen sniffled and swiped at her wet cheeks.

Daphne grabbed Jen's hand in hers and held it tight. "So, what do you need from us?"

"The only thing I care about is protecting my daughter from him."

"Of course. We'll help." Charlie nodded. "Of course, we will."

"Does Ben know?" Daphne asked.

"No." Jen leaned her head against her aunt's shoulders.

"I know this is hard, but we're going to have to tell him. We'll need him and the DOL behind us," Charlie said.

"I know. I just don't know if he'll want to help. You know how he feels about sorcerers."

"Yeah." Charlie pursed her lips and nodded. "He thinks they're all evil."

"Are they? I mean, I know their power differs from ours, but does it mean they're evil? I mean, if you look at the stereotype of the witch, we're considered evil." Daphne mused. "There are plenty of witches who cast curses and hexes and make questionable potions, but there are more who just would rather connect with a goddess or the universe."

"I didn't think he was evil when I met him, and he used to be so charming. Sharp tongued sometimes, but... sweet too." Jen swiped at an errant tear.

"That could've been a spell," Lisa said.

"Do you think he would try to take Ruby from you, outside of a court of law?" Evangeline asked.

"I don't know. I've gone over it again and again in my head and I just don't know. The only thing that keeps coming back to me is, am I wrong to keep his daughter from him? You know, sometimes she asks me questions about her daddy. What he was like. Why he doesn't come visit her."

A fresh wave of tears swept through her and she waited for them to subside.

Charlie stroked the center of Jen's back. "That's a hard decision, one you don't want a court to make for you. Trust me on that."

Jen blinked hard and remembered Charlie's first custody battle with her ex. Did she really want to put her daughter through that?

"You should really talk to Ben," Lisa said.

"I know, but... what if he hates me for not telling him the whole truth? You've never heard him talk about sorcerers. He *hates* them."

"There's only one way to find out how he'll feel, and honestly, I'd feel better with the weight of the DOL behind you no matter what Mark's real intentions are." Charlie retrieved her phone from her purse and handed it to Jen. "He's number two on my Favorites list."

Jen took the phone and quickly found him in Charlie's phone Favorites. She hovered her thumb over his number but couldn't bring herself to call him. Instead, she opened the contact and clicked the option to text him.

Hi—it's Jen. Can you come to the house? It's important.

Within seconds, he responded. *I'm on my way.*

CHAPTER 10

J en paced the back porch while she waited for the familiar rumble of Ben's truck. The sultry night air wrapped around her body and sweat gathered on the back of her neck. In the yard's darkness, crickets sang, and a strong breeze blew off the water. The rustling of the trees between the house and the tributary that fed into the river added to the evening music.

The others had all gone home, and she'd put a sleepy Ruby to bed and left her father in the living room watching television.

After a few minutes, she took a seat on the porch swing. The chains creaked, and she rocked herself back and forth, letting the motion soothe her raw nerves. The pending fight with Ben played out in her head—along with all the different outcomes. None of them ended well. Oh, what she wouldn't give to have Charlie's gift to see the future. To know for sure that no matter what, Ben loved her and would stand beside her.

Headlights flashed across the yard, and the growl of the FJ40's diesel engine grew louder. Jen left the swing and walked to the edge of the top step. He gave her a wave once he exited his truck. Once he made it up the stairs Jen grabbed hold of him and didn't let go. He chuckled and hugged her close. "I missed you too."

She shivered against him despite the nearly eighty-degree temperature of the night air but said nothing.

"Hey. You okay?" Ben whispered against the top of her head.

Jen hugged him tighter. "I am now."

"What is it?" He peeled Jen from his arms and cupped her chin. Jen pressed her hand against her face and met the concern in his eyes.

"I need to tell you something, and I'm terrified because I think you might hate me."

"Hate you? That's unlikely. I can't think of anything you could do to make me hate you."

"You say that now—" She tried to joke, but it sounded flat.

"Seriously, Jen, you're scaring me."

"I'm sorry." She took his hand in hers and led him over to the swing. "We need to talk."

"Those are never good words," Ben muttered.

He took a seat on the swing, and she sat next to him.

The chains squealed and the joist overhead groaned a little. "Daddy really needs to oil this swing."

"Sure." Ben nodded. His body stiffened with anticipation. She could feel him staring at her, drawing a protective wall around himself. Jen swallowed hard and met his gaze. She shoved her hands beneath her thighs and let her arm brush against his.

Ben let out a nervous laugh, breaking the tension. "This is your show."

"I know." She nodded and let her gaze drift to the dingy gray floor of the porch. "I'm just trying to figure out where to start."

"The beginning's always a good place," Ben joked and nudged his weight against her.

"Right," she said in a breathy whisper. She stared deeply into his eyes with a look that conveyed love and need and fear. "Tell me one thing first."

"Okay." Ben's face registered alarm.

"Do you love me?"

He cracked a puzzled smile. "Of course, I do. You know I do. What's going on?"

"Good." She let out a breath of relief and her body relaxed a little. "I had a surprise visitor today at the café."

"Okay." The line between Ben's brows deepened.

"Ruby's father came to see me. He wants to meet her. To get to know her, and he's threatening legal action if I don't allow him visitation."

Ben planted his feet firmly on the ground. "Can he do that? What does Lisa say?"

"That if I fight him on it, he could petition the court for a paternity test and sue for custody. Lisa wants me to talk to one of her lawyer friends that specializes in child custody cases."

"We won't let that happen." Ben draped his arm around her shoulder. "I'm here for you, okay?"

"I appreciate that." Jen leaned her head against him and breathed him in. "I need to tell you something about him. Something I should've told you a long time ago."

"It's okay, Jen. There are things I've never told you about my exes, too."

Jen let out a stuttering breath, like a release valve letting off steam. He was on her side. Why had she ever doubted that?

"I know, but he wasn't just any ex. We were engaged."

Ben's face hardened. "You were going to marry him?"

"Yeah. I thought I loved him until I found out the truth." Jen studied Ben's face for a moment. She braced herself for the fight. "Mark's a sorcerer."

Ben didn't blink. "I know."

"I know I should've told you. I know how you feel about sorcerers," Jen rattled on before what he'd said registered. "Wait. How did you know?"

"You mentioned his name once, and you were kind of vague about whether he was a witch, so I ran a background check on him."

"You... what?" Jen's voice rose half an octave and her cheeks flooded with heat. "You spied on me?"

Ben sputtered for a moment. "I didn't spy, exactly. I just wanted to know what we were dealing with."

"You didn't think to just... I don't know... ask me?"

"I think you're focusing on the wrong thing here."

"I don't think I am. Here I was afraid you were going to be all self-righteous and angry at me, but honestly, this is something like Mark would do." Jen hopped off the swing and faced him. She folded her arms across her chest.

"Hey. Just wait a minute." Ben held up a hand in defense. "This isn't something I did to you. It's something I did for you, so I knew how to keep you safe. To support you."

"Bull hockey."

"Bull hockey?" Ben mouthed. Shadows from the overhead porch light deepened on his face, stressing his disbelief. "What the...? Are you kidding me? I'm the one who should be mad here."

Jen gritted her teeth. "You should be mad? You're not the one whose privacy has been invaded. You know what? I can't even look at you right now."

"I can't believe this." Ben stood up and towered over her. "Why did you even call me here?"

"I called you because some weird things have happened around here lately, and because I thought I needed you and the DOL to protect me from the big bad sorcerer. But really, it looks like you're the one I need protection from." She hugged her chest tighter.

"What kind of weird things?"

"It doesn't matter."

"Yes, it does, Jen. Now please tell me what kind of weird things."

"My protection jars keep getting broken, and someone broke a few of the sigils on the house."

"Broke them? How?"

"Probably with blood and a reversal incantation, if I were to guess," she snapped.

"Why didn't you tell me this before? I could've had my team come in and investigate. Did you reset the protections?" He took a step closer.

"Of course, I did," Jen scoffed and stepped back. "Do you really think I'd leave my daughter and father unprotected?"

"That's not what I meant."

They stared at each other for a moment in the dim light of the porch. "Do you think Mark did this?"

"I don't know. He was never one to get his hands dirty. He always had assistants and other people around him."

"Did he... did he charm you? Not just in the normal way, but do you remember thinking maybe you were under a spell when you were together? Did he want you to get pregnant with Ruby?"

"What? No. If anything, he didn't want me to get pregnant. After I told him, he became very distant. I thought he was going to suggest I have an abortion."

"But he didn't?"

"No, his mother..." Jen swallowed hard, "intervened. She thought having us around would be useful. Those were her words. Useful."

"Useful," Ben muttered. His jaw tightened. "How did you get away? Sorcerers don't like to lose things they think belong to them."

"His brother got me out in exchange for a pendant Mark had given me. He said if I gave it to him, he'd ensure Mark would never find me."

"And yet here we are."

"Yep, here we are." Jen rocked on her heels.

"Are you checking the protections daily?" Ben walked to the top step of the porch and his gaze swept across the property.

"Twice a day."

"Good." Ben let out a heavy breath, but his body remained stiff. "I'll call Athena in the morning and have her set up a protective detail for you, Ruby, and your dad. We'll make sure that he can't bring harm to any of you."

For the first time Jen wished she could see his aura the way Lisa and Daphne could. Had it changed from the soft periwinkle they'd talked about to something else? Something darker?

"I don't know how to fix this, Jen," he said so quietly she almost didn't hear him.

The back of her throat tingled, and she could practically taste the salt of the tears threatening to pour from her and drown her.

"I don't know either." Her voice cracked.

He nodded his head, and his entire body swayed. "I'll make sure you have a protective detail by the end of the day tomorrow."

Some angry part of her almost spat the words *don't bother*, but she knew better. She needed people looking out for her and her family. As much as she wanted a few spells to protect her, she knew it wouldn't be enough.

"I'm going to walk the property. Reinforce what I can..."

"Fine." Jen let a chill fill her voice, then turned to go into the house.

"You know, for what it's worth, I don't regret checking him out."

"Aren't you lucky? I have more regrets than I know what to do with right now."

Ben grimaced and shook his head before he took the stairs slowly, thoughtfully, one at a time. Jen watched him until he disappeared into the woods to check on her protections, then sat down on the swing again and wept into her hands.

CHAPTER 11

C harlie flipped on the light to the spacious office
she shared with Ben. He had found the space
and rented it so they both could work from
Palmetto Point instead of making the trek to Charlotte
each day. Not having to face a daunting nearly three-hour
commute each morning and evening lifted an enormous
burden off Charlie. And she could get just as much work
done in their little office space using her computer. Ben
made for a good office companion most of the time. She
set her leather tote bag down next to her desk and glanced
at the digital clock on the wall. The red numbers glowed.
8:03 AM. It was unusual for her to beat Ben to the office.
And she couldn't remember him ever being late, not that
three minutes past was late. It made her wonder about his
talk with Jen the night before. Had it gone well? Maybe
they'd spent a late night talking, figuring out what to do

about Mark. She took a seat at her desk and unzipped her tote, then retrieved her laptop. The sparsely furnished office had two desks that faced each other. Ben had gone all out and gotten electric standing desks, so they could sit or stand as they pleased. Ben often stood while he worked —answering emails, taking part in conference calls with the little Bluetooth headset he bought for himself, and making hard decisions that Charlie couldn't imagine handling.

Charlie preferred to sit most of the time, and she didn't like conference calls. She pressed the button on the laptop, and it whirred to life. After a few minutes, she logged into the DOL network, and her partner in most things these days, Athena Whitley, texted her using the company chat.

Morning. Is Ben in yet?

Nope. He probably just stopped for coffee.

Charlie didn't want to raise any suspicions, and it was none of the Athena's business (or hers for that matter) what had really happened between Jen and Ben last night.

This an emergency? Charlie probed.

No. Nothing like that. He just asked me to look something up and I wanted to let him know what I found.

Anything related to our mole case?

Nope. All the leads are dead for now. I guess we'll just have to wait until something breaks.

Until something broke meant another witch would have to die at the hands of the witchfinders. Charlie leaned forward and rubbed her forehead to quell the throb starting behind her eyes. She hated that they couldn't figure this out. Whoever the mole was, he (or she) had covered his (or her) tracks well.

How are you this morning? :D

Even in text, Athena sounded chipper.

Doing okay.

Still having reaper dreams?

Charlie took a slow breath. Last night's dream flashed through her mind. A young man in a prestigious university, unable to handle the pressures from his parents and peers, stepped onto a stool, put a noose around his neck, then kicked the stool out from beneath his feet.

Yes. Pretty much every night.

Ever since she had discovered her fate—that she would become a reaper when her human life ended—dreams about death had plagued her. Every night she would witness death at work. She had no way of knowing who they were or where they were. And she had absolutely no way of stopping it. The weight of this wore on her some days, heavier than other dreams. She longed for dreams about things she could control, things she could affect.

I'm sorry to hear that.

Thanks. I appreciate that.

I'll ping you later.

K.

Charlie closed the chat app. Her phone chirped with a

familiar ring tone, and she dug her phone out of her tote. It surprised her to see Scott's number, and a flutter of panic filled her chest. She pressed the green icon.

"Hey, Scott."

"I have a problem," Scott said with no niceties.

"Hello to you too," Charlie said, not willing to let him frazzle her. "What's going on? Is Evan okay?"

Scott sighed and lowered his voice. "I found him sleep-walking this morning. That spirit he encountered yesterday convinced him to follow her into the woods. If I hadn't woken up to the sound of him talking to her, who knows what would've happened."

From the sound of Scott's breathing, Charlie pictured him, phone to his ear, pacing back and forth. Dread plucked a cold string in her chest.

"I'm a little out of my depth here, Charlie. What the hell do I do?"

"Okay. Back up a second. What spirit?"

"Evan didn't text you?"

"No, he didn't."

"Christ," Scott muttered.

"You're freaking me out. What is it? Why should he have texted me?"

"He encountered a spirit yesterday. A girl not much older than him. He said he saw her jump off Guilford's Peak."

"What the hell, Scott? Why didn't you call me? Seeing

something like that could push an adult over the edge, much less a kid."

"He and I talked about it in depth over dinner. I thought..." A scratching sound filled her ears, and she imagined him running his hand over several days worth of stubble on his face. "I thought I had it under control. I also thought he was going to text you about it."

Charlie clamped her mouth shut for a second. She didn't want to say anything too critical. They'd agreed to be more cordial and supportive of each other. To present a united front in dealing with Evan and his teenage shenanigans. And if she was being honest with herself, she didn't know how she would've handled it either.

"All right. I'm sure you did the best you could. Tell me everything that happened."

Scott walked her through Evan's encounter, and the tenderness in his voice as he talked about his son's sensitivities softened Charlie's heart. He was trying. Really trying.

"Do you think she tried to influence him? I mean, beyond wanting his help?"

"I don't know. Evan won't talk to me about her, which is why I'm calling you. He's being a sullen teenager just now."

"Can I talk to him?"

"Sure. Evan," Scott pulled the phone away from his face, his voice distant. "Your mom's on the phone."

"I told you not to call her," Evan whined in the background.

"Well, I did, and now she wants to talk to you." The phone rattled with the switch of hands.

Evan huffed, "I'm fine."

"I'm glad to hear that," Charlie said. "Your dad is just worried about you, that's all. And I am too. Seeing someone die would be traumatic for an adult, Evan."

"I knew she was a spirit. I knew it wasn't..." He paused for what seemed an eternity. "I knew it wasn't real."

"Nobody's saying it wasn't real, Evan. You and I both know that spirits are very real. Your dad said you were sleepwalking. It's been a while since you've done that."

"Yeah." Evan let out a shuddery sigh.

"Can you tell me what happened?"

"Nothing, really. She wanted to talk, and I didn't want to do it in the tent with Dad sleeping. I kept thinking this has to be a dream, but I guess it wasn't."

"What else did she say to you? Did she give her name? Or tell you what she wanted?"

"Her name's Michelle. She didn't tell me any more than that. But she's worried. The man who hurt her, he has another girl. She wants me to help get this other girl away from him."

"That's great information, sweetie. Did she tell you the other girl's name?"

"Um..." Evan went quiet.

"It's okay if she didn't."

"No, she told me, I just wanted to get away from her when she dragged me into the woods. Something with a J —Jenna, maybe? Or Jenny. I don't remember. Dad woke me up about that time."

The door opened behind her, startling her, and Ben ambled into the office space. His sandy brown hair tangled to one side of his head and red tinged his blue eyes. Dark purple shadows beneath his eyes finished the ensemble of sleeplessness. He set his leather messenger bag down on the chair and pressed the button to raise his desk to standing height.

Charlie ignored Ben while he set up his laptop. "It's okay, sweetie. Can you tell me what she looked like?"

"What do you mean?"

"I mean, did she look like she was old-timey? You know, from a different time?"

"No. She looked like she could go to school with me. She had on a white t-shirt and a pair of shorts. Bloody though. Her head looked..." Charlie could almost hear him shiver on the other end of the line.

"It's okay, honey. You don't have to tell me."

"No, it's okay. It looked like somebody had hit her with something heavy. Her forehead had a deep dent in it."

"That must've been really scary." Charlie used her most soothing voice.

"I don't know if it scared me as much as it shocked me, you know?"

"Yeah, I know." Charlie had grown used to the spirits

that came in and out of her life. Some part of her hated that this was happening to her son. That she couldn't protect him from them.

"What would you like to do about it, Evan?"

"What you mean?" Evan sounded wary.

"Do you want to help her? Or do you want her to go away?"

He let out a long, weary sigh. "I hate that she's suffering." His voice dropped to a whisper, "I... I *feel* it. You know what I mean?"

"I know exactly what you mean. Maybe you should let me do some digging. And for now, if she appears to you again, tell her to leave you alone."

"That's all I have to do?"

"Yep."

"And she'll just leave me alone if I tell her to?"

"If you're firm about it, she should. Tell her you've given her information to an adult who investigates stuff like this. Remind her you're just a kid, and you've done everything you can for her. If she's persistent, tell her to go away anytime she shows up and do your best to ignore her. I'm pretty good at finding people. Or at least finding out about them. And I have some resources I can use."

"Okay."

"No matter what happens, I don't want you going after her, Evan. Okay?"

"No problem. I'm really don't want to go anywhere with her."

"Good. Just make sure she doesn't trick you. Sometimes spirits can do that."

"She's not going to trick me. I won't let her."

"Good. Let me talk to your dad, okay?"

"Sure."

"Hey sweetie, you can handle this. And I love you to the moon and back."

"Love you too. Thanks," Evan said sheepishly. "Dad, Mom wants to talk to you."

"Well?" Scott said, back on the phone again.

"I told him what to do. He is to tell her to go away if she bothers him again, that he's let an adult know, and they're handling it."

"Great. I'm assuming you're the adult," Scott quipped.

"Haha. You're hilarious." Charlie rolled her eyes, relieved to sense the tension between them had dissolved. "Listen, you should do the string trick."

"The string trick?" Scott asked.

"Remember when we would go camping with Evan when he was a two or three, and he figured out how to unzip the tent? We'd wake up, and he'd be outside wandering around the campsite? I can't believe you've forgotten."

"Right," Scott said. "We tied a string to him when he fell asleep so that if he tried to go outside, it would wake us up."

"Exactly. Surely you have some bungee cord or something you can use."

"Yeah, I do. That's a great idea, actually."

"I will take that. You going to be okay?"

"Yeah, we'll be fine. Listen, thanks for, well, you know."

"Yeah, sure you're welcome for, you know," she teased.

"Now who's being funny?"

"I'll see you on Saturday," she said. The line went dead, and she put her phone next to her computer within easy reach. The laptop obscured Ben's face, but his heavy fingers on the keyboard piqued her interest.

"Morning, Ben," she said.

"Morning," he grunted.

"You sound like you could use some coffee. You want to run down to the café with me, and we'll get some coffee and a muffin?"

He stopped typing. "No, thank you."

"So I take it things didn't go very well last night?"

"How do you know about last night?"

Charlie cocked her head to one side and shrugged.

"Of course. You all had a coven meeting. I should've known."

Charlie ignored the comment. "Are you going to assign her a protection detail?"

"I'm doing that as we speak."

"That's great."

"I don't want to talk about it," he mumbled.

"I didn't say anything."

"You were saying something with your eyes. And I don't want to talk about it."

"Sure," she said and left it at that, organizing her to-do list.

Ben went back to typing his email, and when he finished, he closed his laptop.

"Yeah, I don't think I can do this today."

"Do what?" Charlie asked.

"Just work. I need to get out of here."

Charlie sensed the turmoil inside him. It boiled beneath the surface like a soup made of jealousy and anger and an overwhelming sense of sadness. Defeat. Like he had given up.

"You can't run away from this, Ben," Charlie said. "No matter what you think you know about Mark or what you think Jen feels about him, she adores you. And you adore her."

"Yeah, I don't know about that."

"Is he dangerous?" Charlie asked.

Ben shrugged. "He's a sorcerer. He has a tremendous amount of power at his fingertips. Literally. His family skates a line of what's legal within the magical community, but we've never been able to prove anything. And," he sighed. "I found nothing on him that showed he was dangerous."

"What about blood magic and sacrifices? Wasn't it you that said that's the way the sorcerers like to work?"

"It depends on the sorcerer. And whatever their goal is."

"Okay. That's not what I thought you were going to say."

"Listen, I'm going to assign extra security to Jen, but she's a big girl, and she can take care of herself. She made that extremely clear to me last night."

Ben unplugged his laptop and put it back into his bag. "I'm going to work from home today, so if you need anything just ping me."

"Sure."

Ben turned and walked away from his standing desk, and Charlie watched him until he disappeared around the corner. What the hell had happened last night? Charlie unplugged her computer and packed up her tote bag before she headed out to get some answers at The Kitchen Witch Café.

CHAPTER 12

Ben set up his laptop at the table near the front window of the coffee shop across the street from the Carmichael Inn. It wasn't really an inn, but a new boutique hotel at the very edge of West Ashley, a suburb of Charleston. Even across four lanes of highway, he had an unobstructed view of the parking lot. All he needed now was a room number, which hopefully Athena would have for him soon. His phone buzzed on the table. He picked it up and quickly answered the call.

"What have you got for me?" Ben asked.

"You were right," Athena chirped. "He's definitely staying at the Carmichael Inn. Looks like a nice place. Has a water view."

"Yeah, it does. I'm looking at it right now. Can you tell me what room he's staying in?" Ben asked.

"That took a little more maneuvering, but he's in room

214. And based on his credit cards, he's got company in an adjoining room and a rental car from Hertz. So look for a yellow front tag."

"Great. You're the best," Ben said.

"Aww, thanks, boss," Athena said.

"And as usual, let's just keep this between you and me, okay?"

"Sure thing." Athena took a breath. "You should probably know that Mark Stonehill is not the only Stonehill in the area."

"Tell me," Ben said.

"Devon Stonehill—who we have a warrant for, by the way—boarded a plane yesterday evening and flew to Charleston. He hasn't checked into a hotel yet, so I don't know where he's staying, but I'll keep an eye out."

"I wonder what he's doing here?"

"I don't know. They're brothers, and they both work for their family business. So..."

"Right." Ben scrubbed the thick stubble on his chin. Was Devon here to help his brother take Jen and Ruby away? He suddenly lost his taste for the blueberry muffin he'd bought.

"Let me know if you want to pick him up, and I'll send a team. He's very slippery. We've never been able to catch him."

"Yeah, I know. Thanks."

"No problem."

The line went dead. Ben scanned Carmichael's

parking lot, which looked to be full of rentals, several from Hertz. He would just have to do this the old-fashioned way—watch and wait and hope for a break.

* * *

THE RINGING IN MARK'S EARS BEGAN ALMOST IMMEDIATELY after he stepped into the hot shower. "Dammit," he muttered and shut off the water.

He grabbed a towel from the stack on the shelf over the toilet and dried off quickly, then said a few words to discharge the incantation for the alarm that only he could hear. He wrapped the towel around his waist and threw another one over his shoulders.

He knocked on the adjoining door to Bridges' room. "Bridges, can you step in here, please?"

Bridges opened the door and looked shocked to find Mark wrapped in towels, his dark hair dripping wet.

"Boss?" he said.

"I set up an alarm enchantment around the hotel, and it just went off."

Confusion clouded Bridge's taut face. "I didn't hear anything."

"I'm the only one that can hear it."

"Right. You must teach me that one someday." Bridges pursed his thin lips. "What would you like me to do?"

"Do a quick perimeter sweep. I set the alarm broadly for witches, sorcerers, and other creatures that might be within 300-square yards. It could be nothing, but I don't like to leave things to chance."

"Yes, sir. I'll be back in half an hour. Don't leave the room, please," Bridges said. He disappeared back into his room, and Mark heard the outer door close.

Mark moved close to the sliding glass door to the balcony overlooking the marsh. He lifted the sheer curtain to the side but didn't get too close. The marsh grass rippled in the breeze, and sunlight glinted off the steel-colored water snaking through the field of green. He lifted the towel from his shoulders and scrubbed his dripping hair with it.

Mark recalled the picture Bridges had shown him of Jen sitting on the lap of a man, her boyfriend. A witch and a DOL investigator. Ben Sutton. A name he was already familiar with because his uncle Bertram had killed the man's parents. Mark tried to imagine how that might have haunted Ben Sutton. How it might have driven him to become an investigator to find the man who had wounded him so deeply. How somewhere in the back of Ben Sutton's mind, he might blame all sorcerers for his misery.

If he'd been in Sutton's position, he knew he'd want justice. Or at least revenge. And if he were in Sutton's position and a sorcerer came to town, his girlfriend's ex, Mark knew what he would do. He'd want to check out the threat and diminish it as quickly as possible. Why wouldn't Sutton do the same thing? Then a thought flashed through his head—something that happened to him often. His mother called it intuition. Whatever it was, he trusted his gut more than any person on the planet. He couldn't shake the image of Jen crying in the dark, angry, and heartbroken.

He stepped back into the shadows of his room and dressed quickly. The way he saw it, he had one chance to make this situation work for him, and he'd do whatever it took to ensure he got his way.

CHAPTER 13

Charlie walked into The Kitchen Witch Café and scanned every face, looking for Jen. At eight-thirty in the morning the café bustled with diners — mostly tourists this time of year — devouring muffins, pancakes, and omelets with sheer delight on their faces. The scent of maple and bacon hung in the air, and Charlie's stomach growled. She made her way to the lunch counter and took a seat closest to the cash register. It was usual for Jen to wander around the restaurant at this time of day, refilling coffee cups and chatting up the customers. Where was she? But Charlie wouldn't let herself worry just yet.

Sometimes Jen worked the afternoon shift and early evening shift; maybe she had switched with someone. Dottie, a long-time server at the café, came from the kitchen with a fresh tray of food. Her wild salt-and-pepper hair formed a messy bun on the back of her head, and a faded blue bandana held any stray hair off her face. She nodded toward Charlie. "I'll be with you in just a moment."

"No worries," Charlie said.

A moment later, Evangeline emerged from the back. She wrapped a black bistro apron around her waist before she noticed Charlie. She smiled, and a spiderweb of wrinkles stretched across her cheeks.

"Hey, Charlie," Evangeline said and drew closer. "I wasn't expecting to find you here this morning."

"Work's a little light this week. Thought I'd get some breakfast and check on Jen. She here?" Charlie said.

"'Fraid not." Evangeline shook her head. "She called and said she was going to be late. I take it things didn't go well last night."

"Yeah, Ben came into the office a little evasive and gruff. He looked like he hadn't slept much."

A thoughtful expression crossed her aunt's face.

"He said he was going to assign a security detail to Jen. So, she, Jack, and Ruby are protected at least."

"I'm less worried about her protection. I feel like we can do that. I am concerned about her heart being broken."

"Yeah," Charlie nodded solemnly. "I know what you mean."

Evangeline pulled an order pad and pen from the pocket of her apron. "What can I get you?"

"I'd really like a tall glass of iced tea. And..." Charlie glanced at the chalkboard menu on the wall behind the counter. "I'll take the banana nut pancakes with maple bacon."

"Sounds good." Evangeline scribbled down the order, then clipped the receipt to the shiny stainless steel ticket wheel before she spun it and called, "Order up."

She filled a glass with ice and freshly brewed sweet tea, then placed it in front of Charlie. She leaned one hip against the counter. "So how are you doing? Evan's with his dad this week, right?"

"Yeah, they're trail camping in the mountains of North Carolina. You know how Scott is. He loves anything adventurous."

"And I guess Evan likes it too?"

"Oh yeah. He loves being outdoors, and they're doing hard trails this year. So he's excited about that."

Her aunt narrowed her keen blue eyes as if studying her. Charlie traced through the condensation on the glass with her thumb.

"Is everything okay?"

Charlie smiled aimlessly at Evangeline. "With me?" she said as if she hadn't understood the question. "Oh, I'm fine. Nothing new. Tom's good." Charlie referred to her boyfriend. She bit her bottom lip and knew her aunt would see right through her if she lied, even if it was by omission. She cleared her throat. "Scott called me this morning. Evidently, Evan encountered a..." Charlie glanced around to check the proximity of other people before she whispered, "spirit."

"I hope it doesn't disrupt things for him."

"Me too. He was really looking forward to this trip. I told him how to get rid of her. I'm just hoping she listens. You know how sometimes..." she dropped her voice again, "spirits can be a little persistent."

"Indeed, they can," Evangeline said.

Charlie took a sip of her tea. "How about you?"

"Nothing much with me. You know Jen wants to expand the business. We're offering catering now, and we have our first job this week. It's a pretty big job for the Chamber of Commerce."

Charlie straightened in her chair and smiled. "That's exciting."

"It is. It's just a lot of extra work. We've had to hire more servers, just for catering. Anyway, Jen's very enthusiastic about it."

"You don't seem very enthused," Charlie observed.

Evangeline let out a nervous laugh and fidgeted with her hands. "It's not that. Sometimes change is scary even for somebody like me who's seen a lot of change." She expelled a deep breath. "Jen seems to have her hopes pinned on expanding. I think it'll work. If it were up to her, she'd have franchises all over the south."

"She always was ambitious," Charlie said. "And don't worry. Jen always does well at these kinds of things."

"I know." Evangeline pressed one hand against her

belly. "Hopefully, this whole thing with Mark won't get in the way."

"It won't. We'll make sure of it," Charlie said as confidently as she could. She hated to see her aunt worry.

The bell sitting on the counter of the pass through rang out, and someone in the back called, "Order up."

Evangeline smiled, all trace of worry disappearing. "That should be your pancakes."

A moment later, Evangeline placed the large plate in front of her. Charlie dug in with gusto. If she couldn't quell the anxiety still bubbling in her chest, she could at least quell her hunger.

CHAPTER 14

Evan's father walked to the edge of the trail and looked out over the valley below. A bolt of lightning streaked across the overcast, gray sky. Thunder cracked in the distance, and the air smelled of electricity.

"Evan, let's take cover before it rains." His father gestured to a place in the woods, not too far from the trail. Evan followed him, and they quickly set up a make-shift lean-to from a tarp, bungee cord, and two of the tent's fiberglass poles. Once they'd built the shelter, they took cover, huddling close to wait out the storm.

"I guess Mom was right." Evan wrapped his arms around his knees and peered from beneath the tarp at the thick, blackening clouds overhead. Heavy raindrops fell, thumping against the leaves of the trees and the tarp.

"About what," his father asked.

"She told Miss Cora it was going to rain and that I should take rain gear."

"I told Cora to pack the rain gear." His dad sounded a little defensive. "I like to be ready for all contingencies."

"Right, I know." Evan smiled.

"It's really coming down." His father looked up at the tarp covering them. The edges of it whipped against the wind. Evan shivered a little and pressed his shoulder against his father's for warmth. His father glanced at him. "You know, I'm really proud of you."

Evan met his father's eyes, unable to hide his shock. "You are?"

"Yes. I am. We've had some challenges this week, but you've handled them pretty well. Better than a lot of grown-ups I know. I just... I just wanted you to know that."

Evan looked down at his knees and smiled, unsure how to feel or what to say. "Did mom tell you that Cousin Lisa's getting married?"

"No, she didn't. Lisa is the redhead, right? The no-nonsense one."

"Yeah." Evan chuckled.

"So, she's getting married," his father mused.

"Yep. Her boyfriend asked her at the summer solstice bonfire. It was kinda cool. Romantic."

"Romantic." His father shook his head. "What do you know about "

"I know a few things," Evan countered. "I've been going out with Rachel for almost six months now."

"I see. Should I be planning your wedding next?" his father quipped.

"Whoa! I just want to get to high school and then maybe junior prom."

"Good. I'm glad to hear that. Rachel's a nice girl, but we almost never end up with our high school sweethearts."

Evan nodded. He heard a hint of sorrow in his father's words.

"Did you have a high school sweetheart?"

"I did. Her name was Laura Foley. We were crowned prom king and queen. She was a lovely, sweet girl."

"Was she as pretty as Mom?"

"Nobody's as pretty as your mom." His dad nudged him with his arm. "But Laura was prom queen for junior and senior prom, if that tells you anything."

"Hmm." Evan rested his chin on his knees, and for a second, he imagined prom in two years with Rachel. He needed to send her a text with a picture from one of the waterfalls he and his dad had trekked to this week. He was sure she'd like that. From the corner of his eyes, a shadow flickered. An icy chill skittered across his arms and shoulders, pulling him out of his thoughts about Rachel. His chest felt heavy. "She's here."

His dad turned his head slowly and the nostalgic expression on his face melted away. "The girl's spirit?"

Evan nodded but didn't look directly at her. She materialized completely and sat down next to him. Dark brown blood stained her t-shirt and face. His father leaned forward and looked in both directions. "I don't see her."

"Trust me, you really don't want to," Evan said, concerned for his dad. He blinked and swallowed hard before forcing himself to turn his head and look at her. Half of her face looked as if a stone or brick had crushed it. Her jaw hung in a strange angle, and one eye had swollen shut. Evan's stomach turned sour, and he squeezed his eyes closed.

"You really, really don't want to. She looks worse."

"It's okay, Evan." His father placed a hand on Evan's arm. "Remember what your mom said to do."

Evan nodded and squeezed his eyes shut. "Go away. I told the authorities about you. They're looking into it now. I can't do anything more for you so... please just go away." When he opened his eyes, he found her face so close to his he'd swear he could feel her breath—do spirits breathe? He'd have to remember to ask his mom. A white film covered her blue eyes, and he couldn't stand to look at her anymore but couldn't make himself look away either.

"What happened to you?" he whispered.

She opened her mouth to speak, but her jaw only wagged, and her face turned gray with deep purple shadows filling in the crescents around her mouth and below her eyes. Evan shut his eyes again.

"Breathe, Evan." His father's hand tightened on his arm. "She can't hurt you. In through your nose and out through your mouth." Evan slowed his breathing and focused on his father's words.

The scrape of her icy fingers on his cheek made him want to open his eyes and run out into the thunderstorm. It took every ounce of self-control to stay rooted in place.

"He did this to me. He'll do this to her. Please, Evan." Her voice whispered through his head like a leaf scratching across the pavement. "Please help us."

"I am helping you," he said, his voice a hoarse, nervous whisper. "I called my mom. She works with the police. They'll find you. I swear it, but you've got to leave me alone now."

She pressed her palm against his cheek, and his entire body broke into goosebumps. "Please don't leave me there."

"I've done all I can for you. Now... go away. Go away, or I'll call my mom and tell her to stop looking for you."

The lie tasted terrible and bitter. Hateful. A scream filled his head, the most deafening wail he had ever heard in his life. He pressed his hands to his ears, trying to shut it out, but it only got louder. The cry came from somewhere inside him.

"Stop it! Just stop."

As suddenly as her scream began, it ended. Evan opened his eyes and glanced around. She'd disappeared. He searched in all directions, trying to find her, but found no flicker. No shadows. No icy mist. He let out a shuddery laugh.

"You okay?" His dad squeezed his arm gently again.

"Yeah," he said, his voice breathy. "I think it worked. I don't see her or feel her anymore."

His dad wrapped his arm around his shoulders and hugged him tightly to his side. Evan couldn't remember the last time his dad had hugged him.

"You did great."

His father's words warmed him more than his hug. "I can't believe that worked."

"Maybe now we can just concentrate on the hike and having a good time together."

"Yeah. I'd like that," Evan said.

"The rain seems to be letting up." His dad glanced at the tarp over their heads again. The sound of raindrops had lessened. "Why don't we give it ten more minutes, have an energy bar, and then get back on the trail."

"That sounds great. Can I have the peanut butter one?"

"Absolutely." His dad grinned at him. "I think you've earned it."

CHAPTER 15

Mark poured himself a cup of hot coffee and grabbed the last blueberry muffin from the display of baked goods. The continental breakfast provided by the hotel had pretty well been picked clean by 9 AM, but most of the business guests had left for the day, which meant Mark had the place to himself. He scooped up a morning paper left on the table by another traveler. It would give him a feel for the town. If it had been his choice, he would have stayed downtown in one of the fancier hotels. But he wanted to be closer to Jen. Even so, the edge of West Ashley was still a thirty-minute drive to Palmetto Point.

"Let me go you goon," a familiar voice echoed across the cavernous reception area, drawing Mark's attention from the morning headline. He'd settled in the far end of the lobby where they set up breakfast in the morning, a snack midafternoon, and cocktails after five for the patrons.

Bridges had hold of his brother's arm and forced Devon forward. Bridges leaned close and whispered something into his brother's ear. A shocked look crossed Devon's face, but he shut up.

Mark gritted his teeth. What the hell was Devon doing here? How had Devon even known he had come to Palmetto Point? He scowled at the muffin and pushed it aside. It wasn't exactly delicious. He rose to his feet and tossed the half-eaten pastry and the nearly empty disposable cup of coffee into the trash. The newspaper stayed on the table, neatly folded for the next patron. The last thing he'd expected was an interrogation this morning, but Devon could ruin his entire plan, and he wasn't about to let that happen.

THE APPEARANCE OF DEVON STONEHILL IN THE PARKING LOT made Ben sit up straight and take notice. He took a small pair of binoculars from his bag to get a better look. What was *he* doing here? Everything Ben knew about the Stonehills and their business suggested that Mark ran the family's business, and Devon was the screw-up. Often in trouble for bad debts, sales of illegal potions, and fraudulent spells, the only reason the DOL had not caught up with him was because of his brother Mark. The DOL had never proved the Stonehill's' network of selling potions and magical arms to other sorcerers, witches, even vampires, werewolves, and the occasional demon. They covered their tracks well. Ben's parents had been after illegal magical weapons when they died, and Ben knew in his heart the Stonehill family had been responsible.

But Mark Stonehill, Sr. had a reputation for ensuring that his family name never appeared as suspects in any crime. Devon seemed to be the thorn on that rose stem, often attracting trouble. Athena had pointed out that Devon Stonehill was slippery. On paper, Mark and his parents looked like model citizens of both the witch world and the non-witch world. They donated to hospitals and charities for children and animals. They picked causes that made them appear to be community leaders. From the background check Ben had run on Mark, he photographed well and often attended charity events in San Francisco.

Ben could see how Jen might have found Mark Stonehill attractive, why she might not have even known he was a sorcerer until it was too late. A pang filled his chest. Jen had the best heart of anyone he'd ever met and always found the good in people, even when they couldn't find it in themselves. That must've been a delicious temptation for Mark Stonehill. Devon Stonehill? Ben wasn't so sure about him. What was he doing here?

When Ben saw the short, twitchy man approach Devon, it shocked him he could take control of the slippery sorcerer so easily. Ben watched as the slender but well-muscled man grabbed Devon by the arm, yanked him forward, and quickly ushered him into the hotel. Any attempt Devon made to fight didn't last long.

Ben closed his laptop, shoved it and his binoculars back into his bag before he took the last sip of his coffee, and tossed his half-eaten Danish into the trash. A thrum in his chest drove him forward. Maybe this would end up as a win—he could take Devon Stonehill into custody on sight because of the outstanding warrants—if he could get him away from Mark and his toady. While he was at it, he'd get a closer look at the man who'd swept Jen off her feet so many years ago and maybe get a whiff of why Stonehill was really here. Ben doubted Mark wanted anything to do with his daughter. He'd never shown interest before now. He had to have an ulterior motive. And Ben was going to do whatever it took to figure it out.

BRIDGES WAS STRAPPING DEVON TO A CHAIR WHEN MARK arrived in the hotel room. He didn't like the man's rough ways much. Devon glanced at his brother and laughed.

"Come on, man, is this really necessary?"

"I don't know Devon, you tell me," Mark countered. "I know what you're capable of so..."

"Geez. I can't believe you'd even think something like

that." Devon squirmed in his chair and yanked at the invisible restraints.

"What are you doing here, Devon?" Mark asked, his voice flat.

"I needed a vacation. Charleston is a beautiful city. The friendliest city, from everything I've read. I like friendly." A grin spread across Devon's lips.

Mark tightened his jaw and rolled his eyes. Typical Devon. Always quick with a lie.

"May I, sir?" Bridges stepped closer to Devon and watched for the signal. Mark clicked his teeth together and weighed his options. There were plenty of ways to make Devon talk, but Devon knew them all and had probably taken magical precautions. That only left one way. Mark detested violence, but sometimes it was a necessary evil.

"Don't get blood on the carpet," Mark said. "I don't want to have to explain anything to anyone, and I don't want a huge cleaning bill."

"Oh Mark," Devon chuckled. "Figures you'd be worried about the bill. So fiscally responsible."

"Shut up, Devon," Mark snapped.

"Don't worry, sir. I've got spells that can get blood out of anything." Bridges ignored Devon's comments.

"Fine." Mark shifted his feet. "Do it."

Bridges balled up his fist and reared his arm back. Devon squeezed his eyes shut and braced for a hit to his face. Bridges landed a hard punch in Devon's gut. Devon's eyes flew open, and he grunted, then gasped for air. Mark flinched and reached to stop Bridges from winding up another punch. "Wait. Just... wait."

Devon dropped his head, coughed, and then caught his breath. "That all you got, short stack?"

Bridges lurched forward as if to punch Devon again.

"Stop," Mark said. He raised one hand, freezing Bridges in place. The man stood still as a statue.

"Shit," Mark muttered. "I didn't want to have to do that, Devon."

"Nobody but Mom makes you do anything you don't want to do, brother. I can't believe you have this guy working for you now."

"How do you even know who he is?" Mark said.

"I've seen him around." Devon eyed the frozen man. "He's a PI, right? I know Gray Garber has used him as muscle before—which is hard to believe by the looks of him."

"He's a lot more powerful than he looks," Mark said, unsure he could believe anything that came out of his brother's mouth. "So are you going to tell me what you're really doing here?"

"I told you," Devon shrugged. "I'm on vacation. I needed a break."

"A break from what?" Mark said. "It sure as hell isn't from work because I know you're not doing anything for the company."

"I have my own things going on," Devon countered, unperturbed, sounding almost bored.

"Right," Mark clenched his jaw and counted to ten. There was no way he would let Devon get the best of him. "I don't know what I'm supposed to do with you. I can't just let you free."

"So, what? You're just going to keep me captive? Like that ever works," Devon said in his snarkiest tone. "I think I've escaped from every single attempt of yours to bind me. Remember when we were kids?"

"Just shut up, Devon, and let me think," Mark snapped.

"There's nothing to think about, Mark. Let me go. I will head into Charleston and check out the architecture, take a carriage ride, maybe see what kind of magical action is going on in this town. There are almost as many sorcerers on the East Coast as there are on the West. Maybe we could expand our business."

"Our business," Mark scoffed.

"Yeah. You take the West Coast. I take the East Coast. Together we could rule the world, brother."

"No thank you," Mark said.

"You're going to have to let me go," Devon said. "Otherwise, I'll just do what I do best."

Mark let out a heavy sigh. He hated that Devon was right. He couldn't keep him captive. "Fine. I'll let you go. But if I get any hint, you are here for anything other than some rest and relaxation, I will end you, Devon."

Devon chuckled. "Sure, brother. Sure."

Mark waved his hand toward Bridges. The man unfroze, shook his head and looked around, disoriented.

"It's all right, Bridges. You're all right," Mark said without apology. "Will you please untie my brother?"

A confused expression crossed Bridge's angular face. "Sir?"

"My brother and I had a nice long chat while you were... um... out," Mark said. "He promises not to interfere with us. To spend his time taking in the city's history, basking on the beaches, and drinking fruity umbrella drinks with the lovely women of Charleston. Don't you, brother?"

"I swear it on father's grave," Devon said.

Mark gritted his teeth at the flippancy in Devon's voice. His brother knew exactly how to push his buttons. "I'm going to hold you to that."

"Of course you will." Devon wiggled his fingers, unable to lift his arms from the chair. "Can you let me out of this now?"

Bridges looked from Mark to Devon and back. Mark gave the man a nod, and Bridges quickly released his brother from his invisible bindings.

Devon jumped to his feet and rubbed his wrists. "Thanks. I'll just be on my way." He pushed past Mark, letting his arm lightly brush against his brother. Accident? Or intentional? Mark veered in Devon's direction.

"I meant what I said, Devon," Mark warned. "Don't get in my way here."

Devon raised his hands in surrender and gave his brother a cocky grin. "I wouldn't dream of it, brother," he said and slipped out the door before Mark could respond.

CHAPTER 16

Ben parked his Toyota FJ40 down the street from The Kitchen Witch Café. He watched Mark Stonehill and his companion get out of the rental car and go inside the restaurant. From his vantage point, he could still see into the large front window. The disadvantage of having such a distinct vehicle was anyone going into the café who knew Ben could easily identify it.

The last thing Ben wanted was to have Jen notice him watching the café. They had enough problems already. If she didn't spot him while she refilled coffee cups at the window table, he risked Mark discovering his attempt at a stakeout. He slid a little lower in his seat and sort of wished he could tail this guy without being seen at all.

A pang of jealousy surged through his chest when Mark and the man accompanying him took a seat in a booth next to the front window. Mark kept looking out at the street and then back at the menu in his hands. What else did the guy have to say to Jen? Wasn't his threat enough?

PEOPLE CAME AND WENT ON THE STREET. A FEW CAST glances his way but walked on by. Had any of them recognized him? Jen knew most of the folks in town. It occurred to him he didn't just have to worry about customers going into the café. Everyone knew Jen. Anyone could out him to Jen the next time they saw her.

Ben squeezed the steering wheel until his knuckles whitened. He couldn't have Jen finding out he'd been surveilling her restaurant. She'd get the wrong idea. Maybe it didn't matter anymore. Maybe he should've told her he ran Mark's name through the DOL databases months ago. However, he didn't regret checking out Mark. He would do it again.

His pulse pinged when the door to the café opened. A woman wearing a black bistro apron with The Kitchen Witch Café logo on it emerged from the café with a coffee in her hand and holding a paper bag in the other. Ben recognized her. Dammit. Just what he'd been afraid of. Dottie, the server who'd worked there forever and knew Ben well.

He sat so low in the truck only his eyes peered over the window. He watched transfixed as she stepped off the sidewalk and looked both ways before she crossed the street and headed straightaway toward Ben. A friendly smile spread across her face when she drew closer to his truck. He knew he couldn't get out of this, so he rolled down his window, and Dottie stopped in front of the driver side door.

"Hey, Dottie, what's up?" He flashed his best smile.

"You got me." she grinned and shrugged. Dottie's plump face sported her usual warm smile, but she squinted as the morning sun hit her eyes while she talked. Ben knew who the two guys were, of course, but he avoided looking at the café. He just gave Dottie a confused grin. "This is for you."

Ben shifted his gaze to the paper go-cup of coffee and the brown bag she had thrust into the window. "I didn't order that."

"Yeah, I know. He sent it." She turned and pointed to the restaurant's front window. Mark raised his hand in acknowledgment.

"Great. Thanks, Dottie," he muttered and reached for the coffee and bag. He tried not to let his disappointment creep into his voice.

"No problem. Have a great day." She turned on her heel and watched for the oncoming traffic before crossing the street and disappearing into the restaurant. Ben considered dumping the coffee out and throwing away whatever delicious food was inside the bag but decided against it. It might be the last time he ever got to drink Jen's coffee or eat her food again. A pang filled his chest while he sweetened the dark roast with two sugar packets. He took a sip and savored it. Then he peeked inside the bag and found a ham and cheese sandwich, a small container of tomato soup, and a serving of still warm peach cobbler with toasted almond slivers on top.

"What the?" All his favorites. Ben put the bag down on the passenger seat and brushed his hands together. "You should've known better than to just follow a sorcerer without taking precautions," he scolded himself. "This won't be as easy as you thought."

A painted sign hanging over the sidewalk caught his eye. The delicate pink and white orchid looked smaller than he remembered. The metallic gold script read: A Touch of Glamour Salon and Day Spa. The spa part was new or was it? He tried to remember if Jen had mentioned it recently.

"A Touch of Glamour," he muttered. "Glamour!" Of course! Why hadn't he thought of it sooner? He scrambled out of his truck, tucking his head down when he crossed the street and passed the café.

Daphne's salon was two doors down from the café, and a bell jingled overhead when he entered her salon. He stopped to survey the scene. The décor struck him as a little sophisticated for this part of the county—the white leather stylist chairs, oversized mirrors framed in chunky black frames, and the charcoal walls—all looked like they belonged in a big city salon. A stylist with blunt cut, chin-length blond hair tipped in black turned to check him out.

"Hi, do you have an appointment?" she asked. The client, draped in a black cape, glanced up at him via the mirror.

"Appointment? Uh... no. Is Daphne here?" Ben could've kicked himself for not remembering Daphne's last name. She was practically family.

"She's in the back." The stylist made no move to get Daphne and went back to combing through her client's wet, curly hair.

"Right." Ben glanced toward the hallway leading to more rooms and a red glowing exit sign hanging over a metal door. Ben rocked on his heels. "I'll just wait."

A few minutes later, Daphne emerged from a room with a box in her hands. A grin spread across her face when she approached him. "Hi, Ben. I didn't expect to see you this morning."

"I didn't expect to be seen."

"I'm sure," she quipped and put the box on the receptionist's counter. Inside, Ben saw neat rows of black and gray bottles.

"What are those?" Ben pointed to the box's contents.

"Just a new line of hair products I'm selling."

"Right." He nodded, not sure what to say next. He couldn't remember being totally alone with Daphne before.

"Oh my goddess, Ben. What's going on?" She giggled and slid the box underneath the counter. "You're like a long-tailed cat in a room full of rocking chairs."

"That obvious, huh?"

"Um... yeah. Now what's going on. Seriously. Are you okay?"

"Yeah... yeah. Sure." He dropped his voice. "I do need your help, though."

"Sure thing. I'm assuming this is about Jen." Daphne quirked one eyebrow.

"Yeah," Ben said.

"Come on." She gestured for him to follow her and called to the other stylist. "Kimi, I'm just going to step out for a few minutes."

"Okay." Kimi didn't look up from her client's head.

The two of them crossed through the salon, past the shampoo stations behind an opaque textured screen and down the short hallway. More rooms materialized than Ben had first realized. Daphne had assigned two of them as massage rooms, and on the right, Ben could see a room devoted to pedicures. Past two chairs, a nail technician bent over a client's feet. Daphne definitely had all the bases covered.

The doors to the other two rooms were closed and clearly marked—storage and manager's office. Even back here, the scent of shampoo hung in the air. Daphne led him through the heavy metal door with the exit sign above it out into the parking lot that ran behind all the buildings on the block. Only a couple of cars had parked in the spaces directly behind Daphne's salon, but the lot behind the café looked nearly full. Ben noted Evangeline's little brown truck, but he saw no sign of Jen's Ford F150.

Daphne spun around and looked him in the eye. "So what's this about?"

For a moment, her question caught him off balance. Would she tell Jen? Should he ask her to keep this private? In the end, he just said, "I need some help with casting a glamour. It's really not my forte. Can you teach me?" he asked. There was no need to play games with her.

"Sure. On one condition," Daphne said with a mischievous grin on her face.

Ben hesitated, unsure where she was going with this. Then he said, "Um... okay."

"You have to tell me everything that's going on. My mom said Jen called in late this morning, and she never calls in like that. Ever."

"Daphne, I—" Ben stammered, trying to think of a lie. "I need the glamour help for DOL business, that's all. It's not about Jen."

"Right, and I've got naturally pink hair." Daphne cocked her head and crossed her arms.

"Daphne." He glanced at the cars behind the café. Jen called in late. What did that mean?

"Look, Ben. You do know I was there last night, right? She called all of us to her house and told us about him. The thing is, she was more scared of how you were going to react than his threats. From what I can tell, it must have gone pretty badly between you two."

"Actually, I'm not the one who got upset. She got mad at me."

"I don't think I believe you." Daphne gave him the once over. "But I don't get that you're lying, either."

"Because I'm not." Ben's face heated.

"Tell me what happened then." She held his gaze and her ground. Dammit, she could be as stubborn as Jen.

Ben swallowed and shook his head and turned back toward the door. "Never mind, this was a bad idea."

Daphne gently grabbed his arm to stop him. "Tell me what happened. I promise I won't judge." Her eyes turned soft. "Why did she get mad at you?"

Ben took a breath, then surrendered to the web of all these witches. "When we first started dating, Jen mentioned Mark's name. I recognized the last name, so I checked him out in the DOL databases."

"And she got mad about that?" Daphne's forehead crinkled with confusion.

"Yeah. She said I invaded her privacy."

"Ohhhh... I see. You didn't tell her you checked him out. That makes sense then," Daphne said.

Ben scratched the ground with his shoe and glanced away again, not wanting to look at her.

"So why are you sitting across the street? Why don't you just go in and make up with her?"

"Because I'm following him."

"Mark? He's there now?"

"Yep. And he already knows I'm staking him out. He sent me lunch and coffee."

Daphne covered her mouth and giggled.

"What? It's not funny."

"It's sort of funny," she grinned. "I wonder what he wants?"

"That's exactly what I'm trying to find out."

"I bet he's using a magic recognition charm on himself," Daphne said.

"I was thinking something along those lines too," Ben said.

"I've used one but never on myself before," Daphne explained. "Only on places or objects to know if they've been touched by magic."

"Sorcerers are very well known for casting spells like that on themselves, so they know when their enemies are near."

"Sure. It's a handy charm to know," Daphne said. "But it's also a little paranoid."

"Yeah. So will you help me? I need to disguise myself, so he doesn't realize it's me."

"Okay, but let me think." Daphne clicked her teeth together and paced. "I'd need to find some way to shield your energy. Just a simple glamour won't be enough if you think he's homing in on you. This may take some research. I'll need at least a day to come up with something."

"Right, I hadn't thought of that."

"Can you come to the salon tomorrow afternoon around one? I've only got one other stylist working tomorrow, and she leaves by noon. That will give me time to consult my books and come up with a plan. And it should give us enough privacy to do what we need to do to make sure that even Jen can't recognize you."

"That would be great," Ben said. "I really appreciate this."

"No worries. I haven't done anything yet," Daphne said. "And I'm not sure that I have anything that will actually work."

"Well, I appreciate it anyway. Jen might be mad at you, you know, for helping me."

"Don't even worry about it. She'll get over it," Daphne shrugged. "We're family. It's kind of a love me no matter what situation."

"That's not a bad situation to have," Ben mused.

"I know," Daphne agreed.

CHAPTER 17

J en drifted into The Kitchen Witch Café, tired to the bone. After a tumultuous, sleepless night, she'd known when the alarm went off at four a.m., she would never be able to rouse herself to open on time. Thank goddess for Evangeline. Her aunt hadn't hesitated when Jen called to ask her to open the restaurant, nor did she ask questions about Ben.

Jen spotted Evangeline at the cash register ringing up a ticket, and she noticed her cousin Charlie and her boyfriend Tom Sharon sitting at the lunch counter eating and chatting with their aunt. Evangeline had pulled her long silver hair up into a neat bun behind her head, and she wore a bright smile when she saw Jen. Charlie glanced over her shoulder and grinned in recognition. Jen couldn't stop herself from giving her cousin and aunt a grateful smile. She waved back.

The feeling of gratitude shifted when she noticed the two men sitting at one of the front window booths. The hair on the back of her neck stood up, and her arms broke into goose flesh at the sight of Mark Stonehill and another man sitting steely eyed across from him. Mark held up one hand and managed a charming grin. Jen tucked her chin and kept moving. She knew she'd have to deal with him at some point, but why did it have to be today?

"How are you doing, honey?" Evangeline asked as Jen approached the counter.

"I'm okay. Sorry I couldn't open this morning."

"Don't you worry about it." Evangeline closed the cash register's drawer.

"Hey." Charlie reached for Jen's hand and gave it a squeeze.

"Afternoon, Jen," Tom said.

"Hey, Tom," Jen forced a smile and tried not to let her eyes wander to the booth in the window. "It's good to see you."

"You too," he said. His warm, golden brown eyes set her at ease. Was that a reaper thing? She made a mental note to ask Charlie sometime.

"So, Evangeline," Jen started. "Do you know how long those two men have been sitting at that booth in the window?" She brought her hand up and raised her index finger to point in the general direction but kept her gesture in front of her chest so Mark couldn't see.

Evangeline looked their way, and a confused expression filled her face.

"I don't know. I don't remember them coming in. Dottie must've seated them. Why?"

Jen let out a heavy breath and folded her arms across her chest. "That's Mark and probably his bodyguard if I were to make a guess."

Charlie made a subtle move to get a better look. "*That's* Mark?"

"Yep." Jen moved behind the counter and tucked her bag in the cubby hole underneath the cash register

"Oh my," Evangeline said, studying him. "He *is* handsome."

"Yep," Jen nodded. "And don't think he doesn't know it."

"Oh, I can see that. He has an energy about him that's rather magnetic, doesn't he?" her aunt observed.

Jen let herself gaze at him for a moment. He raised a hand to wave again, and she looked away quickly to keep herself from getting caught up in his aura. He was definitely magnetic. Her stomach twisted into a knot, and she ignored Evangeline's statement.

"Charlie, did Ben come into the office this morning?"

"He did, but he left soon after. Sorry." Charlie leaned forward with her elbows on the lunch counter. "For the record, he looked like he didn't sleep either, and he was a total grump."

"Great," Jen muttered. She took her black bistro apron

from the cubby and wrapped it around her waist, then checked the pocket for an order pad and pen. She let herself glance at Mark again.

"You know, sometimes I wonder if Mark hasn't cast a spell on himself to make people notice him."

"Well, it must not be working very well," Evangeline chuckled. "Because I didn't notice him till you pointed him out."

"Me, either," Charlie chimed in.

"If you're settled, I'm going to make a bank run," Evangeline announced.

"That sounds great. Thank you. When was the last time someone did coffee refills?" Jen asked as she did a quick survey of the few stragglers left from the lunch crowd.

"Dottie refilled teas just a minute ago, and I don't think anybody's drinking coffee, but of course you're welcome to walk around and check." Her aunt gave her a knowing look. "I know you're itching to go over there and talk to him. You don't really need an excuse."

"I know," Jen bristled at the suggestion.

"I'd like to say that I sensed something nefarious from him," Charlie said. Then she shrugged and peeked over one shoulder. "But I don't. All I sense is a hint of an underlying desperation. Sort of. He's not really that easy to read."

"So, what're you saying? I should take his side?"

"Jen, you take Ruby's side," Charlie said. "All I'm

saying is I don't sense anything dark or evil about him. Maybe he really just wants to get to know his daughter."

Heat spread from Jen's cheeks to her chest, and she fiddled with the pen in her hand. "Well, you don't know him the way I do." Jen sniffed and didn't look at her cousin. She headed to Mark's table without another word to Charlie, slowing when she approached to take a quick scan of the situation. The two men had menus in front of them but no drinks. She pulled her pad out of her apron pocket and poised her pen tip against it.

"Good afternoon." She kept her tone all business. "Has anyone taken your order?"

"Jen. It's good to see you." Mark straightened up in his seat.

"Uh, " She stared at the order pad in her hand to avoid looking into his eyes. "What can get y'all to eat?"

"The pork chop special looks interesting," the man sitting across from Mark said. "Could I get that with green beans and creamed corn?"

Jen scribbled down his order. "Sure thing. And for you, sir?"

Mark sighed and glanced down at the menu in front of him. "I'll take the baked chicken special, with the green salad and oil and vinegar on the side."

"Sure thing." She continued to scribble away. "Any drinks?"

"Just water, please," Mark's companion said.

"Same for me," Mark said.

"Great, I'll get your order in right away." She turned and started away from the table.

"Jen," Mark called after her. He rose from his table and followed her across the restaurant.

Pressure built inside her chest until she thought she might explode. She rounded on him. "What?" she snapped and immediately regretted her tone. She glanced around the restaurant, hoping the few patrons left hadn't noticed. No one seemed to even look her way. Had Mark cast a spell on them? She hated feeling this way. Hated being suspicious. It took up so much energy. "I'm sorry. Is there something else I can get you?"

He towered over her. She had originally loved that about him. His height and the shape of his body had made her feel safe. It was something protective that even now still drew her in. She took a step back.

"Is there someplace private we can talk?" He glanced around at the almost empty restaurant, at the patrons still lingering over their lunches.

"I'm not sure what there is to say? You made your intentions pretty clear the other day, so..."

"I know. That's why I wanted us to talk. I think we got off on the wrong foot, and I'm really sorry about that." His face softened.

Jen bit the inside of her lip and studied his face for any hint of a lie. Or worse, a spell. Charlie said she didn't sense anything dark from him, and Jen trusted her cousin's senses more than her own, especially for people.

Once she had been decisive about Mark. Now something inside her wavered.

"I can't leave. My shift just started."

Mark cocked his head. "Aren't you the owner?"

"My aunt and I are the owners, but she had to run to the bank, and I need to be here at least through the dinner rush."

"When is dinner over?"

"It slows down around nine, and we close at ten," Jen said.

"So, that's when you get done?"

"Like you said, I'm the owner. I'm never done." Jen crossed her arms. "I need to get your orders in."

"Please, is there any chance at all that we could talk after you get off work? I don't care what time it is."

"What about that lawyer you talked about?"

"No lawyers." He held up his hands as if in surrender. "Just you and me."

"I don't know if I'd feel safe with you if I'm being honest," Jen said.

Mark took a step back. "You wouldn't feel safe? Is that why you ran?"

The genuine shock and disappointment on his face puzzled her. She shrugged and shook her head. How could he not know why she'd left? "I know how powerful you are, Mark, and that you can manipulate environments and people around you easily."

"Jen, I never tried to manipulate you. Did I do things

to impress you? Yeah, sure. What guy doesn't when he meets a beautiful woman."

Jens rolled her eyes. "Right."

"Do you honestly think I made you fall in love with me? You think I used a spell or a potion?"

"Devon told me the truth about you."

"Devon. And you believed him?" Mark's jaw tightened, and he stared off over her head. "Of course. That's how he ended up with the pendant I gave you, isn't it? You know what, my brother and his—" Mark gritted his teeth. "interference aren't important. What's important is that we talk, and hopefully, that you'll allow me to meet my daughter."

"Why now? It's been more than eight years."

"I'll explain everything if we can just sit down and talk. Really talk. Please? We can go to the most public place you deem safe. We'll drive separately. And I know you're in a relationship, so—"

"Yes, I am. I love him very much."

"I'm glad you're happy, Jen. I really am."

Jen jutted her chin in defiance. Happy didn't seem to be part of the equation today. She studied his face, searching for any sign that he was lying. There was none she could detect. But he'd lied before. She almost liked it better when he came at her—arrogant and just a little threatening. At least then, she knew where he stood. This about-face made her nervous. Still... did she have the right to cut him off from his daughter completely?

"Fine. I'll meet with you for a quick meal, and that's it."

"Thank you." A smile broke across his face and she let herself bask in it for a second. "I'll take it," he said, sounding almost grateful.

"The only reason I'm doing this is for Ruby's sake. I'll listen to you, but I can't make any promises."

"Understood." Mark's jovial expression shifted to somber. "Where should we eat? This is your town."

"We could go to Salty Dogs Bar and Grill off the Folly Beach pier. They serve food till eleven," Jen said.

"Salty Dogs it is. What time you get off?"

"I'm sure I can get out of here by eight. I'll just have Nancy close up for me. So around eight-thirty."

"Perfect. I'll see you there."

Jen pivoted on her heel, and her spying cousin Charlie and Tom both quickly looked away. Jen rolled her eyes. There would be no use in making up a story. Her cousin would see right through her.

"I'll be out in a minute," Jen said when she passed Charlie and Tom at the lunch counter. She quickly put in the orders for Mark and his friend. She grabbed a tea pitcher and ignored the uneasy anxiety that had wound itself into a tight knot around her heart. If he were sincere (a big if in her mind), then maybe they could work through this. Ruby had been asking about her daddy since she was little. Maybe she could give her daughter the one thing she didn't have—a father. Not just any father, though. A father who shared a power with his daughter that Jen sometimes just couldn't get a handle on. Her hand absently found her sister's Brigid pendant hanging around her neck, and she held it between her thumb and forefinger.

Please, holy goddess Brigid, let this be the right thing for Ruby and our family.

Jen dropped her hand and painted a smile across her face when she approached one of the patron tables. "Would you like some more iced tea?" The man nodded, and Jen didn't wait before she filled the glass and moved on to the next table.

CHAPTER 18

Daphne unlocked the door to her salon and let Lisa inside.

Lisa's first words were not totally unexpected. "Have you lost your mind?"

Jen sniffed and spun the stylist chair to face her sister. "Maybe."

Lisa took the two outfits on hangers she'd brought from home and arranged them over one of the armless chairs in the client waiting area, carefully smoothing out folds that could turn into wrinkles.

"Hey, to you too," Daphne quipped and locked the door before she let down the roller shades, used mainly to block out the afternoon sun and to stop the occasional prying eyes. "Glad to see you're in fine spirits tonight."

Lisa whirled on her toes. "I can't believe we're doing

this at all. Didn't we just meet last night to discuss how dangerous this guy is?"

"Sure. But is he? I mean, we don't really know what he wants or if he's truly dangerous, do we?" Daphne countered.

"Yes, we do," Lisa responded. She put her hands on her slim hips and gave her cousin a death glare. "He made it pretty clear he wants Ruby."

"Maybe he does. But in my experience, people never really reveal what they want right off the bat."

"So, you think he's hiding something?" Lisa scoffed. "How is that better?"

"It's not," Daphne patted Lisa's arm and headed to her stylist's chair. "But the only way to know is to talk to him."

"Good goddess, help us all." Lisa threw up her hands in surrender.

Lisa and Daphne gathered on either side of Jen. A squat, footed jewelry box covered in gold-leaf rested on the glass overlay of the modern ebony stylist station. The gold-painted steel legs of the station matched the three drawer handles that held Daphne's combs, brushes, scissors, and other tools.

"Do you want a quick cut?" Daphne ran her fingers through Jen's short dark hair and met her gaze in the oversized mirror affixed to the wall.

A nervous rumble filled Jen's stomach, and her skin felt electrically charged. In her mind, she could almost see a blue arc of energy forming at Daphne's touch. "No, I don't think so. Maybe some blue fringe?"

"Why not choose a color combo that really sends a message?" Lisa took a seat in the station next to Daphne's. She slipped off her four-inch heels and rested her stocking feet on the chair's steel footrest. "You know, in nature, frogs and insects have evolved color patterns that tell predators they're poisonous. Can you do that?"

"She's not a toad or a bug!" Daphne quipped. "And some guys dig different hair colors, so I don't think it will scare him off."

"Fine. But I want to go on the record as saying I do not like this." Lisa lay back in the chair and folded her arms across her chest.

"So noted, counselor." Jen threw a side-eyed glance at her sister. "If this will keep me from having to go to court and possibly fight him for custody of Ruby, then I'm all for it."

Lisa rolled her eyes. "I would never let it go that far."

"I think a blue fringe would be perfect. It always brings out your eyes," Daphne said, her palms resting lightly on Jen's shoulders. "I also have something for those bags under your eyes."

Jen shifted her gaze and stared at her haggard reflection. The creases around her eyes and across her forehead formed visible stripes. Silver strands threaded through her short black hair. Not enough for it to be salt-and-pepper, but enough for her to notice. Gone was the vivacious young woman Mark Stonehill had found attractive, replaced by a woman with responsibilities, a woman running on maybe four hours of sleep. The only thing keeping her going was adrenaline. The last thing she wanted was to poop out halfway through her meeting with Mark.

"Okay. Fine. Do your worst," Jen teased. "Can you also get rid of these grays?"

"Of course. Do you want them gone for good or just for tonight?"

"I think just for tonight. I'll let you color them next time you cut my hair."

Daphne grinned and squeezed Jen's shoulders. "Deal. I'll be back in just a second. I need to get something from my office."

"Sure." Jen nodded and watched Daphne disappear down the hall. Next to her, Lisa rocked from side to side in the spinning chair, sulking. "You know, Charlie met him this afternoon."

Lisa stopped rocking. "And?"

"She said she didn't sense anything evil from him."

"Oh well, that makes everything better... if he's not evil." Lisa clucked her tongue.

"I'm willing to hear him out. Please... I'd really appreciate your support."

Lisa let out a hefty sigh and glanced up at the ceiling for a second before looking Jen in the eye. "Fine. Just be careful. That's all I'm going to say. Text me from the restaurant... and the parking lot when you leave... and when you get home."

Jen laughed. "All right, Mom, I will."

"Here we go," Daphne said in a sing-song voice. In her hand, she carried a short, round, brushed metal tin. She spun Jen's chair around until Jen faced her, then she opened the tin and plucked two round reusable cotton pads soaked in an intoxicating, rose-scented solution. Daphne closed the tin and set it on her styling station next to Jen's jewelry box.

"Close your eyes and tip your head back a little," Daphne instructed. Jen did as she was told, and Daphne placed a pad over each eye. "These need to stay on for at least ten minutes. Longer is better. You can hold them there if you need to."

Jen pressed her fingers gently against the cool cotton. Within seconds, her entire face relaxed and a sense of calm spread through her body. "Holy mother goddess. What's in this?"

"My best spa treatment. There's a little alcohol-free witch hazel, rosewater, cucumber extract, and a minor spell for banishing exhaustion and stress."

"Well, it's wonderful." Jen inhaled deeply, letting the scent wash through her.

"Perfect. Keep up the deep breaths. I'm going to see what I can do about this tight posture of yours." With deft movements, Daphne placed her hands on Jen's shoulders. Her strong thumbs moved in wide circles as if she were searching for knots. "Lisa, why don't you show us the outfits you brought."

"Okay, but no judgment. I picked the best I could under the circumstances."

"I'm sure they're perfect," Daphne soothed. "You have wonderful style. And we can always zhuzh it up with a glamour to make her look a little badass. Something that says, I'm a strong, independent witch, and I will eff you up if you screw with me."

"Oh-kay," Lisa quirked an eyebrow.

"Not too badass, though. I'm still a community leader and a mom," Jen chimed in.

"Right," Lisa said. "That's not a tall order at all."

Jen let out a moan, and her shoulders tightened for a second and then completely relaxed. "Oh, my goddess, Daphne. You have magic fingers."

"I really should get you and Lisa in to see my new massage therapist, Marina. Talk about magic fingers. She's awesome."

"Between this and these pads, I may not look great, but at least I'll feel good," Jen said.

"Oh, you'll look good if I have any say," Lisa said, holding up one hanger. She spun it around so Jen and Daphne could get a good look at the short black dress that looked like it hugged in all the right places. Lisa opened the oversized leather bag she carried everywhere and retrieved a pair of snakeskin heels. "A little dangerous maybe, but definitely good."

Jen removed the pads from her eyes and inspected the dress. Her mouth hung open. "Wow. That is gorgeous."

"It is. And I'll make sure you feel like a million bucks wearing it," Daphne said.

"I would take feeling like a hundred bucks at this point," Jen chuckled.

"That's the thing, isn't it? When you feel good, you'll radiate that feeling, and people will notice it. Trust me. I make my living this way. I make sure people feel good on the inside so they can see what I do to them on the outside." Daphne patted Jen's shoulders. "That should do it for now."

"Right and a little magic doesn't hurt either," Lisa quipped.

"No, it doesn't," Daphne chirped.

"For the record, I think we're focusing on the wrong things," Lisa said a bit sharply. Daphne's eye's popped wide in surprise. Lisa tempered her tone and said, "I'm more worried about him kidnapping you and holding you hostage until you give him what he wants," Lisa shook out the black dress and replaced it on the back of the chair again and held up a sexy, blood-red dress with a strappy back.

Daphne's mouth formed a delighted O. "That is gorgeous," she gushed. "Where do you wear this stuff? I mean, I never see you in anything except suits and those raggedy Daisy Dukes you wear to Friday night dinner."

"Mainly to work functions," Lisa shrugged. "I hardly ever wear this one because it clashes with my hair."

"We should make your hair blonder, so you'll feel good about wearing it."

"Daphne, I don't want to dye my hair," Lisa said.

"Hello—witch here. You don't have to." Daphne gestured to herself.

Jen giggled at the banter. It felt good to laugh. "You know, I don't think he's going to kidnap me. He's powerful, and if he wanted to do that, he would've already done it." Jen pointed to the dress in her sister's hands. "And while I agree with Daphne, that dress is gorgeous — I do not have the guts to wear something that sexy."

Lisa shrugged. "Probably for the best."

"I think I should at least hear him out. He was really nice and reasonable this afternoon."

"Reasonable," Lisa muttered and shook her head. "You were the one who was scared when he showed up. Are you saying you're not anymore?"

"No..." Jen closed her eyes and tried to sort out her feelings. Was she still scared of Mark? "I don't know what I am. But I don't think he's going to hurt me."

"Great." Lisa rubbed her eyes and pinched the bridge of her nose as if she had a headache coming on. She took a long pause before continuing.

"No matter what anybody else says, I think this is dangerous. I don't like it. Not one bit."

"So you've said." Daphne retrieved a brush and a fine-tooth comb from the top drawer of her styling station. "Many, many times. We get it." She gently nudged Jen's chair to face the mirror again. "I am serious about Marina, Jen. You should make an appointment and let her work some of these knots out. It would do you a world of wonders." Daphne ran the brush through Jen's short hair.

"I know. I just don't know when I'll have time for that," Jen said. "Between the restaurant, adding catering to my business, and now Mark showing up, I don't know if I'm coming or going some days."

"Well, self-care is still important. You don't want to end up a frazzled mess." Daphne switched to the comb and ran it lightly through Jen's bangs. When she finished combing, the bangs had changed to an electric blue. "You have your first catering gig this week, right?"

"Yep. A luncheon for the Chamber of Commerce on Friday." The familiar thread of anxiety for this new venture wove its way through Jen's chest.

Lisa sat back down in the chair next to Jen and chewed on her thumbnail. "Can we at least appeal to Brigid? I know I would feel better."

"And it is all about you," Daphne muttered.

Jen met her sister's gaze in the mirror and grinned. "I think that's a great idea. I'd love that."

Lisa blew out a breath. "Thank you. I also want to put a spell on your necklace. There's already a protection spell on it, but I want to put a tracking spell on it too, just in case."

Daphne cocked her head. "Of course you do."

Jen defended her sister. "It couldn't hurt, Daphne."

Lisa ignored Daphne's little jibes. "Great. I need a candle."

"I have some candles over there, along with a holder and some matches." Jen pointed over her shoulder to the cute navy canvas backpack hanging from a hook nearby. "I also have my pouch of crystals if you need them."

"Perfect." Lisa dug through Jen's bag and then made quick work of setting up a make-shift altar atop one of the styling stations using a square of black velvet that Jen had wrapped around her candles. Lisa laid out a five-pointed star with various crystals, then placed the candle in its holder in the center of the pentagon.

Lisa gestured for Jen and Daphne to join her around the altar. Lisa dragged a match against the side of the box, and for a second, the sharp odor of phosphorus and heat filled the air. Lisa touched the wick of the candle with the flame. When it lit, she blew out the match and shoved it back into the box of matches upside down, the still hot tip facing away from the unlit matches. The three of them joined hands, closed their eyes, and tilted their heads up toward the ceiling.

"Great warrior goddess Brigid, protector, healer, I light this candle and beseech you to prepare us for the battles ahead that we must all face together and alone," Lisa began her prayer. "May we be protected from harm. Especially our sister Jen as she endeavors to protect our dear

Ruby from any who would do her harm or use her ill. Walk with us as you walk over this earth, sharing your power and grace. Keep us free from that which threatens our well-being, especially our sister Jen. So mote it be."

"So mote it be," Jen and Daphne echoed.

The cousins released their hands and stared at the flame of the thin beeswax candle. It would take about thirty minutes for the candle to burn out and finish the request to the goddess.

Lisa raised her hand and wiggled her fingers at her sister. "Now, let me see the pendant. It's time to put that tracking spell on it."

Jen rolled her eyes but didn't argue while she unfastened the delicate clasp and handed over the necklace.

CHAPTER 19

J en climbed out of her truck and straightened the black, linen cocktail dress she'd borrowed from Lisa. A wave of shyness came over her. The dress displayed more curves in public than her normal t-shirts and jeans. She slammed the Ford's door as if showing her determination to just do this, not bothering to lock it. The truck had a longstanding spell on it to keep away anyone who might be tempted to take it for a joyride. Plus, the face of the stereo was missing, a definite disincentive to thieves.

A quick glance around the parking lot made her stomach churn a little. Nearly every space of the packed lot was filled. The place would certainly be crowded. No chance for any funny business from Mark. She put her parking ticket in her purse and slung the gold chain strap over her shoulder—a hard boxy thing covered in burnished black satin and adorned with beads.

Lisa had insisted she take the purse instead of her backpack. It barely held her wallet, keys, lipstick, phone, and the small pouch of crystals she never left home without. Her hand drifted to the pendant dangling from her neck; she touched for luck the Brigid's cross from Lisa's circle of support. The gold pentacle bracelet she wore mainly for special occasions dangled against her forearm.

"Here goes nothing. Keep me safe, Brigid," she whispered and walked past the rows of parked vehicles to the exit.

Jen spotted Mark across the street. He waited for her at the base of the stairs leading to the restaurant on stilts. It adjoined the long pier that stretched out over the ocean. He wore a pair of black jeans, pressed with a crease, and an emerald green polo, chosen, she knew, to set off his piercing green eyes.

A thrum of nerves prompted her to run her hands over her hips, straightening the linen dress one more time. She rubbed her hands over the skirt to secretly wipe the sweat from her palms. She'd have the dress dry-cleaned before returning it to Lisa and was glad she'd rejected her sister's four-inch heels. She'd stuck with her own sensible black flats, which made walking to the restaurant easier.

At 8:15 PM the sun hung low in the sky. If they timed it right, they might even get to see the sunset from the deck of the restaurant. Thick puffy clouds near the horizon had begun to turn purple-gray, surrounded by hues of pink and yellow.

Jen could see Mark rocking back and forth on his feet. He kept scanning the street. He hadn't seen her get out of the truck or noticed her pausing on the sidewalk, waiting for a break in the traffic. Part of her wanted to hide behind a car to see what he would do if she didn't show up. But another part of her wanted answers. Wanted the truth.

She pressed her hand against her belly, looked both ways, and crossed the street, making sure he could see her now. When she came into view, he waved, and a bright smile spread across his handsome, aristocratic face. Goddess help her, even with everything she knew about him, her body reacted to the sight of him. She hated that just the sight of him could still send a pulse of desire into her core.

Ben. She had to remember her relationship with Ben. It didn't matter that he hadn't contacted her since their fight. She still loved him, and she knew he loved her. But she wasn't quite ready to forgive him yet.

It doesn't matter where I stand with Ben. This is a meeting with Ruby's father to get more information and to hopefully make peace. Mark can't have it in his head that he deserves custody. I am not cheating on Ben. This is about Ruby, not me.

Mark took her hands when she approached and held them out to get a better look at her.

"Wow," he said, appreciation lighting up his face. He

looked her up and down, seeming to admire every inch of her. "You're beautiful as ever. I love the blue." He pointed to her bangs.

"Thanks." Jen gently slipped her hands out of his and let them fall to her side. "You look nice, too. In fact, I may be overdressed for this place. It's mainly a bar and grill, not a white tablecloth restaurant. Mostly tourists will be here this time of year."

The words rushed out of her mouth and her cheeks heated. *I am not cheating on Ben. I am only having dinner for Ruby's sake.*

"Whatever it is, it smells great, and" Mark's gaze held hers for a second. "I get to see you."

"Right." She let out a nervous laugh. "Well, I'm starving." She broke his stare and pressed her hand to her belly again, as if to find... what? Stability? Comfort? Strength?

"Shall we?" she said.

She followed Mark to the hostess, standing behind him in the crowded alcove while he gave his name and asked for a table outside for two. She had her eye on a spot in the corner where they could wait until their names came up, but to her surprise, the young woman picked up two oversized menus, flashed a dazzling smile at Mark, and said, "Certainly, sir. Follow me."

She led Jen and Mark past the waiting diners through the main dining room, past the bar, and out onto the deck that adjoined the Folly Pier. They threaded their way through the many tables with open umbrellas and chatting diners until they reached the only vacant table. Holly, as she brightly introduced herself to Mark but not Jen, gestured to the cozy seating as if it had been reserved for them.

"Here you go." Holly pulled out a chair for Jen, keeping her eyes on Mark. "You're so lucky tonight. This is the best seat in the house for sunset." She placed a menu down in front of Jen and then one in front of Mark.

"I'll arrange for water and come back to take your drink orders," she said, and left them to look over the menu, returning, Jen supposed, to the diners she'd abandoned to take care of Mark when he'd stepped up to ask for a table.

The Atlantic Ocean shimmered in the sunlight's last rays, and from her vantage point, Jen saw the clean white sand of Folly Beach stretching to the right and left of the pier.

"Did you make a reservation?" Jen asked as she checked the sheet of specials clipped inside the menu.

Mark didn't look up from the wine and beer list. "I tried, but they don't take them," he said casually. "Would you like to share a bottle of wine with me?"

"Um..." Jen swallowed hard. "Since I'm driving, I'll just stick with iced tea."

"Okay, tea it is." He set the wine list aside and moved on to his menu.

Jen glanced around the deck, full of men and women in shorts and flip-flops. Some tan, some sunburned. At a long nearby table surrounded by six children and two weary-looking couples, Jen overheard one of the school-aged boys say he hated fish.

A busboy came by with glasses of ice water for them and left quickly. Jen took a sip and said, "Huh... this place is so crowded. I'm shocked we got such a good table and so fast, too."

Mark continued studying his menu. Without looking up, he said offhandedly, "Maybe it's easier to seat two people. Most of those in line looked like they were with big parties." He peered over the menu, and the emerald green in his eyes, hooked her for a moment. Jen blinked hard to ground herself.

"Yes, but..." She leaned forward with her elbows on the table and looked him straight in the eye. A brief smile played at the corners of her mouth. "You did this, didn't you? Got us in without waiting and the best table in the house?"

A sly grin played on Mark's lips. "I might've put an intention out into the universe. That's all. Everything else shifted on its own."

Jen chuckled and shook her head. "An intention, right? Sounds more like magic to me."

"It's all magic isn't it?" he asked. "You do it, too. You just put it in the hands of a goddess or nature or whatever it is witches do."

"I suppose so." She studied the menu again.

"Mmm..." Mark mused. "The shrimp and grits look good. How are the sea scallops?"

"Good," Jen said. "Usually fresh."

She closed her menu and set it aside. "In fact, I think that's what I'm going to have. The sea scallops special with grilled asparagus."

"I think I'll try the shrimp and grits."

"Good choice." Jen shifted in her seat and tried to ignore him staring at her from across the table, the same way he had when they'd dated so long ago.

Once the server came and took their order, someone named Annie this time, Jen crossed her arms in front of her and placed them on the table. A flutter of panic filled her chest.

Mark folded his hands together and stared down at them for a moment. "You have no idea how often I think about you."

"Devon was supposed to take care of that." She bit her lower lip. "He told me he'd make you forget me."

"Devon..." Mark made a sour face as if he'd just sucked a lemon slice. "How could you think I'd ever forget you? You were the one for me, Jen. My person."

"Mark," Jen whispered and shook her head. "My aunt would tell you we're not limited to the love of one person."

"I am."

"No. You're not. Or, at least, I hope you're not. It's been almost nine years. And I'm in love with someone else now."

"I know," Mark said.

"I wish Devon had just done what he said he would. It would've spared you a lot of pain."

"My brother's never been exactly trustworthy or altruistic. I'm sure he didn't help you escape out of the goodness of his heart."

"He wanted the pendant you gave me. The one with the strange symbol on it."

"Did he?" Mark narrowed his eyes. "And you gave it to him?"

"I did, and he helped me get out of your mother's house unseen."

Mark chuckled, but Jen sensed there was more pain than humor in it. "So can I ask you why you left? Was I not paying enough attention to you?"

Jen looked away, at the waves breaking against the shore. For a moment, she wished she were walking in the surf instead of having to explain her departure from Mark's clutches so long ago. But facing him was the price she had to pay to keep Ruby safe. She turned away from the power of the sea and said, "Mark, you were always attentive. Always the perfect boyfriend. Too perfect. It's like I was living some sort of fairy tale."

"Then why?" he asked with a plaintive note.

Could she trust that earnestness? "Because I learned the truth." She looked down at her lap for a moment. "Or at least I thought I had."

Mark shook his head as if in disgust. "I know I

should've told you I was a sorcerer up front. But I didn't want you to come into our relationship with some pre-defined notion. I know the reputation my kind has. That we're into blood magic and human sacrifices to pay the price of our magic. I swear on my father's grave, we're not like that. Not all of us anyway."

Jen cocked an eyebrow. "So, you weren't planning to sacrifice me and take the baby?"

Her question threw Mark back in his seat. "What? Oh my god, no. Of course not. How could you even think that?"

Jen had a list of reasons, many of them polished to a high sheen over the years as she reflected painfully on Mark's actions, but now she merely said, "I don't know. I just—I overheard your mother talking and your brother—"

Mark shook his head and sneered at her. "My brother is a piece of shit who doesn't care for anyone but himself. And I'm not sure what my mother would have said to make you think that, but it's not true." His jaw tightened. "Do you know what the pendant I gave you does?"

Jen leaned back in her chair. She suddenly felt very cruel. How could she have made such a leap? "No."

"It protects the wearer from all enemies that might wish to harm the wearer," he said. "It's been in my family for over a hundred years. I gave it to you because all I wanted to do was protect you."

Jen furrowed her brow. Where was this coming from?

She flashed on her life in San Francisco for a brief second. "From my enemies? The closest thing I had to an enemy was Megan Price. She wanted my job as sous chef, but I wasn't in any danger from her."

Mark wagged his head as though he were taking in her explanation. "Fair enough. It was probably just my own paranoia at the time. I was taking on more responsibility in my family's company. I had a lot of people around me, including my little brother, rooting for me to fail."

This conversation was taking a turn Jen hadn't expected. She hadn't planned on Mark making a pitch for her sympathy. "Other sorcerers?"

"Yes."

"Would they've hurt you?" Certainly, she needed to ensure Ruby's safety, but that didn't mean she wished Mark harm. A flood of compassion suddenly warmed her to Mark's predicament back then. Perhaps she hadn't seen things from his perspective. Perhaps she'd got it all wrong.

"Possibly, and the easiest way to do it, I mean for them to get to me, would have been to hurt you."

Jen blew out a breath and wished their food would come. She'd not prepared for the intensity of this conversation like she thought she had.

"Listen, Jen, I do understand your concerns. My brother is very good at seeing through to the heart of people's fears. Then he feeds it up to them, scares the hell out of them, and manipulates them. It must've been terrifying to think I could allow anyone to sacrifice your life. I wish you had come to me, so I could've shown you the truth."

Jen's resolve wavered in the face of this new information. She'd left home that evening determined to hold off any attempt by Mark to insinuate himself into Ruby's life. Now she felt pulled asunder by his vulnerability, his tale of rejection, and pain she had caused.

"I was young and pregnant," she explained, "and more alone than I'd ever been in my life." She shrugged. "So, I ran home. Where I felt safe. Where I knew I could protect myself and my child." Then a switch turned on. Why should she be on the defensive? She had done nothing wrong. She shrugged and something lifted from her shoulders. Some hold Mark had on her as they'd spoken. He'd worked his charm on her, as he had all those years ago when they'd been dating. But now she saw through him, and now it wasn't enough. Now she had Ben and could tell a man with real depth. A man who didn't need spells and sorcery to win her over. She looked at him directly and said, "And honestly, Devon scared the hell out of me."

"I'm so sorry, Jen."

She met his eyes. "Me, too."

A picture of Ruby, happy all these years came to mind. But was she sorry? Really?

"Here we go. Sea scallops?" Jen raised her hand, and the server put the hot dish in front of her, slicing through the tension created by their revealing conversation. The server placed Mark's plate on the table. "And shrimp and grits."

"Thank you. Looks delicious."

Jen unfolded the napkin and placed it in her lap.

"Anything else I can get you? More tea?"

"Sure, that'd be great," Mark said.

Jen picked up her fork and sliced through the succulent mollusk, and the two of them ate in an awkward silence.

CHAPTER 20

After the server whisked their plates away, the setting sun left an indigo sky in its wake. Mark studied Jen across the table. He was failing. He thought he had her for a moment, but in the end, none of his usual charms had worked on her, something he wasn't used to. His charm was usually the one thing he could count on. He couldn't let her slip away so easily. Too much was riding on her and on his daughter.

"So... can we discuss Ruby?"

Jen glanced up and smiled, but it looked forced to him. "Of course."

"Her birthday is next week. Are you having a party for her?"

"We are. It's harder since her birthday is during the summer, but she's having a friend... well her only friend really... over to the house Sunday night for cake and a sleepover. The family is celebrating Friday night since that's when we all get together."

"So, she doesn't have many friends?" Mark leaned forward with his elbows on the table and filed away the information for later use.

"Not really. She's a bit of a free spirit, and sometimes I think she scares the other kids a little, to be honest." Jen shrugged, and a sadness molded her delicate features.

"Does it bother her?"

"If it does, she's never said. She's amazing. Smart. Funny. Observant. But I worry about her being lonely. I always had my sister and my cousins when I was growing up. You know what that's like, I'm sure."

"Are you talking about Devon?" Mark asked. He scoffed to himself.

"Yeah. You're brothers, so at least you weren't alone."

"We also went to school with kids of other sorcerers, so we had an easier time making friends."

"Right." Jen stared past him, her eyes distant as if she were a million miles away. "You should probably know she takes after you."

"She does?" He tried to tamp down his excitement about this bit of news.

"Yeah, she does. Her magic came in when she was a baby. And even now, sometimes she's hard to control. Anytime she wishes for something, it just happens."

"Hmmm... like putting an intention out into the universe and letting it unfold."

Jen sighed. "Yeah. Something like that."

"You know, I can help you learn to control her wishing. It can get out of hand if you don't know how to handle it."

"How would you do that?"

"I can teach you some things. Things my mother used to do."

"Are you going to try to take her away from me?" Jen blurted out. Fully present now.

Was she joking, or had she seen into his motives? "No. I'm sorry if I made you think that. I just want to meet her, maybe get a chance to know her. You're going to need me later, whether or not you realize it. When she's sixteen and comes fully into her power, she could be overwhelming."

"You know, that's what I'm secretly afraid of," she admitted, her voice sounding like a child's. She exhaled, and her tense body relaxed. "I've never told anybody that."

"Thank you for telling me. I know it must be hard. I um... I know your boyfriend is DOL. And I know their stance on sorcerers."

"His parents were killed by sorcerers."

"I'm sorry to hear that. That must've been very traumatic for him."

"It was."

"Does he know who they were?"

"Yes. And what his parents were investigating."

Mark traced a line down the sweat of his tea glass. "Oh?" He held his breath, waiting for her answer.

"They were investigating sorcerers who'd been selling illegal weapons to vampires in the Northwest."

Slowly, he expelled the breath and relaxed. Ben didn't know what his family had done to him. "We're not all like that, Jen. Everything my companies do is on the up and up. We don't sell illegal spells or potions and certainly not illegal weapons."

"What exactly does your company do?"

"We run an umbrella company and have many things in our portfolio. Including the restaurant you used to work at in San Francisco, which you already know. I personally run a business that centers on helping people reach their best life. For the right fee, I will help anyone fulfill their potential."

"What do you do, grant them wishes?" Jen chuckled.

Her laugh sent a thrill down his back. After all these years, she could still do that to him. "Not exactly. I see into their hearts — see what they truly want and what's stopping them. I help them overcome that obstacle."

"So you're a guru then?"

He attempted the practiced smile that he knew drew people into his lair, but then let his lips soften into a more natural expression. What was she doing to him? "No. I'm just a guy who wants people to succeed. I wanted you to succeed when we met."

"So, you... what? Looked into my heart?"

"I did." He chuckled at the memory. "You were this little spitfire, and I saw it all — your dreams of owning restaurants across the country, being a superstar chef, even kids. And I wanted to give it all to you. We could have been happy together, Jen. We could've had the fairy tale." Where was it coming from, this pang, this sudden longing for something lost? It had no place in his plan.

"I know." She stared down at her hands.

"And you gave it all up for Ruby. She'll probably never know exactly what you sacrificed for her."

"It was the right thing to do. I'd do it again. I don't know if I'd want her growing up in a world where wishes are encouraged. She needs discipline first. I mean, the last thing I want is for her to end up like Devon."

"I would never let that happen," Mark said.

"Mark, Ruby and I have a good life here. A happy life, and I want it to stay that way. She doesn't know anything about you."

"Has she ever asked?" He surprised himself at the yearning he felt for the answer.

"A few times. But I've always redirected her attention to something else." Jen licked her lips and reached for her tea. She drained the glass, until the last of the amber liquid was gone, and only ice was left in the glass. "But she's getting older, and I know one day I'll have to tell her the truth."

"Jen, I will do whatever it takes to win your trust. To win her trust." When he entered the restaurant, he'd been so sure of his plan. But something about Jen was throwing him off-center.

"It's not my trust you're going to have to win so much as it is my family's."

"Then let me win their trust." He held his hands up. "I promise. No funny stuff. I know you always hated that."

"I do hate it, and you're likable without it."

A ghost of a grin curved his lips. "I appreciate that." Mark shifted in his chair. "So your boyfriend must really hate sorcerers."

"Yeah, he does."

"Maybe I should meet him, too. Prove to him we're not all evil. We're just people. And I'm sure there are plenty of wicked witches out there, otherwise, he wouldn't have a job, but it doesn't mean all witches are bad, does it?"

"No, I guess it doesn't." Her face softened. "My family has dinner together on Friday nights, seven sharp at my father's house. Every week. I have a luncheon I'm catering Friday, but I'll be home before then if all goes well.

"Catering?"

"Yeah, I'm branching out. Trying to get my restaurant's name out there. I'd like to grow it if I can."

Mark put his elbows on the table, leaned in and smiled. "I can see it now. Franchises of The Kitchen Witch Cafe across the country."

Jen's face lit up as she toyed with her napkin. "Wouldn't that be something?"

"If anybody can make it happen, Jen, you can. I always liked that about you. You would set your mind on something and then do it."

Jen's cheeks turned dark pink, and she shifted in her seat. "Thanks."

"So, who will be at this Friday night dinner?" he asked.

"My sister and her boyfriend. My father. Ruby, of course. My aunt and my cousin, Daphne. I don't know if her boyfriend will be there. Me and you, I suppose, if you want to come."

A sharp pain drilled through the center of his forehead. He couldn't imagine wanting to gather with his entire family every week. The concept seemed so foreign, but he just said, "So, a full house."

"Yes. But we enjoy each other's company. And it's a good way to stay connected."

What else could he say? "I wouldn't miss it. I really appreciate you giving me an opportunity to meet my daughter."

"Sure. We'll see how it goes. But I will not force her to be in your life, and you shouldn't want that either."

"I don't."

"Good. Then you can meet your daughter Friday night. Be prepared to meet her chickens. And probably her stuffed animals." Jen laughed and dropped her napkin on the table.

Mark chuckled. "Sounds perfect."

CHAPTER 21

"Evan."

The voice filtered through his sleeping brain, and he burrowed deeper into his sleeping bag.

"Evan. Wake up."

He groaned and opened his eyes. His heart sped up when he found himself outside the tent fully dressed, hiking boots on, backpack hooked over his shoulders. How was this possible? He'd just been in his sleeping bag. He twisted his hand around his wrist. His father had joined their wrists and ankles together with a thin bungee cord and tied it in a knot. If Evan tried to sleepwalk again, a jerk of the cord would awaken his father. No cord bound his wrist. A pale blue fog clung to the ground, thick and shimmering with an odd light.

I'm dreaming.

Her shadow appeared at the edge of the woods, semi-opaque at first. She flickered, lit by the pale light in the fog. She beckoned him forward, and her voice drifted through his head.

"Come play hide and seek with me."

Evan shook his head. "No. That's a little kid's game. I'm too old for it. Plus, I think you're trying to trick me."

"Why would I trick you?"

"So I'll help you. I already told you. My mom is going to help you. She's an investigator for..."

Was the DOL a police agency? He didn't know for sure, but the ghost didn't have to know that.

"... the police. She's looking for you now. I just want to hang out with my dad and enjoy what's left of our trip. Please, just go away."

"Your mom isn't here. You are. And you can see me." The suddenness of her appearance in front of him startled him, and he took a step back from her.

After putting space between them, she was shorter than him. Blood clumped in her long brown hair forming strings that matched the striped blood pattern on the shoulder of her glowing white t-shirt. An oozing crack in the skin on her head made his stomach turn. He squeezed his eyes shut.

"I don't want to look at you like this. I don't like blood."

An icy finger scraped across his cheek. Her finger. He couldn't stop himself from shivering at her touch.

"Open your eyes," she whispered.

"No." He clenched his jaw.

"Please?" The weight of her sadness washed over and through him, pulling him down into her emotion. "Please, Evan. I promise not to scare you anymore."

"Back up," Evan said, his voice husky with sadness and fear. "You're too close."

"Better?"

Evan waited a beat and finally opened his eyes. She stood three feet away from him now. He let out a heavy breath and stopped shivering. Her straight, sandy hair shimmered in the moonlight filtering through the trees, and he could even make out her pale blue eyes. In life, she'd been pretty. Homecoming queen pretty. Petite and thin, she couldn't have weighed over 100 lbs. The feelings of dread that made him shrink away from her had dissipated, and relief swept through him. "Thank you."

"Please come with me. I have to show you something."

He felt a ping of alarm. They'd warned him she might do this. "I can't. I promised my mom and dad I wouldn't follow you again."

"What will it hurt? You know this is a dream."

Evan glanced around at the campsite again. His fathere snored inside the tent. "Am I sleepwalking again?"

"You're not, I promise." She touched her hand to a drift of the fog, and the thick clouds drew up around him like a misty blanket. He froze in place, and the pressure in his chest made breathing hard. It enveloped him, blinding

171

him for a moment. A little scream escaped from him when something grabbed him by the wrist.

"It's okay, Evan."

Evan opened his eyes and found himself in the yard (if you could call it that) of a decrepit, old cabin. Stilts, on the front of the cabin, leveled it to the angle of the steep mountain terrain. A neat stack of firewood filled the space beneath the wide front porch. Patches of brown scrubby grass broke up the ruddy brown soil, and gray granite rocks jutted in places. An old brown and white Chevy truck sat in front of the cabin. Rust had eaten away at the truck's metal siding, and it looked brittle along the bottom edges. Large patches of the dark, grim substance covered the truck's hood.

Several old tires made an enormous pile on one side of the property along the wall of what appeared to be a barn. From the bottom steps, Evan could see a folding chair like the one his dad always brought to Evan's soccer games. A row of beer cans lined the top of the banister running the length of the porch. More cans were scattered at the base of the porch with distinct holes in them. Bullet holes.

"It's just a dream," he reminded himself. From the corner of his eye, he could see Michelle floating, still looking as she had in life, pretty. Cheerful even.

"Where is this place?" he asked her. "Can you tell me an address or show me a name? Something I can tell my mom. She's an investigator. She can find stuff about this guy, but she can't do it without information."

An icy hand trailed from his shoulder, down his arm to his hand. She lifted his fingers with hers and slightly tugged at him, moving forward without saying a word.

Once they got to the top step of the porch, her voice echoed in his head again, an ominous warning, "Stay quiet. He's drunk this time of day. He should be passed out, but sometimes he's not."

Evan stopped at the front door. "I thought this was a dream."

"It is. I'm sorry I scared you, okay? He can't see you." Her voice whispered across his senses. "But just to be on the safe side. Stay quiet and stay close to me."

He gave her a curt nod, and the next thing he knew, he was inside the house.

Definitely a dream.

Her fingers felt solid against him, distracting him from the man lying on the dingy, brown plaid couch, passed out and snoring. The stench of rotting meat choked Evan. He jerked his hand away from hers to cover his nose and mouth. "I think your friend is already dead," Evan said. The stench made his eyes water.

"No, she's not. I swear. I wouldn't bring you here if she were dead."

"How can I smell this if this is a dream?"

"Please come," she beckoned. Her entire body changed, and the pretty glowing girl melted away, leaving behind only the broken specter still covered in blood. She held out one hand, summoning him down the hall to the place where he smelled that terrible rot. Evan shook his head no and stepped back.

He'd had a few spirit dreams before. Enough that he should've realized he had no control here and no way to stop her from moving him from one place to the other. He blinked and found himself outside a closed door with a padlock on it.

"She's in here." Michelle pressed her hand against the door. "Her name's Jenna Routh. Tell your mom."

Evan nodded. "I will." He looked over his shoulder at a door slightly ajar. In the shadows, he could make out an unmade bed. "Jenna Routh," he muttered. "Got it. What's in there?" He pointed to the room across from the padlocked door.

"Nothing you want to see right now. You need to go tell your mother..." She tried to push him away, but her hands went right through him.

A buzzing filled his head as if he'd stumbled into a hive of bees. His breath shortened, and he couldn't resist the dark crack opening to the other room. He took a step toward it.

"Evan, no. Don't go in there. That's..."

Evan pushed the door open. The hinge squeaked, reminding him of the chains on the porch swing at his Uncle Jack's house. He reached his hand inside, feeling along the wall for a light switch. When he found the switch, it clicked, but the light didn't come on. A fresh wave of the stifling rot wrapped around him. If he stayed here much longer, he'd be sick.

"Evan, we have to go. He's awake." Michelle's voice startled him out of his reverie.

"What the fuck do you think you're doing here, boy?"

Evan spun to find the man, no longer sleeping, glaring at him with nearly black eyes. Astonishment froze Evan to the spot. "You can see me?"

"You're fucking right, I can see you." The man raised a wooden bat. Evan heard the bat scream through the air, aimed at his head. The bat moved in slow motion, but so did Evan. He ducked the dingy, thick piece of carved maple.

A scream clogged his throat. "This isn't real! This is just a dream!" Then his eyes flew open. He jerked himself up, taking his father's arm and leg with him. Evan fought to get himself out of the bungee cords but made the tangle worse.

His father snorted awake. "Whuh-what's going on?" he said drowsily. "What happened? Evan, wait. We're still connected." His father's firm hand grabbed his wrist. The heaviness of his dad's touch broke through his terror, and Evan stilled for a moment before he burst into uncontrollable tears. His father worked the knots loose, freeing Evan.

"Can we go home? Puh-puh-please Dad," Evan

managed through the heaving sobs. His father's arms went around him, pulling him close.

"What happened?"

"Please. Can we just leave?" He continued to weep.

"Of course, we can leave," his father said in a soothing voice that both surprised Evan and calmed him. His father usually hated tears. "We'll leave at first light."

CHAPTER 22

A dense fog settled over the mountain trail and with it a stillness that left Scott Carver's skin tingly and his heart jittery. He hated to admit that navigating the parenthood of a teen was harder than he expected. Was it because Evan was sensitive? Or so sulky? He didn't remember sulking so much when he was Evan's age. His father would never have put up with it.

Scott glanced over his shoulder. Evan lumbered behind him on the trail. For someone who had awoken so terrified, Scott didn't understand why his son wasn't leading the way.

"Come on, Evan," he called with a look back. "Make sure you keep up with me."

"I'm trying. It's just the fog is so thick," his son answered.

"It's not that thick. I can still see you behind me and the trail up ahead," Scott countered.

Why did the boy always have to be so contrary? Scott kept moving, taking care on the worst of the slopes. A crow cawed above his head, drawing his attention, and it shocked him a little when he couldn't see the tops of the trees through the fog. All the more reason to get out of this place. He'd never been in a forest so quiet. Somehow, the girl's spirit must've affected the weather.

Don't be crazy, Scott. Ghosts can't make it rain or foggy. The weatherman had been wrong.

Maybe if they put some distance between this ghost, his son would find some peace. Lord knows they both needed a good night's sleep. Evan had proved himself too old for the string trick.

There had to be some way to shield the boy from his sensitivity. Charlie would not like it, but when they got home, he would sit down with her and discuss how to protect their son. His ideas might be hard for Charlie to hear, but what if this accessibility to the spirits became worse for Evan just as it had for her? That thought turned his stomach. He'd watched Charlie suffer for over ten years—seeing ghosts, hearing voices, thrashing awake from nightmares.

Of course, back then, he'd been too arrogant to understand he'd only made her suffering worse. Sometimes he thought back to when they were married. Could he have made a difference for her if he'd been supportive instead of an asshole? Would they still be married if only he'd believed her?

These questions would haunt him for the rest of his life. She was haunted. Maybe he deserved to be haunted too. He didn't want to push his way on her. Yes, he would have to work with Charlie to protect Evan better from bombardment, but she needed to listen to his ideas, too.

The sound of his footsteps crunching against the gravel beneath his feet and the occasional slap of water from a puddle from yesterday's rain brought him out of his reverie. He stopped and turned.

"Evan?"

Scott's heart leaped into his throat. The dense fog formed a wall so thick behind him, he could barely see through it.

"Evan? Evan Michael Carver, answer me!"

Only the eerie stillness of the woods and the occasional drop of rain still clinging to the leaves overhead answered him. He turned and began up the trail again.

"Evan Carver!" he called every few feet.

He walked another thirty minutes before he realized he was alone on the trail. Really alone. The sharp focus he used when dealing with emergencies at work kicked in, and he immediately did two things.

First, he called the ranger station to let them know that his thirteen-year-old son had gotten separated from him on the trail. The ranger agreed to meet him with a team at his position on the trail, but it would be at least an hour before they could get there.

Once the call ended, Scott took an orange strip of plastic that hunters sometimes used to mark their way through the woods and wrapped it around a sapling just off the trail where Evan had possibly disappeared. Why hadn't he paid more attention the last time he turned around to check on his son?

Dread filled his chest as he thought about the next action to take. He would have to call his ex-wife to let her know that, somehow, he'd lost their son in the woods. He stared down at the phone, took a deep breath, and selected Charlie's number from his Favorites. It rang twice before she picked up.

"Hello?"

"Scott?" Charlie waited a beat. All she could hear was heavy breathing. She pulled the phone away from her ear to look at the caller details again.

"Scott, I know it's you. What's going on?"

"Charlie," Scott said with gravel in his voice. The tone of suffering sent a chill skittering down her back, setting off alarms in her head.

"What's happened? Is Evan okay?"

"I lost him," Scott said.

The image of him raking his hand through his hair

with an expression of near madness on his face popped into her head.

"I don't know what happened. We were coming down the trail, heading home. The fog... god the fog is so thick. It's almost like it swept him away to some other place. I know that's not possible, but..."

"What? Wait a minute," she said as alarm climbed up from her throat. "You're not making any sense. Just slow down and start from the beginning."

She listened to him tell her about Evan's dream and being awakened by him and the intensity of Evan's terror. How he tried to comfort their son.

"Naturally, we left, so we packed up early and started away from the campsite, back toward the trail."

Charlie couldn't believe she was hearing this. A wave of panic swept through her, but she tamped it down to focus on the details of Scott's story.

"The fog is so thick," Scott said again. "Evan kept falling behind. You'd think for someone so scared, he would've moved like his feet were on fire."

Charlie got a vision of the mountain, the fog, but she couldn't see Evan. "He may not have been able to, Scott," she said. "She might be in his head. She might've been slowing him down."

Scott cleared his throat as though emotion had blocked his words. In a split second, he had his voice back. "I didn't think about that. All I told him was to keep up, and when I turned around again, he was gone. Just disappeared into the fog. I ran up and down the trail, but there was no sign of him. Why would he leave the trail?"

"He may think he's on the trail," Charlie said. "Spirits can play tricks on the living sometimes. They can make you see things that aren't there. Make you feel things."

"I can't believe I lost him."

The vulnerability in Scott's voice almost broke Charlie's resolve to stay calm.

"Should've tied a string to his waist and kept him with me." He sounded almost near tears.

"It's okay, Scott. I need you to listen to me now, all right?" She squeezed her eyes shut. "This is not your fault. You don't know how a ghost can affect somebody, and that's my fault. I should have said more to you before you left. Have you called the rangers?"

"Yes. I did. They told me to stay put and it would be at least an hour before they could get there."

"You do as they say, okay? Stay put. Promise me?"

"I promise."

"Good. If she thinks you're going after him alone, she might just get you good and lost, too." This she knew from her own experience with wayward spirits.

"Jesus," Scott mumbled. "How can something dead have so much power?"

"It's going to be okay." Charlie said the words even though they felt like a lie. How could everything be okay until they found her son, preferably alive and unscathed?

"I'm going to make some calls, all right? I'll get on the road as soon as I can."

"I just wanted to get him out of here. Get him away from her," Scott muttered.

"I know. But honestly, she's been so persistent it doesn't surprise me she either tricked him or took him."

Shock sent Scott's voice up an octave. "Took him? How can a ghost take someone?"

"You'd be surprised at what they can do, Scott. Hang in there, okay? I'll text you as soon as I get on the road."

"All right. Thank you."

Charlie's tone softened. "There's nothing to thank me for. I'm his mother. My place is there with you till we find him."

Scott stammered a bit. "That's not what I meant. Thank you for not blaming me. I don't know that I would've afforded you the same treatment."

A burst of affection colored her words. He'd been listening to her, finally. "I'd like to think you would. You've come a long way."

"When we get home with him, we have to find some way to protect him better."

Cooperation. How she'd longed for it in the interest of Evan's well-being. "I agree. We'll do what we can. I'll see you soon."

An image flashed through her head of Scott heading into the woods as soon as they hung up.

"Just promise me you'll wait for the rangers and won't go looking for him by yourself."

She heard his heavy breaths, but he didn't reply.

"Scott?"

"Fine. I promise."

The line went dead. She looked down at her phone; her hand shook a little. Charlie turned to her boyfriend, Tom Sharon, leaning against the counter next to her in the kitchen. A concerned look on his handsome face.

"What's going on?" Tom took a sip of coffee from his favorite cup.

"Evan's disappeared. I think the ghost that's been haunting him is the culprit."

"What can I do?" he asked.

"Can you go with me?"

"Of course. I'll go talk to my sister right now. She can handle the business while I'm gone."

Charlie started making lists in her head. A practical exercise and a means of keeping calm. "Thank you. I'm going to call my family and let them know what's going on and see if Evangeline can feed my cat. I'll have to call Ben and let him know, too."

"Of course. Why don't we meet back here in an hour?"

An hour? "Sure," she said, keeping the impatience out of her voice. Tom was, after all, dropping everything for her. "But sooner if we can."

"Sooner if we can." He squeezed her tighter for a moment and pulled out of the embrace. His human glamour disappeared like smoke, leaving only the black robes of his true reaper form, and then he disappeared completely. Charlie picked up the phone from the counter and debated the best way to communicate with all of her cousins and aunt at once. Thumbing through her contacts, Evangeline's number popped up, and she took it as a sign to call her first. She trusted her aunt could spread the word quickly and also keep any panic to a minimum. Charlie pressed the call icon and her aunt picked up after one ring.

"Evangeline, it's Charlie. I need your help."

CHAPTER 23

The bell jingled overhead, and Tom and Charlie quickly strode inside the cafe. When she'd called her aunt, Evangeline had insisted they come to the café before leaving town. Charlie stopped in the middle of the busy breakfast rush and glanced around to look for her aunt. Jen walked from table to table with the coffee pot in her hand, offering refills. When she noticed Charlie, she waved, but the welcoming smile on her face faded quickly.

"Charlie, what's going on?" Jen asked as she approached her cousin.

"It's a bit of a long story, and I'm short on time at the moment. Is Evangeline here?" Charlie asked.

"She's in the back. I'll go get her."

"Thanks." Charlie moved toward the lunch counter, but every seat was taken. The kitchen door swung open.

Evangeline emerged with a large paper bag and drink carrier before Jen could fetch her. Evangeline signaled for Charlie and Tom to follow her, and Jen trailed behind them.

"I made you some food for the road. There's two breakfast sandwiches and two sandwiches in there for lunch. These are hot coffees." She touched two insulated cups with a C marked on the side in black marker. "These are iced teas. I'm sorry I don't have a cooler with me. Daphne borrowed mine and hasn't returned it yet. "

"No worries," Charlie said. "This is wonderful. Thank you so much, and I've got a chest of ice in the car with some water and fruit, so we'll be fine."

"Is somebody going to tell me what's going on?" Jen said.

"It's kind of a long story." Charlie hesitated and eyed her aunt.

"I was going to tell her but didn't get a chance," Evangeline explained to Charlie, then directed her comments to Jen. "Evan's gone missing in the woods."

Jen's face fell. "Oh, my goddess. Oh, Charlie."

"It's all right. I know what's going on, and I'm sure we'll find him."

"Did he just wander off by himself?"

"He's been pestered by a ghost all week, and I think she's led him into woods alone." Charlie dropped her voice to a whisper. "She's been very persistent."

Jen looked up at the ceiling, anguish searing her face.

"I feel terrible that we can't go with you. But we've got our first catering gig tomorrow, and Mark is here, so there's that." Jen's hands fluttered about like nervous butterflies.

"It's all right." Charlie placed her hands on her cousin's arms to still her. "Tom's coming with me, and I have the full support of the DOL behind me if I need it."

Tom put his arm around Charlie's shoulder. "And I've already made contact with the reaper in the area, and she's going to meet us once we get there," he said.

"What can we do from here?" Jen asked.

"Say a blessing for us?"

Jen grabbed Charlie's hands and pulled her into a tight hug. "Absolutely."

"We're going to be okay, Jen. You have more important things to think about right now. Tom and I can handle this," Charlie soothed.

"Have you told Ben?" Jen sniffed and stepped back but held onto her cousin's hand. She looked Charlie in the face.

"I called him and left him a message. But I'm in touch with Athena at the DOL, and she's already started searching for missing girls in the area. I think the ghost is connected to a killer and she's protecting a missing teen."

"That's great. I'm so glad Athena's there to help," Evangeline chimed in.

"Yeah, the DOL is only a couple of hours away if I need reinforcements. Right now, y'all just need to focus on the situation with Mark."

Charlie squeezed Jen's hand and let it go. Tears wet Jen's cheeks and she sniffled. Evangeline retrieved a fresh tissue from the small packet she always kept in her apron pocket and pressed it toward Jen.

"And you're going to take care of my cat for me, right Evangeline?"

"Absolutely," Evangeline said. "I don't want you to worry about anything here. We'll get everyone together in a circle tonight to help you find Evan."

"Thank you," Charlie said. "That means the world to me."

"We should get on the road, Charlie," Tom said.

"I love y'all," Charlie said.

"We love y'all too, sweetie. Drive safe," Evangeline said.

Charlie nodded and she and Tom headed to the car, her heart full of dread for the long drive and daunting task ahead of them.

CHAPTER 24

E van stopped in the middle of the trail and looked around. This didn't look familiar at all. When had the trail given way to woods? The fog hung so thick he could barely see the shape of his father up ahead.

"Hey, Dad," Evan called. "Are we going the right way? I don't remember any of this."

He listened and waited for a response. The shadowy figure in the fog up ahead disappeared, and a cold finger of panic touched his heart.

"Hey, Dad. Wait for me." He picked up his pace and began to move as fast as he could. A tree branch bit into the side of his calf. He stumbled and landed on wet leaves. Was he off the trail? Terror wrapped around his heart and squeezed tight, and he scrambled to his feet.

"Dad!"

He made a 360-degree turn, scanning in all directions for his father. This was not the trail. How could he have gotten off the trail? He'd been following his father. Sure, he'd kind of gotten lost in his thoughts about last night's dream. The image of the man with the baseball bat kept replaying in his head. But every time he'd looked up, he'd seen his father ahead of him in the fog.

But did you, really? a little voice inside him asked. His entire body stiffened under the weight of his thoughts. His mother had warned him. Warned him that the spirit could trick him. Stupidly, he'd thought there was no way he'd let that happen. Could the spirit have pretended to be his father? Was that even possible?

You already know the answer to that.

"Okay," he said to himself. What would his father do? "Think, Evan. This is not the end of the world."

He picked himself up from the ground and began to rummage through his backpack until he found his water bottle. They had refilled their bottles before they started the hike, and he'd already had two big swallows, not worrying about running out. Which left him now with only about three-quarters of a bottle. He kept digging and came across several packets of water purification tablets floating around the bottom of his pack. They were only supposed to be used for emergencies.

"Yeah, well, I think this is an emergency," he said aloud.

He found a little canvas pouch with the multi-tool his

mother had given him. He quickly started pulling out the attached tools. A very sharp blade, a Phillips head screwdriver, a can opener—which did him no good since he had no cans, but it did have a flat head that could be used as a screwdriver or to pry something if he needed it—a pair of scissors, a smaller sharp blade, and a saw blade. That could come in handy. When he pushed everything back in their slots and replaced the tool in the pack, he spotted his phone.

"Of course," he muttered and grabbed the black-screened device. It came alive once he touched it and found it still plugged into the extra power pack his father had made him bring. The battery read 100% and even had one bar, enough for a text if not a call. His fingers raced over the tiny virtual keyboard. When he finished the message, he pressed the arrow sending the text to his dad. A green line appeared near the top of the screen indicating how long it would buffer before it landed on his father's phone. The indicator climbed to the halfway point and hung there.

"Come on," he said urgently. "You have a bar. There should be no problem with this."

He waited and watched it for a couple of minutes, and when it became clear the text wasn't going through, he tried to refresh it and resend it. The indicator hung up again at the halfway mark, and not long after, a bubble with bold red letters appeared below his text: Undeliverable at this time. Try again? Or Cancel?

"Yes, try again." Evan gritted his teeth and clicked the Retry button. He couldn't take his eyes off the green line.

He tried to soothe himself. "It's okay. It's okay. Sometimes it takes time up here." He sucked in a deep breath. "Just let it do its thing."

But his mind wouldn't just let go and hope for the best. He needed a plan. If he stayed put, eventually, his dad would realize he wasn't behind him and come looking for him. Wouldn't he?

He threw a glance over his shoulder and tried to determine where he'd taken a wrong turn. How far off the trail was he? His heart drummed in his ears. How had he gotten lost in the first place? He'd seen his father ahead of him in the fog. Or, had it been a trick of the eyes? He rested his forehead in his hand and stared at the phone. He hit send, but again the message came back as undeliverable.

His mother's voice floated through his head. Just make sure she doesn't try to trick you. Sometimes spirits do that. Of course. Michelle did this to him. The anger heating his neck and cheeks competed with the icy fear building in his chest.

"I'm not going to help you!"

He spat the words into the nearly silent woods. The sound of water dripping from leaves was his only reply. "My dad will come for me, and then you'll just have to wait for my mom. Or be stuck here forever."

The fog grew dense again, and the damp made him

shiver. He took a seat at the base of a tree, drank two long swigs of water, then properly inventoried his pack. He may as well know how long he could last out here.

Inside, he found one pair of clean shorts and two clean short-sleeved t-shirts—he'd worn his current shorts for the last few days, only changing t-shirts every morning. He'd stuffed his dirty shirts in a zippered compartment separate from the main interior of the bag. He didn't bother to check it, so he continued digging. Everything had settled near the bottom of the pack.

He pulled out the plastic vacuum bag Cora had used to pack his emergency clothes—a long-sleeved t-shirt, a fleece jacket, a pair of jeans, and extra socks. He also had an unopened space blanket and his rain poncho stuffed into its matching nylon bag. He'd snagged the 2-foot length of bungee cord his dad had used to tie them together. It might come in handy. He had packed the knife his mom gave him and his grandpa's compass into a canvas bag so he could find them easily.

He opened the bag and retrieved the box holding the compass. His dad was supposed to show him how to use it. He flicked open the lid and held the brass and glass instrument in his palm. The needle swayed back and forth before finally settling between the N and the E. In real terms, he had no idea what that meant. He closed the lid and carefully put it back into its box and into his bag to keep it safe. When his dad found him (and he would, wouldn't he?), he'd ask him to show him how to use it.

The last bag within the backpack was most precious of all, next to his water bottle. He untied his food bag and peered inside. His stomach rumbled at the delicious scent of the ripe banana. Beyond the bright yellow fruit, four energy bars, a half a bag of beef jerky, a half-eaten bag of granola cereal, and an orange rounded out his collection. His dad had packed all the food that needed boiling water into his own pack along with the propane canister, stovetop and nested pans for cooking. At the thought of his dad, he checked his phone again. Another undeliverable message. He pressed Retry once more, but the error message responded faster this time, as if it were impatient to assure him he was truly alone.

"Dammit," he muttered. Maybe there was something wrong with his dad's phone. That could happen, couldn't it? He wasn't really sure, but anything was worth a try. He jotted off a text to his mother and pressed send. It didn't take long for the undeliverable error to appear. He suppressed the urge to throw the phone away. It might be his only lifeline.

An icy blast of air blew against his neck, and a familiar chill skittered across his senses. The ghostly form of the girl swirled in the fog in front of him, becoming almost solid. Finally, she appeared a few feet away. At least she didn't look all bloody this morning. He didn't think he could stomach that.

He glared at her. "You did this, didn't you?"

"I did," she said.

"What do you want from me?"

"You know what I want, Evan."

"My dad's going to come for me. Once he realizes that I'm missing, my mom will too. And I swear to you she will be able to help you."

"No. That'll take too long. You're the only one who can help me now, Evan."

Her voice was as thin as her form. He could almost see right through her.

"I highly doubt that," he countered. His stomach grumbled again.

"You should eat something. You'll need your strength."

"I don't need any strength. I'm not going anywhere." He folded his arms across his chest and lay back against the tree, refusing to look at her.

"You do if you want to survive in these woods."

"You know my mom warned me about you. She said you might try to trick me." A pulse of anger warmed the back of his neck.

"What does your mother know," she scoffed.

How dare she throw shade at his mother. "She knows a lot," he said, defiant as he sat straighter against the tree. "She can see spirits just like I can. You know if you let me go, I can call her and have her come. Plus, she's a witch. She has abilities that I don't have yet. That I may never have. She could help you more than I can."

"That all sounds nice," she said.

"Great. Then let me go."

"Like I said, that will take too long. He's going to kill her. He's already kept her a week. Two days longer than he kept me."

"If he's the guy in that dream you sent me, he's a pretty strong adult, and I'm just a kid. What do you think I can do?"

"I don't know. You're smart. You can figure it out."

He shook his head. "I don't think so."

"I can make sure they don't find you." She moved so fast and so close to him it startled him.

"Are you serious?" He tried to move away, but he seemed stuck to the spot. "Why would you do that? You're not making it easy to want to help you."

"Evan, she's going to die. And he's... he's acting the way he did before he killed me."

If Evan didn't know better, he'd have thought she was crying the way her lip quivered and her face morphed into a grimace. But spirits couldn't cry, could they? If he ever saw his mother again, he'd ask her. She would know.

"Please, Evan. Please?"

"How do we know that he hasn't already killed her? Can't you stop him somehow? Obviously, you're not help-less, or I wouldn't be here, off the trail. Alone." He gestured to the woods around them.

"Don't you think I've tried? Everything I've done to scare him or stop him doesn't seem to work. He can't see me. You can. Please, Evan. I'm begging you."

Evan slapped a hand against the wet leaves lining the

floor of the forest and gritted his teeth. He picked up the bag of emergency clothes and shoved them back inside his pack, then packed everything else inside, putting his food and water bottle near the top.

"Fine, but if I end up dead, I swear I will never speak to you again."

"Really? You'll help me?"

"How can I refuse? You've basically kidnapped me."

"I know. I'm sorry. I promise I'll do everything I can to keep you safe."

"Have you been protecting her?"

"I've been trying too."

"Maybe that's why she's lasted longer than you." Evan pulled an energy bar from his food pouch, unwrapped it, and stuffed the wrapper back into the bag. Pack it in, pack it out, his father's voice echoed through his head. It hurt too much to think about his dad still on the trail, headed down the mountain. He pushed the thought away.

"I'm going to need water too. No water and I die, which won't really help you, will it?"

"There's a stream not far from here. You can refill your bottle there."

"Great," he grumbled. "Let's get this show on the road. The sooner I help you, the sooner I can go home."

When he finished eating, he took a long swallow of water, then repacked the bottle and got to his feet. He had no trouble moving once he agreed to help her. His phone still in hand, he followed her deeper into the woods.

CHAPTER 25

"**B**e still," Daphne scolded.

"Whatever you're doing tickles," Ben complained and shifted in his chair. He lifted his hand to touch his face and found bare skin instead of his usual heavy stubble. "What the..."

"Just be patient." Daphne gently guided his hand away and touched him lightly on his shoulder. A sense of calm spread through him, followed by the sensation of floating in warm water.

"How'd you do that?" he asked.

"It's something Darius taught me," she said, referring to her boyfriend. He was a well known acupuncturist but also a wickedly talented necromancer. "He's very good at calming people down."

"I assume so in his line of work."

She beamed. "Yep, that's why his clients love him."

"You know, I appreciate you doing this. And I'll be happy to pay you for your time," Ben said.

"Don't be ridiculous," she said. "You're practically family."

"I wouldn't hold my breath on that," he muttered.

"Don't worry about Jen." Daphne fussed with his hair, running a comb through his coarse, sandy brown waves. "I promise you; she will come around. She's just a little distracted at the moment."

"It's that distraction I'm worried about," Ben said.

"You know, if you'd like, I can spy for you," Daphne said.

"I appreciate the offer, but I'm not sure that's such a good idea. I don't completely know the scope of Mark's powers, and I wouldn't want anything to happen to you, Daphne. Nor would I want Jen to turn her anger on you if she ever found out."

"Don't you worry about me. I can take care of myself. Evidently, Charlie met him and said she didn't sense anything evil from him. I'll tell you what, though. From every description of him I've heard, the man is covered in charms. Literal magic charms. He's hiding something. And, of course, Jen doesn't see it. It worries me because I think that's how he got her to fall for him in the first place. Charms aren't very different from love potions."

"I know," Ben said. He frowned. "I worry about the same thing. Do you think she'd listen to you if you told her?"

"I don't know. I think some part of her wants him to be a good man, and so that's what she sees. You know what I mean?"

"Yeah, I do," he mused. "Especially for Ruby."

"I'll know more tomorrow night," Daphne said. "I'll be watching him, no matter what."

"What's happening tomorrow?" Ben asked, alarmed by her revelation.

"It's Friday night dinner, and Jen invited him."

"Shh—oot." He shifted his swearing and tightened his jaw. "I guess I'm not invited then."

"Ben, you're always invited." Daphne stopped fiddling with his hair and put both hands on his shoulder this time.

"I appreciate that, but I don't think Jen feels that way at the moment."

"Have you talked to her? Has she expressly said, do not come to Friday night dinners anymore?"

"No," he mumbled.

"If I were you, I'd show up just like always. Then make her talk to you. At least you'd know for sure one way or the other."

"That's just it, I don't know if I want to know," he quipped.

"Of course you do. It's better than being in limbo. And don't forget—you have two things going for you."

"Yeah, what's that?"

"First, you have the home team advantage. Our family is your turf. We're all rooting for you, not him."

"That's good to know. What's the second thing?"

"You're not hiding who you really are," she said.

"Oh, no?" He slipped one foot onto the floor and turned the stylist's chair around to face the mirror at her station. The tan blond surfer dude staring back at him looked nothing like him except vaguely around the eyes. "What do you call this?"

Daphne laughed back at him, her eyes lighting up when she said, "I call this brilliant, but that's beside the point. You won't be wearing this glamour tomorrow night." She slipped something around his neck and quickly fastened it into place.

"I don't know," Ben said. "I feel like I'm outgunned." He touched the puka-shell necklace she'd put on him. The white shell beads felt cool and smooth against his fingertips.

Daphne gave him a kindly scowl. "He's not all powerful, you know. Stop acting like he's some sort of god. He isn't."

"I can't imagine having all that power and not feeling a little god-like."

Daphne rolled her eyes as she fussed with the tools on her station. "Trust me. He's not nearly as powerful as you give him credit for. If he was, he'd have breezed in here and cast some spell on Jen and whisked her away within hours. I have no doubt he has an agenda, and I don't think it's all about Ruby, either."

Ben shook his head, his surfer waves dancing over his forehead. "I wish I knew what it was. Wish I could expose him to Jen so she'd see it too."

"She'll see. It takes a lot of energy to hide yourself the way he does. Hiding who you are is really hard on the mind, body, and soul. I just wonder what happened to him that made him that way. Somebody must have hurt him very deeply to entrench himself in a butt-load of charms."

"That the official term?" Ben teased.

"Yeah," she chuckled, "it is. You got a problem with it?"

"Nope." He shook his head and grinned. The reflection in the mirror grinned, too, and Ben had to turn his chair away from it. Seeing it smile and laugh using his voice freaked him out a little.

"You know you're really wise, Daphne. People don't give you enough credit."

"I know," she chirped without any pretense. "Most people don't see it. They think I'm just a hairdresser. All they see is pink fringe and unbridled optimism."

"You're right. They underestimate you. I'm sorry if I've done that to you," he said.

"No worries. I'm kind of like a duck. It all rolls off like water, even Lisa and her barbs." She tipped her head. "Most of the time."

"She really can be tough on you."

"Yes—but she would also die for me. And I know that. Just like she knows I would die for her. That's really all that matters, isn't it? She's my family, and that's what families do."

"Not all families," Ben mused. "I doubt old Mark would agree with you on that. From everything I've heard about his mother, she's an ice queen."

"Fair enough. But it's what our family does, and just so you don't forget—that includes you."

"I appreciate that—maybe you can remind your cousin of that sometime. Since she's still not taking my calls."

"Okay, you win. Don't come to Friday night dinner. Give her the space she needs to process everything. She'll come back around."

"You really are an optimist, aren't you?

"Yes, I am. I'm also in your corner." She patted his shoulder lightly and turned the chair to face the mirror again so he could take a good look at his reflection. "I know it's weird to not see yourself in the mirror."

"You're not kidding." He rose from the chair and moved closer to the mirror to inspect her handiwork. She had changed everything from his hair color to his eye color even the shape of his face appeared longer, less round. "Holy goddess," he said, not hiding his amazement.

"I included an extra charm for non-detection. That

way, if Mark does have some sort of magic detector, you shouldn't set it off."

"Daphne, you're a genius. Has anyone ever told you that?"

She shrugged her shoulders nonchalantly. "Every once in a while."

"I don't know how to thank you for this."

"Stop sulking. And be willing to pick up the pieces if he breaks her heart again."

"Let's just hope it doesn't come to that," he said. "Now, can I turn it on and off like a light switch, or am I stuck looking like I belong on the cover of a surfer magazine."

Daphne giggled. "You're not stuck. Here's what you do."

CHAPTER 26

The skies darkened as if on cue, and thunder cracked overhead, shaking the café. The lights flickered, and Jen paused to look at the ceiling.

The kitchen door swung open, and her aunt stood in the threshold. The worry lines of Evangeline's brow deepened.

"That felt very close."

"They were calling for afternoon thunderstorms on channel 5 this morning, so it's not really a surprise. When has the weather ever rattled you?"

Jen continued counting money, writing down totals on a sheet next to the register before she stuffed it into a bank bag. She zipped it up and turned to stare into her aunt's concerned face.

"Normally, it doesn't," Evangeline said, "but my hair is standing up on end. This one feels bad."

Jen surveyed the mostly empty restaurant. The after-lunch crowd cleared out mostly, and now only a few stragglers hung around for coffee and free Wi-Fi. They had at least another hour and a half, almost two hours before the dinner crowd would start to filter in.

"Hopefully, it will be over before we know it."

Evangeline shuddered. "I hope you're right but..."

The bell over the door tinkled, announcing a patron had entered. Jen looked up and saw Mark practically sprinting across the floor.

"You need to get everyone and yourself into an interior room, right now," he said, racing toward the counter, and he half-shouted his urgent message.

"What?" Jen asked, looking to her aunt in alarm. "Why?" she said to Mark. She turned to the customers at the counter who'd turned to check out the commotion.

"There's a tornado warning in the area," Mark said, a little breathless.

"No, that can't be." Jen pulled her phone from her apron pocket and pulled up her weather app. A red banner at the top said tornado warning in effect. Take cover, it said. Stay indoors, and stay away from windows.

"Oh my god. He's right." She showed her phone to her aunt.

Evangeline nodded. She gave Mark a suspicious look. "It's very convenient that you showed up right at the time of the alarm. We'll discuss that later," she said in a stern school marm voice.

"Of course," Mark said, a confused look on his face.

Evangeline stepped out from behind the counter and clapped her hands together, then cleared her throat, a signal for the customers to pay attention.

"I don't mean to frighten y'all. But there's a tornado warning for this area. And we're asking everyone to come with us into the storeroom for now to ride it out. Just as a precaution. I'm sure it will be fine. But rather safe than sorry," Evangeline said with a calming smile.

An older couple took a few last sips of their coffee and pushed away from their table. A young man who had been coming in for weeks with his laptop for two hours in the afternoon closed his computer and stuffed it in his bag. He glanced at the window next to him rattling, the wind kicking up outside. The fear on his face, the recognition of Evangeline's words made him hasten his way to the counter. Another older lady who came in, in the afternoons, to have coffee and pie followed suit. Evangeline led the group along with the cook and two waitresses into the storeroom in the rear of the cafe.

Jen watched after them and waited until the door closed before turning to Mark.

"What are we waiting for?" he asked. She heard the panic in his voice. She couldn't remember him ever sounding so out of control before.

"Did you do this, Mark?" she asked.

"What? Cause a tornado?"

"Yes. Are you messing with the weather?"

"Jen, I have many talents," he said. "But causing a tornado is not one of them. Why would I do that?"

"I don't know," she lied. *Maybe to rescue us and be the man of the hour,* she thought? She remained silent but sent him a penetrating gaze.

Mark said, "Now, are we going to go back there, or am I going to pick you up and sling you over my shoulder and take you back there?"

Just then, the lights went out. The sound of the wind outside roared louder than Jen could remember, except for maybe during a hurricane. She covered her ears, and Mark gently nudged her toward the door just as the front window burst and blew inward. The air swirled fiercely through the restaurant, swinging the door back and forth, almost as if it was chasing them.

Jen led Mark through the shadowy darkness to the storeroom, where they kept sacks of flour and grits, cans of tomatoes, and other ingredients that she cooked with every day. She opened the door to find the others huddled in a corner down on the floor.

For several minutes, the wind shook the building so relentlessly, it felt as if the very walls would collapse on them. Explosions of sound rattled Jen's bones. She covered her ears and closed her eyes. The sound reminded her of a storm or hurricane that she and Lisa and Evangeline and Daphne had gone through when she was around ten years old. It had blown out almost every window on the south side of the house. That storm had come in stronger than anticipated. They sat in the dark waiting. Mark pressed his shoulder against hers.

"Are you okay?" he asked. Jen opened her eyes and nodded.

"I'm fine," she said coldly. She pulled her phone from her pocket and called her father.

It went straight to his voicemail. "Daddy. Please call me immediately when you get this. There's a pretty bad thunderstorm, and I think a tornado just passed the café. We're okay for now, but I want to make sure that you and Ruby are safe. I don't know if it's coming toward you or not. Please call me."

She ended the call and stared at the screen, praying it would ring. When it didn't, she pressed it to her chest.

"I'm sure they're fine," Mark said.

"Are you sure you didn't do this?" she whispered.

"I swear on my mother's name," he said. "No matter what you think of me, I would never put you in danger."

The thick darkness of the room made it difficult to know if he was telling the truth.

The sound of the roaring died down, and after a while, Jen could hear the others breathing more than she could hear the weather outside.

"I think it passed," she said.

Mark rose to his feet, pulled his phone out of his pocket, and used it as a flashlight.

"Jen, why don't we survey things out there to make

sure it's safe enough for everyone to come out." He offered his hand to help her to her feet.

"Okay, good idea," she said. "Evangeline?"

Her aunt radiated a calmness that sent an aura of peace over the small storeroom. "Y'all go on," she said. "I'll wait here with them. Call us if you need us."

"Okay," Jen said.

Mark pulled open the door into the dark hallway. He looked at the freezers across from the storeroom.

"Do you have a backup generator?" he asked.

"My dad has one for the house. I never needed one for the cafe. They're usually really good about getting the electricity back on quickly," Jen said.

"Okay, that's good," Mark said. Jen turned on her phone flashlight and shined it at the ceiling. Water dripped on her head. "Well, that's not good. The roof is leaking."

"Do you own this building?" he asked.

"No, not even remotely. This is a lease," she said, worry tinging her words.

"Well, hopefully, your landlord is insured."

"I'm sure he is," she said. She led him back through the kitchen. She gasped when she saw pots and pans strewn across the floor where the wind had reached the shelves above the stove. Jen walked through the pass through and the swinging door, which had blown back so hard against the wall it cracked, and the hydraulics of it had locked up in an open position.

"This is not looking good," Jen said, dread knotting in her stomach. The two of them made it into the café proper where they found the large picture window across the front wall had blown out. Tables and chairs had tipped over, and many of them had traveled haphazardly across the floor toward the back wall. An inch of water stood on the linoleum floor.

"Be careful," Mark warned. "The floor might be slick."

Jen nodded, her attention drawn to the missing front window. She could see through the open gap other business owners making their way out to the street.

"Oh, my goddess," Jen said and headed outside with Mark close on her heels.

The street looked like a bomb had gone off. Windows in the businesses across the street were blown out. Cars that had not lost windows were crushed under downed trees. Everywhere leaf and other debris covered plastered walls and lawns. Broken branches from nearby trees fell across sparking power lines. Signs hung askew in precarious positions, threatening to drop on passersby. Power lines sagged, and a transformer high on a nearby pole had caught on fire. Smoke curled up from the blackened hulk.

"Daphne," Jen muttered and started toward her cousin's salon two doors down from the cafe.

"Jen, wait," Mark said. "The air still feels electric to me. Don't you feel it?"

"Yes, but," she said, "I have to make sure my cousin is okay, too."

Jen picked up her pace to a jog but came up short when she found herself in front of A Touch of Glamour Salon and Day Spa. The hanging sign swung in the breeze but looked undamaged. Jen leaned in to get a better look through the front window. She cupped her face to block the glare of light.

Darkness stretched through space, but no one sat in the four stylists' chairs. Half-full wine glasses sat perched on the drawers next to each station as if the drinker had put them down in a hurry. Jen knocked on the window.

"Daphne, are you in there?" She waited a beat and knocked again. No answer. Jen moved to the front door but found it locked. She banged on the door and called louder. "Daphne?"

A moment later, Jen saw movement in the back of the salon. Daphne, three other stylists, and four women wearing black capes and in various stages of hair coloring, cutting, or washing emerged.

Daphne quickly made her way across the floor and unlocked the door. Jen launched on her cousin, hugging her close. Daphne gladly took her cousin's embrace.

"I'm fine," Daphne said. "Are you okay? How's the cafe?"

Jen gave her cousin a quick squeeze and then let her go. "The restaurant's a mess, but we're all safe." Jen sighed. "Which is what counts."

"It's amazing that this place is so untouched," Mark said. "Almost as if by magic."

Daphne shifted her focus and eyed him suspiciously. "You must be Mark Stonehill."

"I am. And you are?"

"Daphne Ferrebee. I am the owner of this establishment and Jen's favorite cousin."

Jen chuckled. A little embarrassed. "Daphne. You know I don't have favorites."

"Yes," Daphne said, grinning, "but if you did it would be me."

"Sure," Jen said and rolled her eyes. "So, this must be quite a protection spell you have on your salon. You have to tell me exactly how you did this," Jen said, gesturing to the windows.

"I will," Daphne said.

"Regardless, I'm glad you're okay."

"How's my mom?" Daphne asked.

"Probably worried sick. But she's okay. We all hunkered down in the storeroom. I'm wondering how long it'll take them to get the power back up. I've got a freezer full of food right now for that catering job for the mayor tomorrow. The last thing I want is fifty pounds of crab claws and a hundred pounds of shrimp to go bad."

Daphne made a face. "Do you think they'll still have the luncheon? I mean we just got hit by a tornado."

Jen opened her mouth to argue then snapped it shut. "I don't know. Oh sweet goddess, I hope so, otherwise I'll have a ton of extra food."

"Assuming they get the power back on and it doesn't

end up spoiling. Does Uncle Jack have a generator you could borrow?"

"He does, but we only have one for the house, and if he brings it here, then all the food in the freezer at home will go bad."

"We'll make sure you get a generator, Jen," Mark said. "If that's what it takes to keep your business going. Until you can rebuild."

Jen and Daphne stared at him with their mouths agape. "That's very nice of you. And here I thought all sorcerers were evil," Daphne teased.

"Well, I think that's just an ugly rumor. The same one that says that all witches are covered in warts and kill children to keep their beauty."

Daphne couldn't hide her sardonic grin. "Touché."

Jen broke in and said, "If you're okay, I'm going to head back to the restaurant and make sure Evangeline and the other patrons are okay."

"I'm good. Call me later, okay?"

"You got it."

On the way back to the restaurant, Jen waved at Marcy Holmes across the street, standing in front of her ruined knitting shop.

"Your cousin is very talented," Mark said.

"Yes, she is."

"Are all the women in your family that gifted?" Mark asked.

Jen grinned. "Yes, they are," she said, a note of pride in her voice.

"Then I take it Ruby's magical education is in good hands?"

"Yes, it is."

"Good," he said. "Let's just make sure that her mother's livelihood is in good hands too."

"I appreciate that," Jen said. "The sentiment at least."

"I meant it last night when I said I want to make amends. I want you to trust me, Jen."

"Well, just know that trying too hard won't necessarily win me over either."

"So noted," he said. "Let's get inside off the street. Still feels dangerous out here to me."

"Agreed," Jen said.

CHAPTER 27

The small ranger station bustled with activity. Men and women in olive green uniforms milled around the make-shift table in the center of the back room. From the outside, the building, painted an institutional gray, looked unappealing. But inside, against the log cabin-like walls, rangers had stacked wood from ceiling to floor. An engaging gift shop and reception area in the small front room invited visitors to browse, and signs hanging above the display counters offered information and permits.

The same map they stared at on the table hung on the wall of the gift shop and showed just how massive the national forest truly was, covering hundreds of square miles of mountains and virgin forests. Charlie stared at the map on the wall behind the reception desk as a sick feeling took root in her stomach. Evan was out there somewhere, lost in those trees.

"Charlie?" Scott's familiar voice made her turn.

"Hi," she said, raising her hand. He threw his arms around her and hugged her close, catching her off guard.

"Thank you so much for coming," he said, his words full of feeling.

His desperation poured off of him and flowed through her. The onslaught of his emotions almost made her knees buckle.

"Of course, I'm here. Of course, I am," she said in his ear.

She squeezed him tight for a moment just to regain her balance, then let him go.

He grabbed hold of her hand as if it were a lifeline. "I know, I just..." He shook her hand and then his head.

Charlie put her arm around his shoulder. "It's going to be okay, Scott. I swear to you we will find him," she said. She moved back a little and squeezed his hand. "Is there a ranger around here?"

They stood off to the side in the small alcove that passed for a lobby.

Scott nodded to himself as if trying to pull himself together. "Yes, let me take you to her. Danica is her name. Danica Hart. She's been wonderful. We've already got people out searching the woods where Evan and I got separated. They won't let me search with them right now." He sounded stricken.

"That's probably better, Scott, to be honest. With the way you're feeling right now, you might be more of a hindrance."

He cleared his throat to hide his emotion, Charlie thought. His eyes looked a little glassy, and he nodded as if he were unable to speak.

"Come on. Introduce me to Danica, okay?" she said, taking him out of his misery.

Scott nodded. "Sure. I thought you were coming with someone. I figured at least your boyfriend would be with you."

Charlie glanced around at the crowded ranger station.

"Yeah, he came. But he had something he needed to do first before he joins us."

"What could he possibly have to do?" Scott asked.

Charlie danced around the subject. There was no reason for Scott to know about Tom's true nature. No reason at all she could think of at the moment.

"He has some contacts in this area, and he sometimes works with me. So we're going at it from the ghost angle." She whispered in case some of the rangers were close by.

"Oh, I see," Scott said.

"Have you mentioned any of that to the rangers?" Charlie asked. "What I do?"

"No. God no. Of course not. How would I even explain that and have it sound rational?"

"I know, it won't sound rational. But I'll flash my

badge, okay, and have a talk with Danica about things," she said. "I'll help them understand."

Scott looked worried. "Do you think that's the best idea? I mean, what if they don't take you seriously?"

"I've never had any kind of agency police or otherwise not take me seriously, Scott. We're pretty legitimate." Charlie had dealt with this situation before, and she could make calls if she needed to get verification.

"Okay," Scott said reluctantly. "Okay." He nodded his head. "I trust you."

"Great. Danica?"

"Of course. She's through here." He led her down a small hallway to a tiny back office. It was neat as a pin with no stacks of paper on the desk, just a computer monitor and keyboard. A floor-to-ceiling bookshelf held books on nature conservancy, the native animals, and several volumes on the history of the park.

Charlie could've perused the books for hours, but that was not her purpose here. The petite ranger looked up from her computer.

"Mr. Carver," she said when she recognized Scott. Then she corrected herself. "Sorry, Dr. Carver."

Her long straight hair hung in a ponytail at the nape of her neck. An olive green hat with a leather band and a badge on the front that read national parks ranger perched on a small table next to her desk. "What can I do for you?"

"This is my ex-wife Charlie Payne." Scott gestured to Charlie. "She's come to help with the investigation."

"Please, y'all, have a seat." Danica gestured to a small worn plaid couch against the wall.

"Not to be contrary," Charlie said. "But I actually work for a federal agency, too," she said.

"You do?" Danica asked, looking her up and down.

"I do." Charlie reached into the pocket on the front of her tote bag. She pulled out her credentials and showed them to the park ranger.

Danica took the blue leather case holding Charlie's badge and her vital information.

"What is the DOL?"

Charlie closed the door to the office.

"We investigate and help agencies like the police and yourself with things of a more supernatural vein."

"Supernatural?" Danica asked. The skepticism on her face created deep lines around her mouth. "Ma'am, I'm not exactly sure why you think you would need to be here, other than this is your son that's gone missing. I can assure you that people go missing all the time, and we will do our best to find him. But I don't believe there's anything supernatural going on here."

Charlie tilted her head in a kindly way. She knew she had to use tact with the ranger. "Well, I'm afraid you'd be wrong," Charlie said. She took a seat on the couch and patted the empty spot next to her. "Why don't you come here and let me tell you why I know this is a supernatural matter. It will make working together so much easier."

Danica drew her pointed chin back and didn't move from her chair.

"Okay, then." Charlie leaned forward and put her forearms on her knees. She folded her hands together and began to tell Danica about Evan and his encounter with the spirit in the woods.

Every once in a while, she would look to Scott to corroborate what she said. Thankfully, he complied.

"I know this is difficult to believe," Scott said when Charlie finished. "Trust me, I know exactly how difficult it is." He paused and waited for all of this to sink in for Danica.

The ranger looked from Charlie to Scott. She peered up at the ceiling, and then she said, "So, let me get this straight. This DOL agency is what? Like the X-Files?" Danica asked.

Charlie shrugged her shoulders. "Sure. Sort of. Only no aliens. Just, you know, your run-of-the-mill witches, ghosts, sometimes demons, and vampires. Oh and very rarely, a werewolf."

Danica put her hand up to stop her. "Wait! Werewolves are real?"

"Yes, but not as many as Hollywood would have you believe," Charlie said.

Danica sat back in her chair.

"And you're a witch."

"I am," Charlie said, showing no expression. "I'm happy to demonstrate if you need me to," she said.

"That really necessary, Charlie?" Scott said. He scooted an inch or two away from her.

Charlie cocked her head toward Scott and explained, "He's a little afraid of my ability sometimes. It's grown over the years."

"You can say that again," Scott muttered.

"No," Danica said. "I'd like to see something."

"Sure." Charlie pointed to the green hat sitting on the table behind Danica.

"May I?"

"Sure." Danica handed the hat to Charlie and leaned back in her chair, casting a skeptical look at Scott. Charlie held the hat in her hands and closed her eyes as she visualized the hat on fire. When she opened her eyes, the felted wool began to smoke.

"Whoa," Danica said. "What are you doing?"

The felted wool burst into flames in Charlie's hands.

Danica jumped to her feet and looked around for something, anything she could use to stop the fire.

"Drop it!" Danica said, her voice urgent.

"Fire Burn, Water Douse," Charlie muttered the incantation. A flash of water erupted beneath the burning hat enveloping it until the fire went out and all that was left was a burned smoldering piece of wool.

"Oh, my god," Danica said, staring at the charred remains of her hat. "How did you do that?"

"Magic," Charlie said.

A small breeze wrapped around the hat in her hands and then promptly died down. The hat transformed to its original condition. Danica took it from Charlie's hands and inspected it closely, then she took one of Charlie's hands in hers, turning it over, as if she were trying to find the trick.

"That's crazy," Danica mumbled. "Is this real?"

"It's very real," Charlie said. "And it's also very important that you use discretion. None of your other rangers need to know about this. Do you understand?"

"Of course." Danica put her hat back onto the small table.

"I don't think they'd believe me anyway."

"You'd be surprised how many people believe in ghosts, ma'am," Charlie said.

"No, it probably wouldn't. These rangers are mostly from around here and haints and spirits are a big part of their culture."

"That makes sense. If you don't mind, I'd like to set up my computer. I'd like for us to work together. I need things that you may not have considered. Based on what my son told me, I think we may be dealing with two girls."

"What are the girls' names?"

"I don't have much more than their first names. I'll need to search my databases to see what I can come up with. And of course, I'll share any information with you or the local law enforcement if it ends up under their juris-diction."

Danica inched her chair forward. "So, you think whoever killed these girls he has a home base here? In the forest?"

"I think he probably lives somewhere on the fringes of the national forest," Charlie said. "Maybe his property butts up against it. Or close enough for the spirits to wander away."

Danica looked at her computer screen but didn't make a move to start an internet search.

Charlie continued. "I also need to talk to the local medical examiner. There was evidently a girl found dead here a few years ago? I need to figure out if she's tied to my case in some way."

Danica furrowed her brows. "Right, the girl they found at the bottom of the Guilford's Peak drop off. It was before my time, I'm afraid. I've only been here a couple of years. But there are some rangers who've been here a long-time, and they may be able to answer your questions."

"That would be great," Charlie said. "I appreciate you listening and not immediately dismissing what I have to tell you."

"I'm still not sure exactly what I saw." Danica looked at her hat.

"It's okay. Once we leave, you can forget all about it."

"I'm not sure I'll be able to," Danica said with a wry smile. "It's like asking me to unsee it."

Scott chimed in. "It's a difficult thing to do. I didn't believe for a very long-time. And now that I do. I couldn't forget it, either."

Charlie gave him a knowing smile, then looked at Danica. "Can you accommodate me?"

"Absolutely," Danica said. "We want to find your son as soon as possible. It might be summer, and we don't have to face hypothermia generally at night. But there are animals out there and so many dangers to a boy alone."

"Yes," Charlie said. She feared the forest less than she did the spirit that had taken her son and was leading him to god knows where. "Agreed."

CHAPTER 28

After an hour or so, Mark returned to the café. This time, the man he'd brought with him yesterday morning was helping him wrestle a large box from the trunk of the car. A photo of a gas generator was visible on the side of the box.

Evangeline and Jen's father were too busy at the moment sweeping a path through the rubble to pay much attention to them. The mosaic of shattered glass littered the chaos on the messy floor, but at least Jen and Jack could easily maneuver the large pieces of plywood she kept in the storeroom for hurricanes.

"You know, Jen, your landlord should invest in hurricane shutters for this building," Jack mumbled. They paused for a moment, and Jack switched hands, giving his sore palms a rest from the plywood digging into his tender flesh.

"Sure, Daddy," Jen mumbled, not knowing what else to say. What she really needed was Daphne's spell to protect the windows of her store. When she had a chance, she would have a long talk with her cousin. Jen and her father put down the first piece of plywood in front of the broken window. That's when they spotted Mark and his friend wrestling with the box in his trunk.

"Hold on, Daddy, we need a break. I'm going outside to see what Mark is up to."

"Don't mind if I do," Jack said, wiping his brow. "I could use a glass of sweet tea about now."

"Coming up," Evangeline said, propping her broom against the counter and grabbing a glass from under the counter.

Jen walked out to the parking lot and sauntered up to Mark and his friend.

"You got it in there," she heard Mark say to his buddy.

"Yes, sir, I know, but it doesn't seem to want to come out."

"So, you found one?" Jen said as she approached the car.

Mark looked up from the trunk and flashed a friendly scowl to show how hard he'd been working. "Yeah, we snagged the last one at the store. I guess the storm freaked out a lot of people."

Jen shrugged. "It's understandable. It's mid-July. Hurricane season is ramping up. It's just a reminder that we could face worse in the fall," she said.

"Sure," Mark said. He glanced around at the busy street full of people cleaning up glass and pulling shards of wood out of the rubble. The sound of saws and screwdrivers filled the air like a dissonant song.

"So, if you got it in there, you can get it out, right?" Jen asked, hopeful Mark had come with a solution for her refrigerator full of food that would soon spoil without electricity.

"I'm sure we can." Mark smiled and lightly touched Jen on the shoulder, sending a little electric shock traveling through her. She shivered, but it wasn't uncomfortable.

"Don't worry," he said. "I've got this."

Jen noticed Mark scanning the café through the large broken window.

"I guess your family's here," he said.

"Yeah, they just got here a few minutes ago."

"Is...Ruby here?" Mark had his eyes on the storefront and the grisly looking man standing next to the door staring at him, sizing him up. To Mark, Jack Holloway must have looked like a man who kept fit through physical labor. He had sharp blue eyes like his daughter and his white beard made him look more ominous than like Santa Claus. Mark shuffled his feet. "So, is that your father?"

Jen cast a glance over her shoulder and gave her father a brief wave. "Yep. Don't worry. I won't let him hurt you."

"That's good," Mark said. "He looks like he has strong hands."

"He does, but they're gentle, so don't worry."

"Right," he said.

As if Mark's scrutiny of him was an invitation, Jack ambled up to the car and took a look at the situation in the trunk. He inspected the box and said, "You turned it on its side, didn't you?"

"What?" Mark asked. He looked at the box, clearly perplexed.

"The box, son. You turned it on its side, and then slid it underneath, right? You're going to have to take it out exactly the same way you put it in. Either that or you have to push it through. You have the pass through down in the backseat, don't you?" Jack asked.

"Yes, we do," Mark's friend piped up.

Jack scratched his beard and, without saying a word, shot Mark a crooked smile that let him know the big dog had arrived. "You can probably push it through the backseat and turn it on its side," he said. "You'll have more space inside the cabin of the car to maneuver it, then slide it out the side door." Jack's final nod left no room for an alternate theory.

"Thank you," Mark said. He thrust his hand out to Jack. "I'm Mark Stonehill."

Jack stared down at Mark's hand. "Yeah, I know who you are. And I don't care."

Jack took Mark's hand, shook it, and yanked him close.

"There are three things you need to know about me, son. One, I love my daughters and my granddaughter more than life itself. Two, I'm a medical doctor, and I know how to use a scalpel. And three, I'm not above cutting you up and using you for crab bait. Are we clear?"

Mark's face turned pale, and he stepped back and looked Jack in the eye.

"Crystal clear, sir."

Jack studied Mark's face for a moment longer, then said, "Just as long as we're on the same page. Let's get that generator out and get it going before Jen loses half the meat in the freezer."

"Yes, sir."

After some maneuvering, the two of them got the generator out of the car and carried it into the restaurant. They put it down onto a space that Evangeline had swept clear of glass and debris. Mark looked around at the shambles in the cafe.

"Don't worry," Evangeline said. "Jen will get everything back to the way it was before."

Jen came up and surveyed the mess with him. She nodded. "I know. It's just, we've got a lot of work till then."

Mark let his gaze settle on the child sitting at the end of the lunch counter with her nose buried in a book. He tilted his head and said, "That's her, right?"

Jen looked over at her daughter, a smile inching across her face. "Yeah, that's her."

"She looks just like you," Mark said, almost wistfully.

Jen said, "This is not exactly the way I pictured you meeting her in my head. Sometimes, she looks like you when she gets this determined look on her face. And she scratches her brow the way you do. And every once in a while, I see you in her profile."

"Sure," he said, cocking his head. His voice low and suddenly cautious. "I can see that. Kind of like a shadow."

Jen glanced around and noticed her father and aunt watching them.

She swallowed hard. "You ready to meet her?"

Mark looked at her with an expression she had never seen before. Something akin to terror and excitement all at the same time.

"Yeah," he said. "I think so."

"I'm not going to tell her who you are exactly, just that you're a friend. We'll see how it goes from there, okay?" Jen looked into his face expecting him to challenge her. Expecting a flash of anger. But it didn't come.

"Like I said at dinner last night." He cleared his throat. "It's all on your terms."

"Great," she said. "Let's do it."

Evangeline had already cleared a wide path so Ruby would not come into contact with glass. She had a stack of markers and coloring books and some chapter books that she seemed addicted to reading at the moment.

"Hey, Rubes," Jen said. "I'd like to introduce you to somebody."

"Okay," Ruby said, not looking up from her book.

Jen gently moved in and closed the book in front of Ruby. Her daughter sat up straight and looked into her face, her eyes a little dazed from still being immersed in the story world.

"Mom," she said, her tone showing her impatience. "I was just getting to the good part."

"You can go back to it in a minute," Jen said. "First, I want to introduce you to Mark Stonehill. He's a very old friend of mine."

Mark licked his dry lips and moved in close. He took the seat next to Ruby at the lunch counter. "Hi, Ruby. It's nice to meet you. I've heard so much about you."

Ruby stared at him, and Jen wondered what was going through her daughter's head. Mark shot her a concerned glance over Ruby's head, and Jen shrugged her shoulders.

"What's wrong with your energy?" Ruby said.

"What?" Mark asked, clearly taken aback. "There's nothing wrong with my energy. You can see my energy?"

"Sure, it's like a halo. Everybody has one. Yours is weird."

"Ruby," Jen said, shaking her head. "That's not nice. We don't make comments like that."

"Fine, but it's true," Ruby said. "Are you sick?"

"No," Mark said, sounding unsure how to answer. "I'm not sick."

"It kind of reminds me of Mrs. Lampley at school. She had energy like yours," Ruby said. "She's dead now."

"Ruby Ellen!" Jen said, her cheeks filled with heat. "I'm so sorry, Mark. At no..."

Mark looked up from his daughter and shook his head. "Don't worry about it. I think it's awesome she can see my energy. Maybe it's just because we're a little different, that's all."

Mark shifted on the stool and an unexpected intuition tapped Jen's heart. She would ask Lisa to evaluate his energy later at Friday night dinner. Was he sick? Is that why he came here after all these years?

"Sure," Jen said. "Why don't you two get a little better acquainted? I'm going to talk to my dad about getting the generator set up."

"Sure, I can probably get Bridges to help with that," Mark said.

"No, it's okay. My dad has an old buddy of his who is a retired electrician. He's going to come by and hook it up for us."

"Oh, okay. That sounds good," Mark said. He looked at Ruby nervously.

She had opened her book and continued reading.

Jen turned her back and walked away before casting a furtive glance over her shoulder to watch the awkward exchange between her daughter's father and the headstrong young girl. Jen hoped she was doing the right thing. She hoped more than anything he would see that Ruby needed to be with her mother. She hoped somehow Mark would be a better man than the one inside her head.

CHAPTER 29

Charlie waited outside the ranger station for Tom. Scott stayed with her, grumbling the whole time. "I don't understand why they won't let us help them search."

"Probably because they don't want us to get lost, too," Charlie said. "They know the area. We just have to trust them to do their job."

"Right. Which is why you came barreling in here with your badge, right?" he said.

Charlie took a breath. She didn't want to start arguing with Scott. She knew he was on his last nerve, and she should call up an extra measure of patience. But Holy Mother of All the Goddesses! She was under massive stress too.

Nevertheless, Charlie calmed herself down and smiled at Scott. "I'm not going to be much good out in the woods either," she said, trying for a note of softness. "I can be more effective from here, at least for now."

She eyed the surrounding woods and glanced at her watch. Tom had assured her this wouldn't take more than half an hour. He'd been gone for almost an hour now.

"Why do you keep looking at your watch?" Scott asked.

"I told you. I'm waiting for Tom."

"Isn't that his car in the parking lot right there?" Scott pointed to the black Ford Fusion.

"It is," Charlie said, ignoring his stare.

"Charlie, you're not saying that he went off into the woods by himself. We don't need him to divert resources from our son."

Charlie wished Scott would just focus on Evan and not poke his nose in her business. But Scott was just being Scott. She couldn't change that. Patience, she reminded herself and said, "Don't worry about Tom. He's not going to get lost. It's hard to explain. But trust me, he's fine, and he should be back soon."

A moment later, Tom appeared on the gravel service road that led to the small parking lot. He wore blue jeans with a blood-red polo shirt and a pair of hiking boots. His dark wavy hair rustled a little in the breeze. He stopped for a moment, turned, and a young woman came up behind him.

She barely stood five feet tall, the top of her head aligning with Tom's shoulders. Brightly colored beads hung three to four inches from the bottom of her braids. Even in the dull gray light of day, her sepia brown skin gleamed. She also wore blue jeans, a pair of boots and a black flutter sleeve top that formed a V in front and showed off a round silver and gold pendant.

Tom and the young woman chatted as they approached.

Charlie said to Scott, "Stay here for me, okay?"

"Why?" Scott asked.

"Because I need to talk to them privately. I promise you'll get to say hello, and when you do, please be nice."

"Of course, I'll be nice," Scott said. "When am I not nice?"

Charlie gave him a dubious look. She was grateful when she walked away that he stayed put. Charlie waved to Tom and went to meet him and his companion. She must be the reaper from this area he'd mentioned.

"Hi," Charlie said when she met them halfway.

"Hi." Tom reached for her hand and gave it a squeeze and kissed her on the cheek.

"Charlie, I'd like to introduce you to Monique," he said.

"It's very nice to meet you." Charlie extended her hand.

Monique shook it and returned a bright smile. "Good to meet you, too. I don't get to talk to people very often."

Charlie gave her a quizzical look.

"I see Scott's hovering over you," Tom said.

"He's just worried about it all. I don't think he wants to be by himself. Then he'd have to be alone in his head."

"That's totally understandable," Monique said. "I appreciate your letting me tag along."

Charlie gave Tom a puzzled look.

"Monique is in a unique situation. She's only recently become a reaper."

"And by recent, he means in the last ten years," Monique added.

"But you're so young," Charlie said.

"Yeah, I know," Monique said. "It happened real fast."

"I have a million questions for you," Charlie said. "

"Tom thought you might," Monique said.

"Once we find my son and we finish up here, maybe you and I could sit down and have a chat?" Charlie asked.

"I'd be happy to," Monique said.

"You're a little different than some of the other reapers I've met," Charlie observed.

"Yeah, I get that," Monique said. "You see I was a real people person. Since this happened, I've found it hard to be so solitary. When Tom told me about his family. I was intrigued."

"Of course," Charlie said. "I can see that."

"Scott's watching us," Tom said. "Maybe we should go ahead and acknowledge him."

Charlie threw a glance over her shoulder. Scott stared at the three of them with an expectant expression on his face.

"You're probably right," Charlie said. "Then we'll find some quiet corner to discuss what y'all can do to help."

"That's great," Monique said. A little too chipper for Charlie's taste.

Charlie led them back to Scott and made the introductions.

"Hello." Scott nodded at Tom. The last time they met had been Charlie's first date with Tom, and it had not gone well. Thankfully, Scott had already had two other girlfriends since then and seemed to have mellowed when it came to Charlie's relationships.

"Hello, Scott, good to see you again," Tom said.

"Yes. You, too, Tom."

"This is Monique Alexander."

"Hello, Monique," Scott said, extending his hand.

Charlie sensed the tension building and said brightly, "She's from this area. And knows it very well," but everyone continued to hold their stiff postures.

Monique smiled, but there was something false about it. And Charlie wondered if Monique really did know the area so thoroughly.

"That's good." A look of skepticism that Charlie was very familiar with crossed Scott's face. She braced herself for whatever came next out of his mouth. "But what does that have to do with anything? This is a matter for the rangers. Not some random friend of your boyfriend. No offense."

"None taken," Monique shrugged.

243

"Right," Charlie said. "Scott, I need to talk to Tom and Monique for a little bit. Would you mind going back to the ranger station? Maybe there's an update."

"Charlie," Scott said, not hiding his annoyance. "I think they would've come and gotten us if—"

"Scott," Charlie said, her voice not quite a warning. "Please."

"Fine," Scott huffed. He turned and disappeared into the ranger station.

"So, Monique," Charlie asked, turning back to her. "This is your territory?"

"It is, but like I said, I've only been here about five years. So, although I know it, okay, it's not like I know every nook and cranny."

"Sure. Is there any chance you know of a spirit named Michelle in your book? I know it's kind of hard without a last name, but it's all I've got at the moment," Charlie said knowing the reaper's book held the names of every spirit the reaper was supposed to collect.

"I checked. I don't have anybody named Michelle in my territory," she said.

"Okay, that's a little disappointing," Charlie said.

"I know," Tom agreed.

"I told Tom that I'm happy to help however I can. There are plenty of spirits roaming these woods. Maybe we can contact one of them," Monique said.

"Will they even come to you?" Charlie asked.

"Maybe, if I don't look like, you know, normal," Monique said.

"Monique and I figured that we could travel through the woods in our reaper form, and then when we sense spirits nearby, we would change into hikers," Tom said.

"I'm kind of hoping it'll give me a chance to collect some of these souls. Seeing Tom like this makes me think a friendly face might be able to walk them over to the other side a little easier, if you know what I mean," Monique said.

"I do," Charlie said. "I think that's a great plan."

"And I can keep in touch with you telepathically," Tom said. "To let you know what we find."

"That would be so wonderful," Charlie said. She glanced at the ranger station. "Now, I just have to figure out what to tell Scott about why you won't be here with me."

"Why don't you just tell him the truth, Charlie," Tom said cautiously.

She gave him a horrified look. "You've met him, right? He's having a hard enough time with his sensitive son. I don't think he will be thrilled at the idea of his ex-wife being involved with a supernatural creature."

"It might make things easier," Tom said. "I think you've given him too little credit. It's not as if he's forbidden Evan from pursuing witchcraft or enhancing his abilities. I think you're underestimating your influence on him. He seems softer than he used to be," Tom said.

"You got all that from that little bit of conversation you had?"

"No, it's just something I've observed," Tom said.

Charlie took a deep breath. "I don't know."

"Not that it's any of my business," Monique said, "but maybe Tom is right. This might be a good time since he's surrounded by all these strangers who are looking for his son. He might keep a lid on his emotions."

"Well, he doesn't like to make a scene unless it benefits him, of course," Charlie said.

"Right and having a fit in front of a bunch of rangers isn't going to benefit him," Tom said.

"All right. I'll come clean with him. And you two will start moving through the forest," Charlie said.

"Yes. And I'll stay in touch." Monique gave her a big smile, her slim face bright and welcoming. It surprised her when Monique pulled her into a hug.

"I just want you to know it's going to be okay. Monique Alexander is on the case. We'll find your boy. And I don't mind shaking down these woods for some spirits that have been here too long."

Charlie gave her a squeeze, beginning to warm to the young reaper. "Thank you," Charlie said. "You have no idea how much I appreciate it."

Monique pulled out of the embrace, and she and Tom headed back the way they came. Charlie watched until they disappeared down the road, well away from any prying eyes that might see them transform, even if only for a millisecond.

She turned and faced the ranger station.

"May as well get it over with," she muttered to herself and headed in to talk to Scott.

CHAPTER 30

"I'm sorry, what did you say?" Scott stared at Charlie, incredulous as if she'd somehow sprouted a second head.

"You heard me." Charlie shifted her feet. "And the only reason I'm telling you this is because Tom and Monique are going to comb the woods. She's from this area."

"Wait, I..." Scott scrubbed his face with his hands. She knew this tell. It signaled his anxiety like a fire alarm. "I don't think I understand, Charlie. You're telling me the Grim Reaper is real, and you're dating him?"

"First of all, Tom is not the Grim Reaper."

"All right. Death then," Scott said.

"He's not death, either. And that actually will piss him off if you say that," Charlie said. Sometimes she had the feeling she was talking to an adolescent when communicating with Scott.

"God forbid we piss off death," Scott said. "Listen, Charlie. I'm beyond stressed and exhausted from not sleeping very well this week, thanks to Evan. I really don't think I can handle any of your supernatural bullshit today."

"My what?" Charlie put her hands on her hips. "I hate to break this to you, but we are steeped in supernatural bullshit. Our son was kidnapped by a ghost."

"Yes, and that's hard enough to deal with. I don't really think I can handle your love life on top of that."

The anger that had bubbled up faded when she took a step back and really looked at him. She'd never seen him so broken before. If this had been some medical emergency, he would've been cool and calm, maybe even detached. But it wasn't. She was in her domain now, and he was floundering. Cracking around the edges.

"Fair enough," Charlie said, softening her tone. "I just didn't want you to keep asking me, where's Tom."

"All right, I won't ask. Are you sure it's the right thing for him to be out there wandering around the woods too? What if he gets lost?"

"Well, first of all, he's kinda tied to me. All I have to do is call him, and he'll appear, so it's unlikely he would ever get lost. Plus, he's with a reaper from this territory. And she knows this area."

"What exactly do they expect to accomplish?"

"Well, they're trying to contact other spirits in the woods. To see if any of them have seen Evan."

"Wait. There are other spirits?"

"Yes. According to Monique, this mountain is covered in them, which kind of doesn't surprise me. People lived and died here for at least two hundred and fifty years."

Scott sat down on the edge of the steps leading into the ranger station and ran his fingers through his hair. When he looked up at her again, it was a tangled wavy mass.

"When was the last time you took a shower?" she asked.

"Why? Do I stink?" he said dryly.

"No, you just look exhausted, honey. Tom and I are going to get a hotel room nearby, and you know, you're welcome to use the shower," she said.

"I guess it's not a bad idea to get a hotel room, is it?" Scott said after pondering the idea for a brief moment. "Who knows how long we'll be here?" he mused. "I should probably call my partners and let them know what's going on. Find someone to cover my patients until I get back."

Charlie said, "Well, with any luck, we won't have to worry about that."

"Right. Luck." Scott gave her a wry smile that didn't reach his eyes. "I think we could use some of that about now."

Charlie's phone chirped, and she pulled it from her back pocket.

Athena texting.

How are you doing? Ben told me what's going on. What can I do?"

So good to hear from you. I was going to text you.

At your disposal per Ben.

There's so much I can't even process at the moment what I might need.

I'm only about an hour and 1/2 from where you are. I could come, but I don't want to be underfoot.

Really? You won't be. I've already pulled the DOL card on this and talked to the ranger.

Cool. I've got a go-bag in my car. Just need to pack up my work stuff. How's the Wi-Fi?

Decent so far. Can you still search all the databases you need?

You know I can gurrrl. Plus, you might need some witch backup.

That would be fab if I'm telling the truth. Been thinking about summoning the spirit that has my son. Two witches would be better than one.

You got it. I'll text Ben to confirm I'm going, then I'm on my way.

Thank you. You have no idea how much this means to me.

Of course. What are partners for, right?"

Yes.

A pebble of emotion formed in Charlie's throat. She'd

been without a real partner for a couple of months now. Ben tried, but he had so many administrative duties, she often found herself working alone and a little lonely. *What are partners for?*

"That was Athena," Charlie said. "She's...my partner and a very skilled investigator and, of course, a witch."

"Hooray." Scott lifted a half-hearted fist into the air and didn't hold back on the sarcasm in his voice. "More supernatural to deal with."

"Scott, I know it's a lot, but trust me, you would rather have us around than not. Especially when it comes to stuff like this."

"For Evan's sake, I hope you're right."

CHAPTER 31

After checking into a nearby hotel, Charlie set up her own little command center in her room. The hotel wasn't far from the ranger station and it only made sense to stay out of the rangers' way, and to minimize their exposure to any magic.

Charlie had set up her computer at the two person table in the center of the room's kitchenette. She flipped through the digital files of the missing children's database on her computer. Athena had given her access, and every single picture broke her heart. They all had stories to tell, but she couldn't let them pull her away from her first mission. She must find and bring her son home safely and preferably without a ghost attached. Her stomach rumbled, telling her it was getting close to dinnertime, so she closed the file to head over to the ranger station to find Scott. She didn't expect Tom to return anytime soon, and he had no need to eat anyway. Food was more of a pleasure thing for Tom, something he liked to share with Charlie.

Torrential rains had brought operations to a halt, so when she arrived at the ranger headquarters, activity had slowed. She found Scott sitting at the large command center table with a map in the center showing the national park and the grid search.

"Hey, Scott," Charlie said and turned around an office chair and slumped in it to face him. She noticed immediately that the chair made the backs of her legs tingle a little bit. "It's getting late, Scott. When was the last time you ate something?" she asked.

She knew he'd been staring at that map for over an hour, seemingly not having moved since the last time she had checked in with him. Did he think the map somehow might suddenly reveal their son's location? He glanced up at her, bleary-eyed. "Oh, I don't know," he said.

"Well, I'm getting hungry. We've been working at this for a while, I imagine. What say you and I drive down to the closest town and see if we can get some dinner?"

"What about your boyfriend?" Scott yawned and stretched, and then his arms collapsed in his lap. In addition to some food, Charlie could see he needed some rest.

"He'll be fine. Tom can eat something later if he wants," she said. Several rangers wandered in and out of the station. She dropped her voice, not wanting them to overhear their conversation. Scott had been freaked out enough earlier. She didn't really need to tell him the ins and outs of a reaper's life, that Tom didn't need food or sleep.

The door to the station opened, and a very wet redhead stepped inside and looked around. Her emerald green eyes lit up when she saw Charlie.

"Hey!" she said, waving.

"Hey," Charlie said. She bolted out of her chair to greet her and smiled more than she had since she arrived at the station. "I was beginning to get worried about you."

"It was a little bit of a rough ride, I'm not going to lie," Athena said. "It's really coming down out there."

"Yeah, I can understand that." Charlie hugged Athena and then gestured to Scott. "Athena, I'd like to introduce you to my son's father. This is Scott Carver."

Athena withheld her wet hand. "Hi, Scott. Sorry, I'm still dripping wet. But it's very nice to meet you. I've met Evan a couple of times. He's a great kid."

Scott managed to pull himself out of his chair to stand and nod. "Yeah, yes he is." The defeat in Scott's voice made Charlie pat him on the shoulder.

"We'll find him, Scott," Charlie said.

"Yes, you keep telling me that," he said.

"Listen, Athena's here. Trust me. With two of us working on this..."

"Sure, but that's not going to stop the rain tonight, is it?"

"You said he has raingear. And he's been camping with

us in all sorts of weather. And he always helped set up camp, or a make-shift lean-to, Scott."

"Sure. It's just, it's getting dark, and it's raining, and that would be a lot for a kid to deal with, on top of being lost in the woods."

"He knows we won't stop looking for him. And he's not really alone out there."

"That does not give me any comfort. Does it give you comfort?"

"Well, yeah, in a weird way, it does," Charlie said. "I can almost guarantee you that the spirit is not about to let anything happen to him. She is his lifeline. He is her entire purpose at the moment. So, yeah, actually, if something happens to him, then she may be stuck for eternity, and she knows that."

"I hope you're right, Charlie," Scott said. "I really do."

Charlie couldn't take any more of her ex-husband's pessimism in that moment. She turned to Athena and said, "Scott and I were just discussing going to get some dinner. Have you eaten?"

Athena's eyes brightened. "No, not yet. After the drive I've had, food sounds really good. Then when we get back, we'll need to set up a little command center of our own."

"I'm already on top of that. I checked into a hotel room with a kitchenette, two queen beds and a desk."

"Great," Athena said.

Scott showed a bit more energy at that idea. "I'm sure the rangers here will accommodate us too.

They've been super nice. When this rain stops, they're going to call in a helicopter to resume searching from the air."

"Great," said Athena. "Maybe over dinner, we can discuss some strategies."

Charlie said, "Yeah, I think that's a good idea. Do you want to join us, Scott?"

He shook his head. "No. I think maybe I should just stay here. Sounds like you two have a lot to discuss, and I don't want to miss anything if they come up with a sighting."

"Okay," Charlie said. "That's fine, Scott. I hope you don't think because I'm not sitting around here wringing my hands that I don't care about what's happening to our son."

Scott shook his head and gave her a sad but genuine smile. "No, not at all. If I were in your position, I'd be doing the exact same thing," he said, letting out a heavy sigh.

Charlie put a hand on his shoulder and gently squeezed it. "I know. You're not someone who's used to sitting around."

"There's no reason we can't deputize you and have you help us. The rangers are great. They're doing what they can, but we have different resources. And we don't have to wait for it to stop raining to use them. We can always use an extra pair of hands."

"Athena's right," Charlie agreed.

"I have some ideas about the best way we can aid them," Athena said.

"That's great," Charlie said. "I can't wait to hear them. Why don't we get out of here and get some food, get a little refreshed?"

"I think that's a great idea. We'll get out from underneath their feet. That way we can speak a little more freely too," Athena said.

"Okay," Scott relented. "I'm on board."

"I saw a diner on my way in. The counter looked empty, probably because of the rain. But their sign said they have hot apple pie."

"Pie sounds good," Scott said dryly.

"Yeah, to me too," Charlie said. "Let's get out of here,"

CHAPTER 32

C harlie scrolled through the lists of missing children in the southeast area for the fourth time. Bleary-eyed, she pushed away from the breakfast table in the kitchenette in her hotel room and rose to her feet. Athena kept working at the desk near the front door, her fingers racing over the keyboard of her laptop.

"Have you found anything yet?" Charlie asked, massaging the back of her neck with her hand.

"Yep, I accessed the medical examiner's report for the dead girl found inside the park four years ago. Her name is Michelle Brody," Athena said without looking away from her screen. "I also have some potential runaways that look interesting. A couple could be possible matches for Jenna. I'm compiling a list now." Finally, she looked up at Charlie, as bright-eyed as if she'd had a full night's sleep.

"Great," Charlie said. "I'm going to step outside to get some air and check on Scott."

"That's a good idea," Athena said, her red curls bouncing against her shoulders as she nodded. She'd thoroughly dried out from her soggy drive. "He didn't look very good during dinner."

Charlie shrugged. "I think he's just feeling a little helpless right now, and he's not a man who does helpless very well," Charlie said.

"I gathered," Athena said, giving her friend a wry smile.

Charlie gave her a little wave and headed out of their hotel room onto the long open corridor that looked out over the parking lot. Scott leaned on the railing just outside the front door, his gaze cast toward the mountains and the national park. Charlie slid up next to him, close enough to let her arm touch his.

"Hey," she said, nudging against him. "I thought you wanted to help us read the maps."

"Hey," he said, his voice full of gravel. "Right. It's just..."

"I know. How are you doing?"

"I'm fine. I have a nice warm hotel room. Dry clothes. Warm food. And all the clean water I can drink. Evan may not be so lucky."

"Yeah. I know." She glanced down at her hands and

pressed her arm harder against his. The rain had finally let up, leaving behind a warm, muggy evening. Cricket song filled the night with sound.

"We're going to find him, Scott. I promise."

"I believe you," he said. "I just don't know what sort of state we'll find him in when we do."

"He's a strong boy, and this isn't his first trip into the woods. Have a little faith in him."

"I do have faith in him. It's the bears and every other dangerous thing out there that scares the bejeezus out of me."

"Scott, we've been taking him camping since he was two years old. Evan is a smart, observant kid. I have no doubt that he picked up quite a bit, and that doesn't even count what we taught him directly."

"I know," Scott whispered. "But he's still just a kid."

"I know." She nodded and crossed her arms so she could put her hand in the crook of Scott's elbow. Scott put his hand on top of hers as if he was thankful for the comfort. "Did Evan ever tell you he has a talent for hearing animals?"

"Hearing animals?"

"Yeah. Sort of sensing their thoughts."

"No, he didn't. That's remarkable but... I'm not sure if I should be horrified or not."

"I think it's an excellent talent to have, especially if you're sitting in the middle of the woods, in the dark, surrounded by coyotes, bears, and bobcats."

"You're really not making me feel better, Charlie."

"I'm sorry." She squeezed his arm. "To me, it's much easier to defend yourself against something if you can sense it before it senses you."

"Okay." Scott nodded and pursed his lips. "That's a valid point."

"I know how hard this is for you. You're not feeling very in control right now, and I know that's driving you crazy," Charlie said.

"You know." He suppressed a smile. "I hate when you do that, and strangely I also love it. What is that called?"

"A paradox?"

"A paradox," he echoed.

"I know a way you can stop feeling so helpless."

"I'm listening?"

"You're very good at reading maps. We happen to have a couple of area maps the rangers let us borrow. Athena and I are about to start searching property records."

"For what?"

"It's kind of a stab in the dark, but my hunch is, whoever killed the girl that's haunting Evan didn't do it in a place where he could be easily discovered. I think he must have a cabin or house where he can take these girls."

"So, you think he's hunting them?

"I do." She turned so she could look him in the eye. "What I really wish is that I could talk to the spirit and get more information from her."

"Why can't you? Couldn't you hold a séance or something? Call her here?"

Charlie chuckled. "You know that's actually a good idea."

"Really? I was sort of kidding."

Charlie rolled her eyes. "No, you weren't. You were serious. You just weren't sure if seances were real or not. Which, they are, by the way, but it's not a good method for us. We need something more specific to one person. Something like a summoning."

"That sounds very ominous. The good Catholic schoolboy in me almost made me cross myself."

Charlie laughed and nudged her arm against his. "It's not like that. You have to remember this isn't my first rodeo. It would be helpful if I had more than just two of us."

"Two of us?"

"Yes. Athena and me. Three, five, seven, nine are always more powerful numbers than two. Thirteen is ideal, but I don't know how I'd get that without recruiting rangers, and they were already pretty skeptical of me."

"It's too bad your cousins aren't here," he mused.

"I know, but they have their own lives. Jen has a big catering event, and her daughter's father is in town wreaking havoc. The others stayed to support her. I have lots of resources at the DOL, so it's possible we could gather some other witches tomorrow."

"Could I stand in?" he asked.

"Would you want to? You'd have to set aside some of your skepticism for it to really work."

"Right now, I would set aside anything—my career, even my life—if it meant bringing him home safe and soon."

"You two really bonded this trip, didn't you?"

"He's my son, Charlie. I love him. Of course, we bonded," Scott snapped. He pulled his hand away from hers.

"That's what I mean. Of course, you love him. No one is questioning that, but you've always had a hard time dealing with his sensitivity. Sometimes, Evan has felt misunderstood by you."

"I know." Scott grimaced. "But I'm trying to be more open-minded. Maybe it's better to just accept that I'm walking among mythical creatures instead of fighting it. I don't have the mental energy for it, especially now."

"I completely understand. Accepting it will make your life easier."

"Yes." He hung his head. "I certainly hope so."

The door opened behind them, and Athena stood at the threshold. "Charlie, are you ready to start combing through property records?"

"I am." She let go of Scott's arm and turned around. "Would you mind if Scott helped us? He's great with maps, and he's camped these mountains many times."

"That'd be great. My mother always said many hands make light work."

Scott threw a glance over his shoulder. "That's a very cheerful way of looking at things."

"Athena is nothing if not cheerful," Charlie said.

"I am." Athena grinned and held her hands in surrender. "Feel free to tell me to tone it down."

"I wouldn't dream of it. We could all use a little dose of sunshine about now," Scott said and pushed off from the banister. "What do we need to do first?"

EVAN UNZIPPED THE PLASTIC VACUUM BAG AND FISHED OUT his fleece jacket. The rain had stopped, but a chill had settled around his shoulders, leaving him cold. He removed his poncho, slipped on the fleece jacket, and sealed the vacuum bag. He rolled it the way Cora had taught him to force out the air and make the contents smaller and easier to pack. Once he was warm, he huddled under his poncho again with his back at the base of a tree. His legs ached from walking most of the day. He pulled his legs beneath the poncho and settled his backpack under his knees to keep it dry. He hoped it wouldn't rain again. He hoped more than anything he wouldn't run into a bear or some other animal that might look at him as either a threat or a meal.

The underbrush he'd walked through today had left long red welts in places, and a few had scabbed over. The skin felt hot to touch near the worst scratches. When morning light came, his first priority would be to tend to those wounds. He couldn't risk them getting infected. His dad had drilled into his head that infection was one of the worst enemies on a trip into the woods. Even more so than animals. Or hunger. Only dehydration trumped infection.

His father's voice echoed through his head. "Rule number one, Evan. If you ever get lost, you need to find water first. No water, no survival. Understand?"

"What's the second rule, Dad?" he'd asked.

"If you get scratched, tend to your wounds. Don't think they'll get better on their own. There are too many invisible, creepy crawlies out here. An infected scratch could cause blood poisoning, which leads to sepsis. And you can die from it. Understand?"

"Yes, sir," he mumbled to the memory. When first light came, he would dig out his first-aid kit, clean the scratches with alcohol pads, and put some of the antibacterial cream on the wounds.

Rain fell again, drumming against the hood of his poncho. His eyes grew heavy at the thrumming sound. He wrapped his arms around his knees and rested his head against them.

"I need to sleep," he said aloud, unsure the spirit was still with him. It had been a couple of hours since he'd last seen her. Since the rain first started and the darkness enveloped them.

"I know," her voice floated through his head.

"I don't want to be eaten by anything tonight. Do you understand?"

"I do. I'll stand guard over you, but I need to go check on Jenna first. I'll be back."

"You better be," he muttered, without lifting his head. No answer. He fought against the chill that wanted to consume him, even though it probably wasn't that cold. He wished he were in his bed at his mother's house, curled up with her cat Poe and one of his video games. Penny, the ghostly chicken that hung around his mom's, would be perched on his footboard snoring, even though she was dead and didn't really need sleep anymore. The thought of the auburn feathered chicken drew a smile out of him. Maybe when he got home, he could talk his cousin Jen into making some macaroni and cheese just for him. She made the best mac and cheese he'd ever tasted in his life. Way better than anything out of the box or that his mother could make. But he'd never tell her that.

"Evan?" The spirit's voice floated through his head.

"That was fast."

"I know you're tired, but we need to keep moving."

"No. Absolutely not. I cannot go any farther. It's dark and dangerous and raining, and I'm so tired. You don't need to sleep, but I do."

"It's just, he's..." She flickered and appeared before him.

"He's just what? Do you honestly think I'm going to be

able to get there in time to save somebody? Especially with no sleep and barely any food?"

She opened her mouth as if to argue and flickered again, looking behind her. "Wait. Someone's here."

"What?" Evan sat up straight and tried to look in every direction, but the moon hid behind the clouds, and the darkness pressed in on him.

"Who's here?" he called.

She hissed, "Shut up!" at him and disappeared. "I'm going to get rid of them."

"No! Don't." Evan hopped to his feet. "I'm here!" he called into the deep gloom of the surrounding forest. "Please, if you can hear me. I'm here."

He stilled his body and listened carefully. After a few moments of silence, his heart sank. Maybe it wasn't a person. Maybe it was another spirit. He sat back down at the base of the tree and drew his knees up beneath his poncho again, along with his bag. The only thing stronger than the feeling of defeat was exhaustion. He wrapped his arms around his knees, hugging them to his chest and leaned his forehead on his arms, and waited for sleep to take him.

CHAPTER 33

"I remember that tree," Evan said. His entire body ached from walking most of the day. The heavy cloud cover made it impossible to know the time of day and he was reluctant to turn on his phone. The battery charger he'd brought had mysteriously died and his phone only had 30 percent left on the battery, so he'd turned it off. "Are we walking in a circle? I thought you wanted to get there as quickly as possible."

Michelle materialized next to him and fell in line with his step. "We're not walking in a straight line. But don't worry, we'll get there in time."

"What does that mean?" Evan said.

"Shush," the ghost whispered. "Lower your voice. We're being followed."

"What?" Evan stopped in his tracks and scanned the

woods. *Please, let it be another person.* "Hello! Help me! I'm lost!" he called frantically into the forest.

"Evan!" Michelle warned sharply. "I said, shush."

An invisible hand clamped around his neck, squeezing just enough to make it hard to breathe. Evan groped at his neck with his hands, struggling to free himself from the unseen culprit scratching at the tender skin of his neck. Then, as suddenly as it started, the invisible hand released him.

Evan coughed violently until he caught his breath and then gently touched his neck. Something sticky and warm smeared against his fingers. When drew his hand away he found blood and in the gray gloom of the forest it looked almost black.

"Great, more scratches," he muttered. His neck ached where she'd wrenched his throat and tried to take him down.

Michelle chastised him. "See what you've done now?" He didn't look up. He wasn't interested in being scolded after something had tried to kill him. "That's all your fault," she snapped. "If you'd just listen to me."

Evan threw an angry glare her way, then dropped his backpack to the ground and kneeled to find his first-aid kit. His legs and arms were now covered in scratches from pushing through the heavy underbrush between the trees for half the day. He took his last alcohol pad and held it for a second before putting it back. It would be better to save it for now, just in case.

In case what?

He shivered and didn't want to think about having a worse wound. Still, he needed something to clean the new wounds, and his first-aid kit was growing woefully depleted as the day progressed. His hand brushed against a clean t-shirt as he dug through the pack. An idea flashed through his brain. He grabbed the shirt and the multi-tool.

He opened the knife on the tool and sliced the fabric, ripping a couple of strips from the bottom. Then he soaked the cotton with some purified water from his bottle.

It was almost as good as alcohol. Hadn't he heard his dad say something like that? At least, he hoped so. The damp cloth felt cool and soothing against his neck, though it stung a little. That had to be a good sign. When he finished cleaning the area, he retrieved the half-empty tube of antibiotic cream and squeezed out only a thin strip of the stuff onto his fingertip. He spread it as thinly as he could across the two scratches on his neck. When he was done tending to his wounds, he packed everything back into his pack and started to get to his feet.

"Stay down," Michelle ordered. He'd been so absorbed in his first-aid, he'd almost forgotten she was there. But then some invisible force pushed him down, and he landed hard on the ground.

"Why?" He brushed the leaf detritus from his hands.

"There's a reaper that's been combing the woods. I think she's looking for me."

"A reaper?" Evan asked, trying not to let any emotion show in his voice. Did that mean his mom might be in the area? A spark of hope lit inside his chest. His mother's boyfriend, Tom Sharon, was a reaper. Although he'd only seen him in his reaper form once, it was enough to scare him. What if Tom had come along too? He knew from eavesdropping that if his mother called aloud for Tom, he would just show up. Would that work for him too?

"Tom!" Evan called. "Tom Sharon! If you can hear me..."

All of a sudden, he couldn't open his mouth. It was as if his lips had been sewn together. He slapped his hand against the forest floor, but nothing happened. He was stuck again. He wished he had never told Michelle he would help her.

"Shut up!" Her voice drifted through his head. "I'm sorry to do this to you, Evan, but I need you."

Evan gave her the most hateful stare he could muster, but she didn't seem bothered. After a few moments of silence, he tried to open his mouth again, and this time his lips moved freely.

"That's it," he said with a flash of anger. "I'm done, Michelle. You're on your own," he said. "You can't keep doing this to me. It's a free country."

He rose to his feet, thinking it was a lame thing to say to a ghost, but what did she expect? He almost expected her to push him back down, but she didn't. He slung his pack over his arms and adjusted it on his back to evenly distribute the load. Then he began to walk away from her, back in the direction they had come.

"You're going to get lost that way," she called after him.

"I don't care," he said. "Anything is better than being with you. I'll take my chances."

"Evan, please wait. I'm sorry." She suddenly appeared in front of him, startling him. He gritted his teeth and stopped in his tracks.

"I hate when you do that and I don't care if you're sorry," he said. "This is not the way you treat people if you want them to help you." He didn't believe she would ever help him, so he was going to find his father on his own. He moved forward to sidestep her, but she flickered and appeared in front of him again, blocking his way. This time he didn't let her stop him, and he walked straight through her.

A fresh icy shiver washed over him when his body encountered her. Michelle made an indignant sound as if she couldn't believe he had just done that. Every five feet or so, she flickered in front of him, trying to block him from walking. Evan was determined. He either side-stepped her or walked right through her.

"You're not going to stop me," he said. "I'm pretty sure my mom is here. She's going to come for me."

A thunderous clap startled him. He hunkered down and tried to find the source. It didn't sound like gunfire. A familiar creaking sound drew his attention and transfixed him to the spot. The top of a pine tree had snapped off and hung by a strip of thin green wood. The splintered top swayed almost directly over his head, creaking in the slight breeze blowing through the tops of the trees. Wet, green pine needles rained down on him. Another crack echoed across the forest, and the treetop began its fall.

"Evan! Look out!" Michelle screeched.

The sound of the branches catching on the surrounding trees awoke Evan from the shock holding him in place, and he darted away as quickly as he could. When the huge branch finally hit the ground, Evan turned and surveyed the scene, his chest still heaving from his sprint.

The broken treetop landed almost exactly where he'd been standing.

"Holy goddess," Evan mumbled. "Are you trying to kill me?"

Michelle materialized next to him. "What? I didn't do that."

"Right," he said, sneering at her. He leaned over with his hands on his knees and tried to catch his breath.

"I didn't," she said softly, almost pleading. "I swear. I don't want to hurt you. I don't want anyone to get hurt."

"Then stop trying to hurt me. When you choke me or seal my mouth, it hurts me."

"I'm sorry," she whispered. "I swear to you, I won't do it again."

"And you really didn't do this?"

Michelle stared up at the broken tree. "No way I have that kind of power."

"My mom would say different," Evan said.

"Really?"

"Yeah. Spirits, like you, you're just energy, and you have a lot more power to affect the physical world than you think."

"How?"

"All it takes is focus. My great aunt taught me if I really focus my energy on something that I want to happen, then I can make it so."

"Cool. And you think I can do that? Even though I'm dead."

"Yeah." He sighed and looked around at the forest. Even the birds weren't singing anymore and the quiet was eerie in the fading light.

"It's going to get dark soon. I should make camp. Will your friend last till we get there?"

"I don't know. I hope so," she whispered.

"All right. I will keep helping you, but you have to swear that you're not going to hurt me anymore." He hoped it wasn't a mistake to trust her again.

"I swear it." She held one hand against her nearly translucent chest and the other in the air, making a pledge to seal her words.

"Good. Let's find a place for me to set up for the night. I'm getting tired."

"There's still a lot of light left," she chided.

"Yeah, well, I have to ration the food I have left, or my energy will run out sooner."

Michelle rolled her eyes. "Fine. We'll break for now."

"Do you know if there's a stream nearby?" he asked. "My water's getting low."

"Let me see what I can find," she said and disappeared before his eyes.

CHAPTER 34

Jen made peeling and slicing the cucumbers she had picked from the garden that afternoon a meditation. Slowly and methodically, she dragged the vegetable peeler across the prickly green skin of the fat, sausage sized cuke, casting the strips into a bucket of veggie refuse, eggshells, and coffee grounds she'd collected this week to go into her compost pile. Lisa sat on the counter in a green tank top and jeans shorts within arm's reach, and she stretched across the counter and snagged a fresh slice of the cucumber.

"These are so good I could eat the whole plate by myself." Lisa reached for another slice, and Jen smacked her hand away.

"I have more in the garden. You're welcome to go pick one and slice it up for yourself," Jen scolded. "I need these for the salad."

"Okay, okay. Sorry." Lisa held her hands up in surrender. "Why're you so testy?"

"No reason," Jen lied and avoided looking her sister in the eye. "You know you could help. That head of lettuce isn't going to turn into a salad by itself."

"Fine." Lisa hopped off the counter and went to the sink to wash her hands, then grabbed a towel to dry them. "When is Evangeline getting here?"

"Oh, my stars, Lisa. You should at least know how to make a salad," Jen snapped. "Poor old Jason's going to starve."

"First off, I practically live off salad, so I know exactly how to make one. And second, Jason is perfectly capable of cooking for himself. If he doesn't feel like cooking, he can order take out for the both of us. That's exactly what I do. Sheesh."

"I see." Jen rolled her eyes. She cringed at the judgmental tone in her voice but didn't know exactly how to stop it.

Lisa gathered the tools she needed—a cutting board, one of Jen's knives from the knife block on the counter, and the salad spinner hidden away in the lower cabinet. Lisa picked up the large head of romaine and turned it over. "This lettuce looks great. Did you grow this, too?"

"No, I picked that up at the market. It's too hot right now for lettuce. Maybe I'll plant some in the fall." Jen finished slicing the cucumbers and pushed the plate aside.

Lisa sliced off the lettuce's root and plopped it into Jen's refuse bowl before she sliced through the crisp green leaves and chopped them into bite-size pieces.

"So, are you going to tell me why you're in such a bad mood or not? Is this because your big catering gig got canceled?" Lisa asked. She scooped up the lettuce and put it into the spinner's inner colander and then gave it a good washing.

"I told you, no reason," Jen said. "And it didn't get canceled. It got changed into a fundraiser. Which was for the best considering a tornado had just hit part of downtown."

"And I smell a lie. Or at least a cover up." Lisa scowled. "Plus, your energy's a weird yellow color. Not your normal color at all."

Jen blew out a heavy sigh and rinsed the peeler in the sink before dropping it into the dish drainer on the counter. "Fine. If you must know, it's because Ben isn't coming."

"Did you invite him?"

"He is always invited," Jen said.

"Then how do you know he's not coming?"

"He texted me about an hour ago and told me he wasn't." It was hard to keep the hurt out of her voice.

"I'm sorry, honey." Lisa reached over and touched her sister's arm.

"It's all my fault. I was so mad at him the other night, and now I just..."

"You just want to make up." Lisa shrugged and placed the colander back into the spinner. She put the lid on tightly and pulled the ripcord, and the colander spun inside, casting off water from the freshly washed lettuce.

"It's totally understandable. You miss him. Have you thought about just swallowing your pride and calling him to talk? Texting leaves too much room for misunderstanding."

"I know." Jen's shoulders sagged a little. She retrieved a large wooden salad bowl and put it on the counter next to Lisa. "It's probably for the best he's not here, with Mark coming tonight."

"You may be right," Lisa said. She opened the spinner and dumped the lettuce into the bowl. She started arranging the cucumbers on top of the lettuce. "Are there any tomatoes?"

"Yes, right there in front of your nose." Jen pointed to the basket full of small cherry-sized tomatoes in all different colors next to the huge heirloom beefsteak tomatoes. "They need to be rinsed first."

Lisa just grinned. "If they'd been a snake, they'd have bit me. What else do you want in the salad?"

"I grated some carrot earlier. You can add that too if you'd like."

"Okey dokey," Lisa said. "Do we need to make anything else? Coleslaw?"

"Nothing I can think of. There's banana pudding in

the fridge, and Evangeline said she was bringing enough potato salad for an army."

"Our army's a little low on troops today. Have you heard from Charlie?" Lisa dumped the basket of tomatoes into the spinner's colander and rinsed them well.

"I haven't. I'm hoping Evangeline will have some news. I can't shake this unsettled feeling I have in my stomach. I hope they find Evan soon," Jen said.

"Yeah. Me too. I wish we could've gone with her."

"I know. It's weird that Ben's not with her. At least then I'd know he's working hard on something and not out there hating me."

"You are impossible to hate Jennifer Ellen Holloway."

Jen couldn't help but smile and quipped, "Right back at you, Lisa Marie Holloway."

"Aww...there's so much love in here," Daphne called out, and the screen door slammed behind her and she quickly closed the back door to keep the air conditioning inside. She set the pie dish in her hands on the table and opened her arms wide. "Come on, group hug, witches."

Jen chuckled and let herself be pulled into Daphne's side. "You're hard to hate too, Daphne."

"Thank you." Daphne kissed Jen on the cheek. Lisa didn't say anything, but Daphne kissed her on the cheek too.

"All right, fine. You're hard to hate. Is that what you wanted to hear?" Lisa grumbled.

"Yes, it is." Daphne said with a self-satisfied grin. "I

stopped at Mama's before I came over and she sent this. What would you like me to do with it?" She pointed to the large pie she'd set on the table.

"What is it?" Lisa asked and peeled back the foil covering the dish.

"Key lime pie with a sugar cookie crust," Daphne said. "Mama wanted to know if you have any whipped cream to serve with it."

"Yes, I do," Jen said.

"Well, there goes my diet." Lisa frowned and closed the foil.

"Daph, can you put it in the fridge, please?" Jen pointed to the white side-by-side refrigerator inside the pantry.

"Sure." Daphne grabbed the pie box.

"So why on earth are you on a diet, Lisa?" Jen leaned against the counter and folded her arms across her chest.

"I went into Maureen's Wedding Shop the other day and tried on a couple of dresses. Both in my normal size, and they were too tight."

Jen scoffed. "Too tight? You're skinny as a rail."

Daphne chimed in. "They probably want you to buy a corset too." She exited the pantry and joined them. "You should just buy the dress you want and have it altered to fit your body and not worry about all that size nonsense. Forget dieting. You have a great figure. And I'm sure Jason would agree."

"Thank you," Lisa said. "I appreciate that."

"Can somebody please help me?" Evangeline called from the back porch. Daphne quickly opened the screen door and let her mother inside.

"Jen, I hope there's room for this in your refrigerator."

Jen peeked at the long tray covered in aluminum foil. "There should be room on the bottom shelf."

"Thanks," Evangeline said. "I'm so glad Jack is manning the grill outside. It's so hot today I didn't want to heat up the kitchen."

"Totally agree." Lisa slid in next to her aunt at the refrigerator and pulled all the salad dressings from the door.

"Thank goddess, we've got plenty of veggies too." Jen plucked a softball-sized red tomato from the counter and made quick work of slicing it into thick slabs. She arranged the pieces on a plate and sliced up a second one.

"Those look beautiful, Jen," Evangeline said, closing the refrigerator.

"So, have you had any word from Charlie?" Jen asked.

"Not really. She texted me about her cat, which reminds me I need to step over there and feed her. But other than that, no news on Evan." Evangeline frowned at her nieces, conveying her worry.

"I'm sure she'll let us know something soon," Jen said.

"You're probably right, but unless you have objections, I think I'm going to head up there tomorrow and see if I can help out."

Jen shook her head. "No objections at all," she said and placed the last slice of tomato on the plate.

"I wish we could go with you," Lisa said.

"I think y'all have your hands quite full, so it's better that you're here."

A knock on the door drew their attention, and Daphne went to answer it.

"Hello, Mark," Daphne said and held the door wide. "C'mon in. You're right on time."

Mark stepped into the kitchen and gave Daphne an incandescent smile. "Hello. Daphne, right? We met yesterday." He nodded as if she were royalty.

Daphne grinned, clearly enjoying his attention. "Yes, we did. I hear you were quite the hero."

Mark shook his head. "No, it was nothing. Jen's the real hero."

Daphne said, "Hey, everyone. Look who's here." She gestured for Mark to follow her. "Mark, I think you know everyone here, right?" she said.

Lisa, Jen, and Evangeline said, "Hey, Mark."

"Hello, everyone."

He stood in the center of the kitchen in an open-collared shirt and jeans with a knife crease, radiating his usual charm by eyeing Jen. "I have to disagree, Daphne, Jen was the real hero. She's the one who suggested to the mayor they turn the luncheon into an impromptu fundraiser for the victims of the tornado. She even donated all the food she'd made."

"It was nothing," Jen said, her cheeks heated with embarrassment. She shrugged. "It was the right thing to do."

"And it doesn't hurt that all the local news channels picked it up," Lisa remarked.

"You looked great on camera, by the way," Mark said and winked at Jen.

"So, what've you got there, Mark?" Evangeline pointed to the box of beer he held in one hand.

"Oh right, I wasn't sure what to bring, so I've got beer and wine. I figured the Merlot would be nice with the steak." He lifted the bottle of wine in his other hand.

"Indeed." Lisa reached for the bottle. "I'll take that for you. I'm Lisa, by the way."

"Nice to meet you," Mark said.

"I think that's very thoughtful of you," Evangeline said. "You can put the box on the table for now."

Mark nodded and the bottles rattled when he placed the container down. "So where's Ruby? I didn't see her outside."

"I think she's in her playhouse with her nose in a book."

"Great, I've got something for her too."

"Mark, you didn't have to do that," Jen said, sounding apprehensive.

"It's not much." He shrugged. "Let's just call it an early birthday present."

"You're making me nervous. What is it?"

"It's a puppy." Mark gave her a sly grin.

"Mark! No. She is not ready for that responsibility." Jen protested.

Mark laughed. "It's not a real puppy. Just a stuffed animal. You said she collected them, so I thought she might like that."

Jen let out a breathy laugh of relief. "She'll love it. Thank you."

"So, Mark, where is your friend?" Evangeline asked.

"My friend?" Mark asked. He seemed to be looking for a spot to sit or lean or stand that wouldn't be in the way of the food prep in the kitchen.

"Yeah," Evangeline said, mopping down the sink. "The one who helped you bring the generator."

"Oh, Bridges. He stayed at the hotel. He didn't want to intrude since this is more of a family affair."

"He would have been welcome," Evangeline said.

"That's very gracious of you," Mark said.

"Evangeline," Jen said, removing her apron. "Can you take over getting the food down to the table? I'd like to give Mark a little tour and introduce him to everyone."

Evangeline put the sponge under the sink and said, "Of course, honey. Y'all go on."

Jen hooked her hand in the crook of Mark's arm and ignored the exchange of looks between her sister and cousin. "Come on, I'll show you around, and we can check the playhouse for Ruby."

* * *

"KNOCK, KNOCK," JEN SAID AND POKED HER HEAD THROUGH the open Dutch door of the playhouse that her father had bought for Ruby. In the year and a half since Ruby'd acquired the playhouse, she had turned it into a little haven. She'd talked her grandfather into installing a hanging rattan chair where she curled up to read. She'd long outgrown the small table and chairs that had come with the playhouse, and Jen had helped her replace them with a bookshelf that held all her favorite books. There was also a beanbag chair on the floor in case she felt like playing games on her tablet instead of reading.

When Mark and Jen ducked to enter the playhouse door, Ruby sat swinging in her chair with her legs extended and her feet on the ground so she could move herself back and forth while she read her book.

"Hey, Rubes," her mother said. "You got a visitor."

"Okay," Ruby said.

"Ruby," Jen said, shifting her tone to a more serious parental tone. "Honey, I need you to put the book down now, okay? It's rude to read when someone's here talking to you."

Ruby scowled and closed her book.

"That's better," Jen said. "You remember Mark, right? From yesterday?"

"Yeah," Ruby said. She sat up on the edge of her swing chair.

"Hi," she said to Mark.

"Hi, Ruby." Mark kneeled. Jen studied his body language and compared to the ease with which he spoke to the women in the kitchen, Mark sounded a little artificial and strained. "How are you?"

"I'm fine," Ruby said.

Jen said, "Why don't you come out of the playhouse, so you and Mark can get to know each other a little better."

Ruby's long dark hair hung in one long braid over her shoulder. She reached up and ran her fingers over it nervously. "Why would I want to do that?" she asked.

"Ruby, that's not very nice," Jen said.

"I don't mean to be rude," Ruby said. "I just I don't understand."

Jen exchanged glances with Mark.

"I hope you don't mind. I think Ruby and I need to have a little talk."

"No problem," Mark said. He smiled and rose to his feet, then waggled his fingers in a brief wave. "I'll see you later, Ruby. I guess I should go hang out at the grill, with your dad."

"That's a great idea," Jen said. "We'll be out in a little while."

Jen watched him walk out and took a seat on the beanbag.

"Mom, he's weird," Ruby said. "I don't want to spend any time with him."

"Okay," Jen said. "Can you at least tell me why you think he's weird? Has he done anything that made you feel uncomfortable?"

"No. Not exactly. I just get a weird feeling from him."

"What kind of weird feeling, honey?" Jen leaned in to listen to her daughter. She trusted her instincts. Had Mark crossed a line?

"I don't know. Just the way he looks at me."

"I'm sorry, honey," Jen said. "How does he look at you?"

"I don't know, like I'm food or something," Ruby said.

"Like food?" Jen echoed. What did that mean?

"Yeah, it's kinda like that story. Remember, when I was little, how you used to read to me about Red Riding Hood. The wolf had eaten the grandma, and Red Riding Hood said, "My, what big eyes you have." And the wolf said, "The better to see you." And then Red Riding Hood said, "My, grandma what big teeth you have." And then the wolf said, "The better to eat you with."

Ruby shivered. "That's sort of how I feel when he's around."

"Sweetie, are you sensing Mark wants to hurt you?"

"I don't know." She shrugged and then seemed to think about it. "No. I guess not. He's weird. That's all."

"I see." Jen shifted, and the plastic beads inside the beanbag made a swishing noise. She crossed her legs in front of her into a half-lotus position, trying to get more comfortable. "Honey, there's something I need to tell you about Mark."

"He's not your boyfriend, now, is he?" Ruby asked.

"What? No. Why would you ask me something like that?"

"I don't know. Because Ben's not here? And you want me to talk to Mark."

"Oh. Well, Ben couldn't be here because he had to work," Jen said.

"He did?"

"Yeah, he did."

"I like Ben." Ruby gently rocked her swing back and forth with her feet. "He's nice to you. And to me. And he's funny."

"Yeah, he is." Jen smiled. "For the record, I like Ben too. And he is still my boyfriend."

"Good. Then," Ruby's brow furrowed, "what did you want to tell me about Mark?"

Jen sighed. "I know this is kind of scary and out of the blue, but you know how you're always asking me about your daddy?"

"Yeah." Ruby eyed her mother with caution.

"Honey, Mark is your daddy."

"Oh," Ruby said. She bit her bottom lip and leaned back in her swing chair, partially hidden behind the cushion.

"Ruby?" Jen leaned forward but couldn't get a good look at Ruby's face. "Are you okay?"

"Sure, I guess so," Ruby said, but Jen wasn't convinced.

"Can you talk to me about what you're feeling?"

"Are you sure he's my daddy?" Ruby asked. She looked around the playroom but not directly at Jen.

"Yeah, I'm sure," Jen said.

"Hey, Jen," Evangeline's gentle voice called through the open door. "I'm sorry to interrupt, but the steaks are ready. Everything's on the table. Are y'all ready to eat?"

"Sure," Jen said and put her hand on Ruby's foot. "We'll be there in just a minute."

"Okay, honey," Evangeline said before she left.

Ruby spun herself around the swing chair until she faced away from her mother. "I'm not hungry," she said.

"I know this is not exactly what you were expecting to hear today. And I know it's kind of a shock. But it would be very rude for you to not at least sit with us while we have guests."

"I'm just not hungry, Mama," she whined in a baby voice she hadn't used in years.

"Come here," Jen waggled her fingers at Ruby. Ruby stuck out her tongue and rolled her eyes but climbed out of the chair. Jen took her hand and pulled her onto her lap. "We have freshly sliced tomatoes. You can eat all you want," Jen said. "And there's banana pudding for later. Your favorite. And Mark brought you an early birthday present. So that's exciting, right?"

"I guess," Ruby said, sounding a little resigned.

Jen kissed the top of Ruby's head and rocked her a

little. "I know this is scary. It's kind of scary for me too. But he just wants to get to know you a little. He won't be here for long, I promise. He lives far away."

"Is he going to try to take me away?"

Jen hugged her daughter tightly. "No."

"Promise?"

"I promise."

"Okay, I guess we should go eat then." Ruby grunted and climbed out of her mother's lap.

Jen held her hand up. "Help me up, honey." Ruby took it and helped pull Jen to her feet.

"These old bones are getting too old to sit on the floor like that," Jen laughed. She held fast to Ruby's hand. "Come on. Let's go properly meet your daddy."

Ruby nodded but showed no enthusiasm.

RUBY SAT QUIETLY NEXT TO HER MOTHER. OCCASIONALLY, she looked up from her plate of vegetables to give Mark a suspicious look. Mark showed patience and returned her scowls with smiles. Sometimes, Ruby just stared at him so hard she seemed to see through him. Mark wondered what sort of mental capabilities she might have. Jen had whispered in his ear just before they all took their seats that she had told Ruby the truth about him.

He hoped more than anything, he would get a chance to spend some time with her to get a better feel for her abilities. If he could do that, he could understand what motivated her. And what it would take for Ruby to want him in her life. And more importantly, what it would take to get Ruby to pledge her allegiance to him and his organization, and not his mother's, on her sixteenth birthday.

So far, Jen had shown no interest in rekindling anything romantic with him. And perhaps that was all right. He didn't need her, necessarily. Although wresting the child away from her would be difficult without that type of connection. Mark glanced up from his nearly empty plate and gave Jen a smile.

"I hope you saved some room for dessert," Jen said to him across the crowded dinner table. "I've got banana pudding and a key lime pie, thanks to you, Evangeline."

"Oh, it was nothing," she said. "I'll be glad when we get everything back in order at the restaurant. I don't like having a lot of time on my hands."

"I agree," Jen said.

"So, Ruby," Mark said. Ruby sat up as if she'd been goosed.

"Yes, sir," she said.

"You don't have to call me, sir," he said. "That's what people called my dad."

Ruby looked from him to her mother. "Is that true?" Ruby asked.

"No, you still need to call him, sir. Because around here, that's simply good manners," Jen said loud enough to make sure Mark heard the words good manners.

Mark held up his fingers. "Of course. I'm sorry. I didn't mean to tread on your parenting style."

"What did you want to talk to her about, Mark?" Jen asked.

"Right. I just wanted to know what Ruby wanted for her birthday? You turn eight next week, don't you?"

"Yes. I do. What I really want is a dog," she said, giving her mother a sideways glance. "But I'm probably not going to get it."

"Ruby, sweetie. We've been over this. It's a lot of responsibility."

Ruby sat up tall and called up a bright smile. "I'm responsible. I would make sure the dog had food and water and that we played outside. I've already been reading books about how to train a dog," she said.

"Have you, now?" Jack Holloway said from the end of the table.

"Yes, sir," she said, smiling at her grandfather.

"What kind of tricks would you teach a dog?" Mark asked.

"Well..." Ruby stared off into the distance as if she were collecting her thoughts. "I would teach it to sit and to stay and to come to me when I called him or her."

"Are you picky about if it's a boy or girl?" Mark asked.

"Not really, I guess. Although, I'd like a girl dog," she said.

"That's great," Mark said.

"Please don't get any ideas," Jen said.

"No worries. I'm just asking questions, that's all. Making conversation."

He turned back to Ruby. "Are you going to have a party?" he asked.

"My friend Bella is going to come over and spend the night on Sunday. And granddaddy said we could sleep out in the playhouse if we wanted to."

"That's very exciting," he said. "You wouldn't be scared?"

"No," Ruby said. "Why would I be?"

"I don't know. If it were me, I might be scared to sleep out there. I might be afraid a monster would get me."

"Monsters aren't real," Ruby said. "But creatures are real. And we don't have to worry about them much because we have protections."

Jen cleared her throat and leaned in quickly and whispered, "Remember that's not polite dinner conversation. We don't talk about creatures."

"Yes, ma'am," Ruby said.

"You have a lot of rules to follow, don't you Ruby?" Mark said.

"What's wrong with rules?" Jack Holloway asked from the end of the table.

"Oh, nothing at all, sir. That's not what I meant."

"Exactly, what did you mean?" Jack eyed Mark as if he were a venomous snake that might bite and infect his granddaughter with his poison.

"I just meant she has a lot to remember. And she's

doing a great job." Ruby's lips curved up a little and then flattened again. It was the first sign of a smile Mark had seen on the girl's face since he met her.

"Do you like chickens?" she asked.

"Chickens? I love chickens," Mark said. "Your mom said that you have a whole flock of them."

"Yeah, I do. I mean, they give us eggs. But I love them. And they love me."

"I'm sure they do," Mark said.

"Of course, you can't teach a chicken to sit or stay or come when you call them," Ruby said, and Mark got the feeling she was directing the comment at her mother.

"No, I suppose you can't," Jen said.

"Maybe after we have dessert, you'd like to meet my chickens." Ruby shifted her gaze and met Mark's eyes.

Mark couldn't stop the grin from crossing his face. "I would love that. Thank you, Ruby." Mark met Jen's approving gaze, and she gave him a slight nod.

Jen turned her attention to her daughter. "Ruby, would you like to come help me serve dessert?" Ruby looked up at her mother and nodded her head.

"Great! Who wants dessert?" Jen asked and rose to her feet.

CHAPTER 35

Mark ambled into his hotel room, replaying the night's events at the Holloway's Friday night dinner. The girl was much brighter than he expected and very advanced in magic for her age and training. When Mark gave her the stuffed animal, a plush brown dog she named Chloe, he showed her how to make the dog come alive, almost as if it were a real puppy. She surprised him by picking up the trick with ease.

But how surprising was it, really? She was his daughter, after all.

By the time Jen shuffled her off to bed, Ruby had the stuffed animal following her up the steps. He knew it would take more than just a stuffed animal, though, to win her allegiance. It might take years. He wondered why his mother had not tried to contact the girl. The way he saw it, she needed Ruby's allegiance more than he did.

And his mother was greedy. She wanted the power all to herself. Even above her sons. He'd resisted going to Jen's family night dinner and agreed only to spend time with Ruby. But the evening had turned his head around about the bonds possible among siblings and parents. It had been flat out strange to be with a family that so obviously cared for one another. They traded only friendly barbs and teases over dinner, none of them intending to wound. They all laughed and touched one another, hugged and kissed each other's cheeks.

It had been many years since he had wondered what it would really be like to have a family. If Jen had not run off scared, would they have married? Had more children? He loved her once, and the attraction still held. Was it true for Jen as well?

He moved into the room and slipped off his shoes before waving his hand above the light switch. He jumped back, startled, jamming his hip into the credenza when he saw his brother sitting in the armchair near the window.

"Devon! What the hell?" Mark said. "How did you get in here?"

"How do you think?" Devon held up his hands and waggled his fingers. "Magic. I've been breaking past your security spells since we were kids."

He crossed his legs and leaned back in the chair, making himself more comfortable. "So, how was dinner with the fam?"

Mark gave his brother a dark look. "Dinner was fine. How did you even know?"

Devon shrugged his shoulders. "I hear things."

Mark sharpened his voice. "I told you to stay out of my business, or I would kill you."

Devon smirked. "You've been threatening to kill me for years." He put his elbow on the arm of the chair and propped up his head with two fingers. "It's really hard to believe you at this point."

Mark put his hands on his hips and stood over Devon, his shadow swallowing up his brother in the dim light of the room. "What the hell do you want?"

"What I want is for you to peck Jen on the cheek and say your goodbyes to Ruby."

Mark shook his head in disbelief. "Are you working for Mother?"

"Are you kidding? Do I look like I want a dagger in my back?"

"Ruby's almost eight. The age of confirmation. I can't just ignore that."

Devon scoffed. "Of course, you can. She won't have to pledge her allegiance to anyone until she's sixteen," he said. "And if she picks up some pointers from her old Uncle Devon, then she'll never pledge her allegiance to anyone other than herself."

"Do not even think about it," Mark said, his voice a warning.

"Right, or you'll kill me," Devon said. "But if you do, it creates a whole other problem."

Mark gestured wildly with his hands. "Why do you even care who she pledges allegiance to?"

"I don't," Devon said.

"Bullshit," Mark said. "You didn't get on a plane and fly three thousand miles because you don't care."

"Maybe I just don't want her to have to go through what I went through."

"Empathy?" Mark sneered. "Really? That's an interesting strategy. I didn't think you were capable," Mark asked.

"Yeah, empathy. You should try it sometime." Devon uncrossed his legs and rose from the chair. He walked to the window and stared out into the dark night.

"What do you really want, Devon?"

Devon turned and faced his brother. "What I really want is for Mother to die and her allegiances to die along with her. Think about all that power, the vacuum she'd leave. You and I could run the companies the way we see fit."

"I already run the companies," Mark said.

"You don't do shit without Mom's approval. You're a thirty-six-year-old baby."

"Shut up," Mark said.

"You know what I find interesting?" Devon said. "You've pulled out every charm you know, trying so hard to win Jen and Ruby over, and they're not having it. That little witch is a lot spunkier than I ever gave her credit for," Devon said.

"How would you even know that? Have you been spying on me?"

"Maybe," Devon said. He retrieved something he'd been concealing in his hand, holding it so his brother could see it. "But evidently I'm not the only spy in the family. I see you've been taking pictures of Jen and her family, and her boyfriend."

"Give me those," Mark said lunged for the photos and Devon held them over his head and danced out of Mark's way.

"Nope." Devon held up Mark's photos and ripped them in half, then ripped them in half again. He scattered the pieces on the carpet.

"Get out," Mark stared down at the torn paper fragments.

"So, where's your toady?" Devon asked.

"I don't know. He wanted to go to the beach," Mark said. "Said he'd take an Uber."

"Whatever," Devon said, sounding bored. "I remember where I saw him, by the way, in case you're interested."

"I'm not." Mark said.

"I think you are," Devon said. "Turns out, he works for Bartholomew Randall."

"Who cares?" Mark said. "He had impeccable references."

"I'm sure he did. On paper, I have impeccable references. You're asking the wrong question as usual, brother," Devon said.

"And what question is that?"

"Where does his allegiance lie?"

"You think I didn't check that out?" Mark asked. "You must really think I'm an idiot."

"No. I don't think you're an idiot. I do think that sometimes you don't see the complete picture. You only pay attention to your little corner of Mother's syndicate."

"Right, like you do. That's why you're so damn successful." Mark's voice dripped with sarcasm.

"I get by. And mostly, I like my life. It's interesting," Devon said. "Can you honestly say the same?" Devon waved his hand over the pieces of torn photographs. When he finished, he picked up the reconstituted photos and handed them to Mark in the same condition he'd found them.

"Just watch your back, brother." Devon patted his brother on the chest. "And lighten up. That will take you much further with Jen than any of your so-called charms." Devon pushed past Mark and headed to the door. He turned before walking out of the room, a smug look on his face.

"And watch your back. You may be Mother's favorite, but she's not above eating her young if it means more power for herself."

The door slammed behind him, resounding through

the room. Mark looked down at the photos that Bridges had brought him, barely a week ago now. He pressed the photo of Ruby and Jen against his chest before he placed it on the dresser and walked around the room to tighten his security spells.

CHAPTER 36

Evan awoke with a start. In his dream, he heard a growl just before the bear rushed him. The darkness of the night receded with the dawn, and he sat up straighter against the base of the tree. His neck ached, and he stretched from side to side, trying to alleviate the stiffness. During the night, he kept waking up hearing things. And now, his body felt heavy and tired, more tired than he'd ever felt in his life.

He sensed the bear's thoughts long before he heard him. His heart hammered against his rib cage when he realized she was close, and he tried to home in on what the beast wanted. It turned out to be a juvenile just looking for food. It had caught wind of something delicious and sweet and had walked nearly all night to find it.

"Crap," Evan mumbled. The banana. He'd been saving it along with two energy bars and the beef jerky. He figured the jerky and energy bars would provide enough protein to keep him going as long as this didn't last more than a few days. If he couldn't find the cabin by early next week, he'd be just like that bear, scouring the forest for food.

No time to waste musing and making plans for the future with a bear on his tail. Evan hopped to his feet and grabbed his pack. It took some doing, but he managed to scramble up the tree, ignoring the very rough bark. He'd worry about the splinters in his fingers later. They wouldn't matter if he died from being mauled by a bear over a banana. Once he got to the first high branch, he breathed a little easier. He was at least twenty feet in the air, but then he looked down, and his heart stopped. Even though he was safe at that height, suddenly he could see the bear below him, grunting and lumbering out of the underbrush. Every few moments, it would stop and sniff the air raising its powerful nose to breathe in deeply.

He remembered his dad telling him a story about a bear breaking the windows of a car and ripping up the seats just because it smelled food. Now, Evan wished he hadn't heard that story.

"Please, Goddess," Evan whispered, "just let her move on." The bear came to the base of his tree and looked up. Evan met the bear's eyes.

He tried to reason with the bear mentally. "Go on then," he said in a thought message. "You don't want this. Keep moving. You'll find something tastier."

He used to practice this type of communication with animals on his mother's cat. But the bear's only thought was for the delicious food. The bear stood on its hind legs and dug its claws into the bark of the tree and grunted louder.

"You're going to make me give you this aren't you?" Evan said aloud.

The bear began to climb the tree, and Evan's heart hammered in his chest. He quickly opened his pack and grabbed the food bag off the top. The bear stopped halfway between the ground and Evan and took another deep grunting breath, just short of where Evan's feet dangled over the branch.

It wouldn't take much for the bear to reach out her powerful claws and grab for him. Evan quickly opened the food bag and found the banana. He held it up, and the bear raised her head and followed the scent.

"This is what you want?" he said aloud. He waved the banana high in front of him so she would be sure to see it. The bear's head bobbed as she followed his motions. Evan turned his head away for a moment when he caught a whiff of her pungent animal scent.

"You want it, go get it," he said and reared back and tossed it to the ground, as far away from the tree trunk as he could. The bear started back down and then stopped. There'd been no time for relief when she began to climb again. Something else in his food bag had caught her attention.

Evan quickly dug out the jerky and threw it out around the trunk of the tree, panic starting to rise in his chest as he frantically tossed the two granola energy bars he had left. Please, he prayed, take these and leave me alone.

As if the bear heard him, she stopped and sniffed the air. Something in the scent satisfied her. She took a deep breath, then turned and jumped to the ground. She used her nose to root around like a pig until she found a piece of jerky. Her mouth smacked with the taste of the delicious dried beef his father had made for the trip. Absorbed in chewing the jerky, the bear began to wander off to find the other goodies he'd tossed to her.

Evan scrambled down the tree and began to run, looking back over his shoulders every few minutes to make sure she wasn't following him. When he was far enough away that he felt safe, he called out for Michelle.

"What are you doing here?" the ghost asked, materializing in front of him.

"I just lost my food," he complained. Anger flashed through him. "I thought you were going to watch over me."

"I was. I am. But I can't be in two places at once," she argued. "I had to check on Jenna."

"Well, that's just great," Evan snapped. "Now I don't have anything to eat, and who knows how far away this place is."

"I'm sorry," she said. "Are you okay to walk? Or do you need more of a break?"

He hooked his hands around the straps of his backpack and hung his head a little. He ignored the rumble of his stomach. "May as well get started. We're burning daylight."

"We're not that far," she said. "It shouldn't take more than an hour for you to walk there."

"That's great. Will you let me call my mom then?" he asked.

"Sure," Michelle said. "Once you get Jenna out."

"Before," he said defiantly and jutted his chin. "Or no deal. I took my chances with the bear."

"Fine," she said. "You can text her when we get to his cabin."

"Thank you." He glanced back at the direction where he'd last seen the bear. "We should probably get out of here before she tries to follow my scent.

"Good idea," Michelle said. She pointed to a path through less densely packed trees. "It's this way."

Evan set off after her, ignoring his aching body. A spark of hope flickered in his heart. He would be able to tell his mom and dad how to find him soon.

CHAPTER 37

Evan plodded on in the early morning light, lost in thoughts of seeing his parents again and eating real food. Not just jerky and energy bars. At this point he'd even settle for some of his dad's powdered eggs. Michelle had disappeared again, but he felt her near. As long as he felt her, he knew he was going in the right direction.

"We're almost there," her voice whispered through his senses. Evan stopped and noticed the thinning trees. He could see a clearing up ahead. Splashes of dingy red paint caught his attention. Maybe it was a barn? He moved forward again, and as he drew closer, he saw the stack of tires he'd seen in his dream. His heart sped up, but he wasn't sure if it was fear or anticipation.

"Be careful," she said. "Stay hidden in the edges of the trees."

"Does he have a gun?" Evan asked.

"I never saw a gun," she said. "Just his hunting knife and the ax."

The suffering undertone in Michelle's voice left him cold. Michelle appeared beside him. Her sudden materialization didn't faze him much anymore, and he wasn't sure if it were just exhaustion or maybe he'd grown used to it. Evan approached the property, following the edge of the trees until he was hidden behind the barn. He peered around the corner at the cabin. Everything about the scene looked almost identical to his dream. Only this time he saw an ax with its blade buried partially in the trunk of a long dead tree near the stack of wood beneath the porch. An image of the man using the ax to split logs flashed through Evan's head. He'd stack them up so there would be fuel to heat the house in winter.

Another image burrowed into his brain. A girl's body on the floor of the barn lying on her back, lifeless. Her throat covered in a mix of fresh and old bruises. A girl he'd never seen before. A familiar man stretched her arm out, stood up and placed his foot on her torso before he raised the ax over his head like a lumberjack and brought it down hard. He gagged at the image, then squeezed his eyes shut, and tried to force the image out of his mind.

Evan squatted down next to the building, out of sight of the porch or any of the windows overlooking the yard.

"Are you okay?" Michelle asked.

"Yeah, I'm fine. I just need to call my mom. Let her know where we are."

"We need to get Jenna out of there first," she said.

"You promised!" Evan said, his voice louder than he intended. He dug his phone out of his backpack and turned it on. The low-power mode message came on almost immediately. How had the battery drained so fast? He'd turned it off to save the power he had left. He raked his hands through his hair.

"Please," he said. "Just one text. And then we get her out."

"You swear to me?" Michelle asked.

"I swear," he said.

"Fine. One text," she said sourly.

Evan thumbed through his Favorite contacts and added his mother and father to the same text. His thumbs danced over the small keyboard as he keyed in, "I'm at a cabin. You need to call the police. A man has a girl here. He killed the spirit who's been holding me hostage."

"Hostage?" Michelle said behind him. "You agreed to come. This is not a hostage situation." She slapped the phone out of his hand.

"I thought you said you couldn't affect anything," he said.

She looked down at her hand dumbfounded. "I can't."

Evan quickly retrieved his phone and brushed off dirt and leaves. When he pressed the button to wake up the screen, all that stared back at him was black glass.

"You drained the battery," he said. "Dammit." He sat down hard on the ground and just stared at his phone. All the hope he had been holding onto, sputtered out like a candle smothered by its wax.

"I should've known you'd do something like that," he muttered.

"Please don't shut down here," Michelle said, sounding a note of panic.

Evan swiped at an errant tear and gritted his teeth. "I'm just a kid. That guy is a grown-up and he's strong. I've seen it. I needed my mom to help us."

"How strong is he going to be against an ax?" she said.

"What?" Evan looked at her, puzzled.

"He left his ax out in plain sight. Wouldn't that at least make you sort of even?"

"I don't know," Evan said. He rested his head in his hands and massaged through his bangs with his fingers trying to work it out. Could he beat the man with an ax? He didn't want to kill anything or anyone. But it would be better going in with a weapon of some sort. He wished for a spell. Any spell that would help him get inside and get Jenna out unseen.

"You always start your spell with an intention," Evangeline's voice drifted through his head. "

"An intention," he had echoed.

"Yes. Basically it's what you want to happen. But it has to be very specific. Otherwise, the universe just might hand you something like it but not exactly what you asked for. The universe will do exactly what you tell it to, as long as you have the right attitude and aren't afraid of doing the work."

"That's crazy," he had said.

"I assure you sweetie, it's not crazy. First, you have to start with what you really want in no uncertain terms and without any negativity. The universe doesn't seem to respond well to negativity. It doesn't understand no."

"Wow," he said.

"What do you want, Evan?" he said aloud, releasing himself from the memory. He peered around the corner and could see the ax resting in the trunk of the old tree. "What is your intention?"

He wished he'd brought a piece of paper and a pen. It always helped to write these things down so he could figure out how to keep a spell positive. Evangeline had taught him that.

"What is your intention?" he said aloud again. "What do you want?"

"Are you talking to yourself, or to me?" Michelle asked.

"Shh." He held his finger to his lips. "I'm thinking."

What do you want Evan?

It took a moment.

I want to get into the cabin unseen so I can get to Jenna.

He closed his eyes and focused on that intention.

Holy mother goddess help me get into that cabin unnoticed so I can get to Jenna.

He blew out a breath and whispered. "So mote it be."

"Okay, you get your wish," he said, "let's scout out the house first. See if we can find an open window or something. Then, I'm going in."

"What about the ax?" she asked.

"I don't... I don't think I'll need it. But we should hide it, so he can't find it."

"Now you're talking," Michelle grinned.

CHAPTER 38

Athena lay curled up in the bed nearest the bathroom, snoring lightly. But that wasn't why Charlie stared up at the hotel's ceiling. Early morning light seeped in around the blackout curtains as she tried to focus on what they needed to do today, but her thoughts clouded with fear. She'd been trying to push it back since Scott first called her with the news that Evan had gone missing.

A soft knock on the door drew Charlie's attention, and she hurried to answer it before the noise woke Athena. The poor woman had worked until almost two in the morning. Quietly, Charlie unfastened the safety latch and opened the door a crack to find Evangeline's smiling face. In one hand, she held a carrier with four coffees and the other a bag from the diner down the street.

"My gosh, Evangeline." Charlie opened the door

wider and let her aunt into the darkened hotel room. She kept her voice low and pointed to Athena sleeping across the room. "I wasn't expecting you for hours."

"I know," Evangeline whispered. "I got a very early start."

Athena snorted herself awake. "What? What's going on?" She pushed herself up to a sitting position and rubbed her eyes. "Everything okay?"

Athena reached for the light on the table between the beds and pressed the switch, turning them both on.

"I'm sorry, Athena. I was trying to give you more sleep time," Charlie said.

Athena stretched her arms out and yawned, arching her back. "Thanks, y'all. Don't worry about it. What time is it?"

"It's about seven-thirty," Evangeline said.

"Oh, my gosh, why didn't you wake me sooner?"

"Because you needed sleep. You didn't get to bed until after two," Charlie said.

"Yeah, well, if you know that, then you didn't either. And you're awake," Athena said.

"I know, but I couldn't sleep," Charlie said. "You were sleeping."

"Well, since we're all awake now, we should probably just get a jump on the day. Right?" Evangeline said.

"Yes, you're probably right," Charlie said. "Whatever that is, it smells delicious."

"It's just some breakfast sandwiches, that's all," Evangeline said.

"Have you brought one for Scott?" Charlie asked, eyeing the bag in her aunt's hand.

"Of course, I did. I brought him coffee, too." Evangeline set the food and coffee on the little kitchenette table and shrugged off her jacket.

Athena rose from her bed and slipped into the bathroom. Charlie sent Scott a quick text before digging into the bag and retrieving one of the wrapped sandwiches.

"Did you eat already?" Charlie asked.

"I don't eat breakfast anymore." Evangeline took a seat at the table. "Just lunch and dinner these days."

"Really?" Charlie said. "Why is that?"

"Just lost my taste for it, I guess. It always seemed to slow me down, so I dropped it."

"You always used to nag us and tell us it was the most important meal of the day," Charlie said, unwrapping her sausage, egg, and cheese on what smelled like toasted sourdough bread. She took a big bite.

"I know, but things change."

Charlie shrugged and took another bite. A firm knock on the door announced Scott's arrival.

"I'll get it," Evangeline said. "You just keep eating."

Evangeline opened the door, and Scott peered around her into the hotel room. "This is the right room, isn't it?"

"Come on in, Scott," Charlie called from inside the room. "This is my aunt, Evangeline. Remember her?"

Scott smiled and offered his hand. "Oh. Yes, of course." Evangeline gripped it and smiled, pulling him into the room.

"Thank you for coming, Evangeline. How nice to see you again. It's been a long time," he said, stepping over the threshold. "Whatever that is, it smells delicious."

"I know, right?" Charlie dug into the bag and pulled out a sandwich. Scott approached her tentatively, as if he were entering alien territory, and accepted the breakfast Charlie held out for him.

A loud ding resounded from the open laptop on the desk next to the window. Athena emerged from the bathroom, her face freshly scrubbed but still wearing her pink plaid pajama pants and white t-shirt.

"Morning, everyone," she chirped.

"Your computer made a dinging sound," Charlie said. She handed Athena the last sandwich.

"Great," Athena said, taking the still warm, wrapped goodness from Charlie's hands. "Hi, Scott," she said, heading to the computer to investigate.

"Holy crap." She looked up at Charlie, her eyes glowing with excitement. "We got a ping on Evan's cell phone."

"Seriously?" Charlie hurriedly balled up the foil-lined food wrapper and dunked it into the trashcan next to the dresser on her way across the room.

"Do we know where?" she said in Athena's ear. Every nerve in her body trembled with hope.

Athena's fingers flew over the keyboard as she leaned forward, squinting her eyes.

"It's gone," she said dejectedly. "I only had the one signal for a few seconds. Not long enough to triangulate his position."

Charlie sat down on the bed next to the desk. She slumped over as if someone had kicked her hard in the solar plexus. "What do you think it means?"

Athena grimaced at her screen. "I think it means that his phone turned on for a few minutes. He must have turned it off to save the battery, or the battery could've gone dead. I don't think it means anything terrible," Athena said.

Charlie leaned forward with her elbows on her knees and rested her head in her hands. Scott sat down on the bed next to her.

"What do we do now?" he asked.

Charlie looked at him, fighting to remain positive. "We keep looking," she said evenly. "Athena's right. It could be anything. At least it came on for however short of a time. I'm going to have to believe that means he's alive."

"I agree," Evangeline said. "You can't lose hope. Have you tried summoning the girl yet?"

"No. I was actually waiting for you. Three's a stronger number than two."

"Yes, it is," Evangeline agreed.

Another knock on the door interrupted their conversation, and Charlie rose to answer it. Tom stood outside with a sheepish grin.

"Is everyone decent?"

Charlie looked at him, not understanding for a moment, her mind still on Evan lost in the woods. Then she chuckled briefly. "Oh...yeah. We're up. Come on in."

He entered, bringing in the smell of pine trees, damp with morning dew. She shut the door behind him.

"I have some news. It's slight, and I'm sorry I didn't come sooner," he said, nodding at the assembled. "My, it's crowded in here. Hello, Evangeline."

"Hi, Tom, sorry I didn't bring you breakfast."

He smiled at her. "No, problem. I'm not hungry, thank you."

"What's your news?" Charlie asked, trying to keep her impatience in check.

Tom turned to her and said, "I could've sworn I heard Evan call me yesterday. Monique and I conferred and tried to widen our search for him. Unfortunately, we came up empty-handed. We didn't run into any other spirits, but we did find this." He retrieved a couple of shredded energy bar wrappers. "I know it's a long shot, but..."

Scott took one of the wrappers and inspected it. "It's the same brand we were carrying, but it's a popular brand. Why is it shredded like this?"

Tom explained, "I saw a young black bear in the vicinity. It could've been its handy work."

"Great," Scott muttered, his expression dark. His

shoulders sagged as he took a seat on the end of one of the beds. He ran his hand over his eyes, then stared down at his shoes.

"Even more reason to summon the spirit," Charlie said. "Evangeline, did you bring everything we need?"

"Yes, I did. It's in my bag in the car."

Scott came to life and rose from the bed. "I'll help you bring your things in, Evangeline," he said.

"I appreciate that, honey, but I'm fine. Y'all should finish your breakfast. We've got a long day ahead of us." Evangeline patted Scott's arm and slipped out the front door. Scott stood in the middle of the room, staring after Evangeline like a lost puppy.

* * *

CHARLIE STARED DOWN AT A BLACK VELVET SQUARE WITH A pentagram printed on it in gold. "I wish we had a little more space."

Evangeline had helped her drag the kitchenette table out of the little dining nook. Charlie used that space to lay out the black velvet, around which they all gathered now.

Scott stared down at the fabric with a worried look on his face. "And you're sure this is not evil?" he asked for the fifth time.

"Absolutely," Evangeline said. "Is that what you're scared of? That we're somehow going to summon evil?"

"I don't know. It's just... The way I was raised this would be considered..."

"I know what it would be considered. Why don't you just watch for now." Charlie patted him on the shoulder. "I promise you. We're not summoning the devil. Or anything evil. Just a spirit. We need answers, and I think she has them."

"Are we ready?" Athena asked.

"Yes," Evangeline said. She retrieved the book of matches from her pocket and lit the white candles in Charlie's and Athena's hands, then lit her own. The three of them each set their candle down in the holder at their feet, raised their faces to the ceiling, and clasped hands to begin the ritual.

EVAN SCOUTED THE PROPERTY, STAYING HIDDEN JUST INSIDE the tree line. He saw high up on the side of the cabin an open window. He studied it and decided it would take some climbing to reach it.

"Michelle," he said, keeping his voice low. She materialized beside him. "I need you to be my eyes and ears. Can you go into the house and tell me where he is? And where that is in the house?" He pointed to the window.

"That's his bedroom," she said and then shuddered. Evan felt her pain and got a quick glance of an image of her lying on the man's bed. He was sitting on top of her, his knees pinned her arms to her sides, and his hands wrapped around her throat, squeezing until she squeaked, and her feet squirmed. Then he'd let her throat go and laugh in her face and start choking her again.

Evan took a deep breath and pushed the image away. He couldn't do anything about the way the man had tortured Michelle, but he could stop him from killing Jenna.

"Do you think he's in there now?" he said.

"I'll go see. Wait here," Michelle said and dissolved before his eyes.

A few minutes later, Michelle returned.

"We have to hurry," she said, out of breath and agitated.

What had she seen? What could cause a ghost to run out of breath? A million questions whirred through his mind, ratcheting up his fear.

"Where is he?" he asked, a little breathless himself now.

"He's in the living room passed out on the couch."

"I don't understand. Why must we hurry so much then?"

"He bought new sheets," Michelle said matter-of-factly.

"Okay." Evan shot a quick look at the cabin. "I don't know what that means."

Michelle said, not hiding her impatience, "He has Jenna chained to a wall with handcuffs around her ankle."

"Okay, but I still don't get it."

"Tonight, he'll play his sick little choking game before he rapes her one more time, then he'll bathe her before he strangles her for good. He uses the old sheets to wrap her body and make the bed with the new ones. Then he'll chop her up and bury her."

"He didn't chop you up?" Evan immediately regretted asking.

"No, I wasn't really dead. He strangled me and I must've passed out because I woke up in the barn, wrapped in his old sheets."

"How were you still alive?"

"I don't know, I just was. Then I ran into the forest and got as far as the trail you were on. But eventually he caught me, and he hit me with the ax." She closed her eyes. Pain streaked her pale translucent face. "I remember floating above my body as he dragged me up to that peak where you first saw me and dropped me over the side of the cliff. It was nearly dawn and the sky was all pink. I love the sky when it's that color."

Evan covered his mouth with his hand. "Oh, my goddess. Michelle, I'm so sorry." His chest tightened, making his lungs feel heavy. "I figured it was bad, but... I need my mom. She'll know what to do. She can bring the police."

Michelle whipped back and forth as if she were pacing. "I told you, she won't get here in time. Jenna will be dead before then."

She gave him her plan. "We should at least try. Please. There's an old ladder in the barn. You could use it to reach the window. I'll go inside and let you know where he's at and if he starts to move..."

Michelle stared down at her hands and a static popping sound skittered from her fingers. "Something's happening?"

"What do you mean?" Evan asked.

"I don't know, but all of a sudden, I feel weird. Something's wrong... I can't... I don't know what's going on."

She began to flicker.

"Michelle," Evan said, not bothering to hide his alarm. "Michelle, what's going on?"

"I can't stop it... it's pull—"

Suddenly, Michelle disappeared completely.

"Michelle?" Evan stared at the place where she had been standing, halfway expecting her to rematerialize.

"Michelle, you come back here right now." No response.

Now what? Evan racked his brain to figure out what had happened. This wasn't Michelle's usual disappearing act. She never hesitated to materialize before when he called her.

Maybe the reaper got her. He wasn't sure exactly how they collected souls.

He looked around the grubby yard, into the trees, up at the window in the cabin, but he saw nothing helpful. His breath came in frightened gasps, and he began walking to and fro, pacing as Michelle had, but it didn't help him come up with any ideas.

"Michelle, if you can hear me, please come back. I need you."

Nothing. He called her name several more times as loudly as he dared, then walked into the woods. He sat down on a large granite rock between some trees.

"I guess I'm on my own," he said, trying to tamp down his fright. If his stupid phone hadn't stopped working, he'd call his parents, but it was dead. *Dead. Jenna will be dead soon, too, if you just sit here. Yeah, no kidding.*

He walked to the edge of the woods but stayed in the shadows. The open window on the back of the house beckoned to him. He thought of Jenna shackled inside, awaiting her fate. He couldn't just leave her there. Another thought came to him. Maybe the guy had a phone inside. Maybe.

Do you even know your mother's phone number? No. Not by heart. He never had to dial it. It was programmed into his phone. *What about 911?* Yeah. That would work. If he could get to a phone. But getting to a phone meant getting inside.

There's a ladder in the barn. Something had whispered that thought into his brain.

He said it again, this time aloud and then blew out a heavy breath.

"No one is coming for her. Or for you, unless you get into that house and find a phone."

The realization sank into his bones.

"Get up."

His body didn't move.

"Get. Up. Now."

He stuffed down the fear threatening to paralyze him and forced himself to get to his feet, even though he felt as though he had a thousand-pound weight on his chest.

"Now move," he said. Putting one heavy foot in front of the other, he headed toward the back of the barn.

* * *

"So mote it be," Charlie said and opened her eyes.

Tom waited in the corner by the door, a look of concern lined his handsome face.

"Maybe I shouldn't be here," Tom said. "It might frighten her away."

"You're fine," Charlie whispered. The energy in the room shifted. The air crackled and the smell of electric ions stung Charlie's nostrils. "It's working."

The shadow appeared in the center of the circle like a wisp of smoke. It formed from the bottom up, flickering in and out. Charlie silently uttered the words, *Thank you, spirit*, repeatedly, until the girl took an almost solid form. Only her legs and hands remained translucent.

Once she appeared, she turned in a circle as if taking in all of the faces surrounding her. Terror molded her features.

"Where am I?" she said, sounding disoriented.

"It's okay, Michelle." Charlie held up her hands to show she meant no harm. "My name is Charlie Payne."

"How did I get here?" The spirit's voice sounded strident. She tried to move but found herself stuck inside the circle. "What? What is this place?"

"I know it's a lot to take in," Charlie said gently. "And I'm sorry I had to bring you here this way."

The girl tugged on her legs. "Why can't I just leave?"

"Because I summoned you here. You can't leave the circle for now."

"Oh, my god. You have to let me go."

"Not until I ask you some questions. Have you seen my son? His name is Evan Carver."

"Of course, I've seen him," she spat out. "You have to let me go. I have to get back to him."

"Where is he?" Charlie asked. "Where's my son?"

Michelle snapped, "He's trying to get into the house. He can't do that by himself. I need to be there. You have to let me go."

"What house?" Charlie asked.

"The house where he's keeping Jenna. You have to let me go. Please. Otherwise, they will both end up dead."

"Charlie," Scott said. Charlie threw a quick glance over her shoulder at him. He rose to his feet and balled his hands into fists at his side. A look of panic shadowed his face.

"It's okay, Scott. I've got this," she said and made a

motion for him to sit down. Then she turned her attention back to Michelle.

"Tell me where he is so we can get him. We can get your friend out safely."

"I don't know where they are. They're in a cabin. You have to let me go."

"A cabin? You know where it is. You took him there."

"Through the woods, yes. But I can't tell you an address. Oh, my god." She bounced on her nearly invisible feet back and forth. It reminded Charlie of someone who needed to relieve themselves.

"If he dies. It's on you. Not me. I'm supposed to be his eyes and ears. I had everything under control until you captured me. Why did you interfere?"

Charlie ignored Michelle's accusations, focusing only on Evan. "Tell me what you know as fast as you can, and I will let you go."

"The man lives in a cabin. There's a road, and before you ask, no, I don't know what it's called. He has a truck. White, I think, only it's rusted pretty bad. And there's a barn. There's a ladder in the barn." Her voice broke. "And if you don't let me go, he's going to kill Evan and Jenna. Then he'll chop them up and bury them where no one will ever find them. Just like he's done to all the others."

"Look at me," Charlie demanded. The spirit seemed startled by Charlie's tone of voice. "You know where I am now, and you know what my energy feels like. I'm going to let you go so you can help my son. But you're going to find out exactly where he is – look for a mailbox number or some piece of mail – anything that tells you an address. Do you understand me?"

Michelle nodded.

"Then you're to come tell me, as soon as you find the information. Do you understand?"

"Yes," Michelle whispered. "You're scarier than I thought you'd be."

"Damn right, when it comes to my son." Charlie picked up the candle in front of her and blew it out. "The circle is broken. You're free to go. Just remember what I said."

The spirit nodded and then flickered for a second before she disappeared.

Charlie turned to Athena. "Did you get all that?"

"Yep. Cabin in the woods with a barn and a rusted truck. And there are other girls. Easy peasy."

Athena sat down at the desk and began to search the state and county databases.

CHAPTER 39

The city restored the power to The Kitchen Witch Café during the night, and Jen rose early to see what she could salvage of the food stores in the freezer and refrigerator. She printed off a checklist of her current inventory from her laptop and brought it with her to the restaurant.

When she arrived, she crept in through the back door and started the hard work of sorting through the damaged foods. She'd gasped in disbelief when the full impact of the destruction hit her: the ingredients inundated by flooding, the overturned shelves that emptied canisters and bags of essentials onto the floor, such as her 100-pound sack of Jasmine rice. Her list grew as she included what she could save, what she couldn't.

She had to call the insurance company first thing Monday morning; she would need their help if she wanted to rebuild. She wedged open the back door and used her father's hand-truck to carry the three 50-pound bags of flour damaged by water leaking into the pantry.

A knock on the back door got her attention as she loaded up the last damaged bag of flour. She peeked around the corner down the hall to find a man she had never seen before standing in the doorway.

"Hello, can I help you?" she asked.

"Jen, I need to talk to you," he said.

"Say that again?" she said, confused. He sounded exactly like Ben but looked like a surfer dude, a complete stranger.

"Jen, it's me," Ben said and insisted again, "We have to talk."

Jen tamped down the part of her that wanted to bristle and throw a petulant fit. That's not adult behavior, she reminded herself, so she gritted her teeth and said as sweetly as she could, "I need to get this rotten flour out of the storeroom, Ben."

"Do you need some help?" he asked.

"That would be great," she said, secretly wanting to throw something at the wall. "But first, you have to tell me why you're wearing a glamour."

Ben looked around at the parking lot behind the building and then ducked inside. "You're not going to like it."

"Okay," she said. "Let me be the judge of that. Tell me what's going on."

Ben walked toward her, and, sounding contrite, began his story. "I've been following Mark since he arrived. I've also been following his brother."

"Devon is here?" Jen asked.

"Yes, I am," Devon said as he slipped from behind Ben, joining him inside the corridor. He took one look at Jen's hand-truck and said to Ben, "Hey, you said nothing about having to do manual labor."

Ben snapped, "You're lucky I haven't cuffed you and taken you in."

Jen shook her head. "I'm totally confused," she said, stepping back from the last of the bags of flour. "But as long as you're here, I have a bone to pick with you, Devon Stonehill. You were supposed to keep your brother from ever finding me. Remember?"

Devon gave her a sheepish look and said, "I know. And I did, for a long-time. But that was before he met Bridges. That guy is a slippery son of a bitch. He makes me look downright easy to catch."

"You weren't that hard to catch," Ben said.

"So, I'm still confused," Jen said. She wiped her hands on her apron and brushed her sweaty bangs off her forehead. "Why do you look that way, Ben?"

"Sorry, Jen. I had to use a disguise for my undercover work," Ben said. "Glamour be gone." Suddenly, the glamour melted away and dissipated like mist in the sun. Ben's natural appearance returned, including his five o'clock shadow.

Jen's heart skipped a beat, and her irritation with him melted away when she saw once again his handsome boyish features. "I am so glad to see your face," she admitted.

She had a powerful urge to throw her arms around him and kiss him, but she'd never do that in front of Devon. Plus, Ben still had some explaining to do.

"Me, too. I mean, I'm glad to see your face," Ben stammered.

"We still need to talk," Jen said.

Devon cleared his throat and interrupted them. "Agreed. Everybody here needs to talk," he said. "If you two lovebirds would tone it down a bit, then I could be on my way."

"Why are you even here?" Jen crossed her arms and glared at him.

"There's so much you don't even know," Devon said. "And to be honest, my motives for being here are totally selfish. Neither my mother nor my brother needs more power."

"You're talking in circles," Jen said, flustered by his dramatic nonsense.

"It's kind of a long story. Is there a place to sit down?"

"Well, everything is still a mess."

Devon gestured toward the dining area beyond. "I don't really care," he said, not masking his impatience.

Jen led them down the hallway into the dismantled

restaurant, Devon continuing his story behind her. "I made my deal with Mr.? What's your name again?"

"Ben Sutton," Ben said, irritation in his voice.

Jen looked from Ben to Devon. "You did? Why?" she asked.

"The real question should be why did I make a deal with him," Ben said.

Jen still looked puzzled. "Why did you?" she asked.

"Because he can help me take down his brother's and mother's organizations. I'm sorry to say this, but Mark and his mother are both criminals," Ben said. "We granted Devon immunity if he will give us information to convict his family."

Jen drew her brows together. "What? No. Y'all are restaurateurs. I used to work for one of your father's restaurants," Jen said, her face a mass of confusion.

"Sorry, Jen," Devon said, looking down at his shoes for a moment before he faced her with the truth. "That's just a cover. A way to launder money from their organizations. My parents and my brother are magical weapons dealers. Although my mother also dabbles in curses and illegal potions. And, good old Mark, well, he manufactures addictive charms. Officially, it's known as the Crystalline Syndicate. My uncle is the one who killed Ben's parents."

Devon took a seat in a booth Jen had cleaned up along the back wall of the restaurant. She and Ben took a seat across from him.

Very little light filtered in through the boarded over

windows, and only half the fluorescent lights worked. The other half had exploded when the tornado struck the transformer.

"Oh, my goddess, Ben. You finally have a name." Jen said. She reached over and gave his hand a squeeze.

"I do. And with Devon's help, we're going to bring them down. I just wanted to be the one to tell you."

"This changes everything," she said. "Mark had me fooled. I was about to let him into Ruby's life."

"He can still fight you on that," Devon said. "Unless you have something to hold over him. Something that would embarrass him."

"What are you talking about?" Jen asked.

Devon and Ben exchanged glances, and Ben gave him a nod. Ben stretched his arm across the back of the booth behind Jen.

Devon retrieved two photos from his front pocket and slid them across the table. "They're going to speak for themselves, I think."

"This is inside my house," Jen said, horrified.

"Yep. My brother is spying on you. Or, I should say, his toady is spying on you, although, honestly, the jury is still out on that one. I'm not sure where his true allegiance lies," Devon said.

"It doesn't matter. He's been spying on me. Why?" She curled her lips as if she had tasted something sour and pushed the pictures back at Devon.

"He needs you, or I should say he needs Ruby. She's the linchpin in his grand plan."

"What do you mean?"

"When a sorcerer turns eight, they go through a confirmation process. Basically, their parents vow to educate the child in the way of magic. They then make a promise on the child's behalf that when the child turns sixteen, he or she will pledge their allegiance to one of the dozen or so families that run the sorcerer world. Over the next eight years, the kid learns everything about that family and their organization and how they will fit in. They are taught the ways they can contribute to their benefactor's power. As you can see, the organization figures out how they can gain from any gifts that a certain soon-to-be-eight-year-old might have."

"Oh, my goddess," Jen said. She covered her gaping mouth with her hand. "Was he planning to take Ruby?"

"No, I don't think he was going to physically take her away from you, but he was going to try to win her over. She evidently impressed him."

"Well, she's not allowed to pledge allegiance to anybody. She is only eight years old."

"I agree," Devon said. "When I was eight, they made me pledge my allegiance to my mother. Now, of course, that can change before you turn sixteen. Let's just say I wasn't an easy kid. And my mother was not nearly as kind and loving as you are."

"How do you know that?"

"I kind of make my living as a spy. I infiltrate organizations and then get intel and take it back to whoever's hired me."

"Are you doing this for some person who's hired you?"

"Partly," Devon said. "Yes. Partly. I must admit, though, it'd really be great to take down my mother and brother. They've done nothing except cause ruin and..." Devon shook his head. "It doesn't matter anymore. Truly, I don't want anyone to hurt your daughter. I don't want you to get hurt, either. I like you, Jen. You were actually nice to me."

Jen reached across the table and tapped his forearms with her fingers. "Devon, I don't think I was really that nice to you."

"Trust me. You were. Luckily you weren't around long enough to get the full Stonehill treatment." Anguish filled his eyes for a second before he seemed to shake it off.

"I'm sorry your life has been so painful," Jen said.

Devon looked at Jen, a tinge of embarrassment in his expression. "I'm sorry to tell you this, but I watched you last night. That's how Ben caught me. I should've known he'd have a security detail. From everything I've seen, you are the love of his life."

Jen blushed and cast a grateful look Ben's way. He pulled her closer.

"You and your family had Mark there with his charms trying to impress everyone. I saw something in your face, though, and in Ruby's. You weren't buying it. You seemed to see right through him. And let me tell you something about my brother. He hates that."

Jen looked away, deep in thought for a moment. "He tried to win Ruby over with a stuffed animal that walked and barked and acted like a dog," she said. "And when I tucked Ruby in, she still had reservations about him."

"Smart girl," Devon said. "Sounds like she takes after her mother."

"Oh yeah, she does," Ben said, smiling.

"She misses you," Jen said, turning to Ben. "She was afraid that Mark was going to be my boyfriend. And she told me last night that she likes you. You make her laugh."

"Well, I like her too." Ben grinned.

Jen wanted more than anything to hug him right here in front of Devon. But she knew that would have to wait. For now, she had bigger things to worry about. She reached for the photos and took a long look at them.

"What do you want me to do?" Jen stared down at the image of her reading to her daughter in her father's living room. Her stomach turned, thinking of how Mark had violated her privacy, her intimate time with her daughter.

"I want you to call Mark and tell him that y'all need to talk," Ben said.

"And once he's here?"

"My team and I will take care of him," Ben said. "Are you okay with that?"

Jen knitted her brows. "Are you going to make the

charges stick?" Her question was more a demand than a query.

"I will do everything within my power to make that happen," Devon said. "And then I'll start working on my mother. No kid should be devoured by her machine. Especially not my niece."

"Let me get my phone. It's in the back office," Jen said. "And then I'll call him."

Ben leaned across the table, speaking in earnest now, as though time was not his friend. "We should probably go over a plan first. Make sure all Jen's ducks are in a row, if you know what I mean?" Anxiety colored his haste.

"Do you want me to call Lisa and Daphne?" Jen asked.

"Sure. We can use every witch on the ground we have," Ben said. "There is no way that Mark Stonehill is going to go down easy."

CHAPTER 40

E van crawled in through the window as quietly as he could. A stale mustiness hung in the air, and he wondered if this guy had ever cleaned in his life. Beer cans littered the floor, but he paid them no attention. The only thing that caught his eye was the dingy beige phone on the nightstand. He crawled across the floor and lifted the receiver, holding his breath and trying not to make a sound. Then he punched in the numbers 911, his heart pummeling in his chest at the noisy old-fashioned handset. The phone rang twice before the operator picked up.

"911. What's your emergency?"

"My name is Evan Carver," he managed in a stage whisper. "I've been lost in the woods for the last two days, but listen to me, please. I'm in this man's house. He's got a girl tied up. I think he's going to kill her. If he discovers me, he'll kill me too."

"I can barely hear you, son. Where are you?" the operator asked, his voice dead calm. "Do you know the address?"

"No, I don't," Evan whispered hoarsely. He glanced at the partially open door. "I can't stay on the phone long. He might hear me."

"Can you get out of the house? Or is there a safe place you can hide until the deputy arrives?"

"I can't. I promised to get her out, too. Can you please send someone? As soon as he figures out she's not there, he's going to come after us."

"Okay, just listen to me, son. Don't hang up. I'm working on getting your location, and I'll have a sheriff's deputy on his way as soon as possible. Don't panic. Just listen to me. Do you know if he's armed?"

"I... I don't know for sure. Michelle told me he has a hunting knife. And...a baseball bat."

"All right. Just stay with me, okay," the operator said.

"I'm sorry. I can't." Evan gazed down at the receiver and remembered the operator's words. He laid it quietly on the floor, between the nightstand and the bed. He couldn't wait any longer. They didn't have time. He had to get Jenna out.

He crawled on the floor through the darkened room, past dirty laundry, and more beer cans. As he scanned the room, he saw beneath the rumpled bed, dust bunnies gathered in the corners.

Once past the bed, he got to his feet and crept to the door and peered into the hallway. It was empty. At least that was in his favor. He wished Michelle were here. He really needed her now. Something caught his eye leaning against the wall next to the door. It was long and cylindrical. The baseball bat from his dream. His breath quickened at the sight of it. *It's just a bat, Evan. Geez, calm down.*

Some instinct reared up inside him, and he grabbed the bat. He felt the weight of it in his hands, felt the cool, smooth wood against his palms.

The man couldn't bash his head in if he didn't have the bat, could he?

Michelle had said the man was passed out on the couch. But how long would that last? His father and mother drank wine occasionally with dinner, but he'd never seen them drunk, nor had he ever been drunk.

Dylan McKenna had brought a bottle of his dad's whiskey to school when they were eleven, and Evan had tried it. The horrible dark gold liquid had tasted awful and burned his throat. He couldn't see why anyone would drink it. How tired would the alcohol make a person? What if the guy woke up?

Doesn't matter. You have the bat. That's your advantage. Still, he wanted to know exactly what he was dealing with. He choked up on the bat and edged along the wall. The man's snoring resounded through the living room. Sawing logs, his dad would've called it.

Evan chanced a glance around the corner. The man was on his back, stretched out on the couch. His arm covered his eyes. An old pizza box and more beer cans littered the coffee table. He'd kicked off his shoes near the front door. A sports channel blared on the television.

With the bat still in his hand, Evan backed down the hall until he reached the door across from the man's bedroom. That's where Michelle said Jenna would be. The guy had padlocked the door to make sure no one could come in or out. The heavy-duty lock hung above the dingy fake brass doorknob. He had to get that off before he could rescue Jenna, but how would he do that without a key?

He'd watched his mother unlock doors without her keys plenty of times, but he never really paid attention to the spell. Evangeline's words drifted back to him.

Focus on your intention, Evan. The words are just a conduit. They can help you do anything if you tie them to your intention.

What was his intention? To unlock the padlock. Unlock the padlock. Unlock. Could it really be that simple? He wrapped his hand around the heavy-duty padlock, closed his eyes, and focused.

He tried to get a feel for the locking mechanism— what it would sound like when it released; how it would feel when he gently pulled on it and it opened.

"Unlock," he whispered and tugged. It didn't budge. He blew out a breath, checked the hall, listening for any sign the man had awoken. When he was sure the guy was still asleep, Evan concentrated on the lock again. This time he visualized the outcome of what he wanted—the open lock in his hand.

"Unlock, unlock, unlock," he whispered and tugged again. The lock pulled down with a click. Spurred on by his success, he turned the doorknob and pushed the door open a couple of inches. The girl scrambled off the mattress on the floor and curled herself up into a ball in the corner of the room. She whimpered and pulled her dirty t-shirt over her bare legs.

"Hey," Evan whispered and pressed his finger to his lips to keep her quiet. He pulled the door closed behind him and leaned the bat against the wall. A dim ray of light from a dirty window fell in a creepy yellow pool in the middle of the floor. It wasn't much, but enough to scan the room and see what was where.

"It's okay. I'm here to get you out." He held up his hands to show he meant her no harm. She peered through her fingers, and he could see the bright green of her eyes. Her dark auburn hair frizzed in wild curls over her shoulder and looked matted in a few places.

"You're just a kid," she said in a hoarse whisper.

"I know," he said. "But right now, I'm the best you've got."

He slipped his multi-tool out of his pocket and held it up for her to see. She squirmed closer to the wall.

"I'm just going to check out the chain," he said. He squatted down next to a heavy-duty anchor bracket affixed to the wall. He fingered a long piece of dog tie-out chain wrapped around the bracket and saw it held another padlock. Attached to the other end was a pair of handcuffs, one of which had been clamped around the girl's ankle.

"I'm Evan, by the way," he whispered.

"I'm Jenna." She watched him but didn't meet his eye.

"This isn't going to work," he muttered. Even with his tool, it would take too long to unscrew the anchor from the wall. Prying it off the wall would make too much noise.

"I'm going to have to try getting the handcuff unlocked. Is that okay?" She nodded her head. He inched closer to her. "It'd be easier if you could extend your leg, okay?"

She nodded and did as he suggested. He inspected the keyhole of the handcuff, aware of her eyes on him. He switched to the Phillips head screwdriver on his multi-tool and pretended to use it to break into the handcuffs.

Again, he focused his intention, visualized the outcome, and mouthed the words, "Unlock, unlock, unlock." The handcuff clicked open, and he gently slid it away from her ankle. She pulled her leg up and rubbed her hand over the bruised area.

Evan heard her gasp in relief and looked up at her face. Tears welled in her eyes.

"How are you going to get us out?" she asked, her voice quaking a little. "There's no back door."

He was a bit overwhelmed himself but also understood their peril, their need to get out of the house.

"There's a ladder outside his bedroom window" he said. "We can get out that way. Do you think you can stand?" he asked.

"I think I can stand," she said, uncertainty in her weary eyes, "but I might need help."

Evan rose from the floor and held out his hand to help her to her feet. The door creaked behind him.

"What the fuck do you think you're doing here, boy?"

Evan's breath caught in his throat. He'd heard that voice before, in his dreams. He turned slowly just in time to see the nearly toothless man choke up on the bat and rear it back as if he were ready to hit a home run.

"Evan! Watch out!" Michelle's voice rang through Evan's head.

Evan raised his arm to defend himself. The girl backed herself into the corner. She turned her nose against the wall and made a soft mewling sound.

"You think you can come in here and take what's mine?" The man's ghastly sunken face reminded Evan of a skeleton.

"Help me," Evan said, directing his words at Michelle. "Just focus."

Michelle let out a keening scream and charged at the man knocking him off balance.

"What the hell?" The man staggered to the side a bit, then looked around, his eyes wide as he swung the bat at empty air. Michelle grabbed the bat and yanked it out of the man's hands, then flung it onto the floor.

"How do you like that, asshole?" Michelle screamed at the man. She charged at him again, pushing him until he hit the wall. "Go, Evan!"

"What the fuck?" The man slurred his words, clearly still drunk and befuddled by the invisible hands holding him against the wall.

Evan grabbed Jenna's arm, yanking her out of the corner. The man bared his yellow-brown teeth at them when they passed him. In a frenzied move, the man broke free from Michelle's ghostly grip. Evan and the man dove for the bat at the same time, but Evan was faster.

Jenna screamed and jumped behind Evan. The bat whistled through the air when he swung it with all his might. A loud crunching sound made Evan cringe when the bat connected with the man's wrist. He howled in pain, hugging his arm to his chest, cursing them as they slipped past him into the hallway. Evan and Jenna raced through the house and out the front door.

"The truck," Evan said breathlessly. He pointed at the dingy vehicle. They crossed the yard, and within a few moments, climbed inside and locked the doors.

"Do you have the keys?" Jenna asked. Her gaze darted to the front porch. "We have to get out of here."

"I don't have the keys," Evan admitted. He'd only seen the truck as a safe place to hide from the man. "I don't even know how to drive. Do you?"

"Yeah, I do. Oh god," she moaned, sliding down low in the seat and rocking herself in fear. "He's coming."

Michelle materialized between the two of them on the bench seat of the truck. "We have to get out of here."

"Right, like I hadn't thought of that," Evan snapped at the spirit. "How do we do that without keys?"

Jenna turned her frightened gaze on him. "Are you okay?" Could she see Michelle? Apparently not. He sensed her wondering if she had just traded one bad situation for another.

"I'm fine. I'm just talking to myself, that's all. I do that sometimes. It doesn't mean anything."

The man barreled across the yard, with the baseball bat in one hand, the injured hand cradled against his chest.

"We need to do something fast," Michelle said.

"Yeah, no kidding," Evan said. He stared at the ignition. Could he set an intention for a key?

"Michelle," he asked, "do you think you could start the car?"

"My name is Jenna," Jenna said.

"I'm sorry. You're right," Evan said, forcing a smile.

"I don't know. It's kind of complicated, isn't it?" Michelle said.

"Not if we do it together. We could both focus our energy on it at the same time."

"Would that work?" Michelle asked.

"I don't know, but I'm willing to try," he said.

Jenna backed against the door. "Okay, you're really starting to freak me out. Who are you talking to?"

"I'm sorry." Evan held up his hands. "This might freak you out even more. But I'm talking to a ghost named Michelle. She's the one who brought me here to find you. He killed her too." Jenna's eyes widened with horror, and she started whimpering again. "I promise. I'm not crazy, and she's not here to hurt you," he said, but it didn't seem to put her at ease.

The man's scream startled them both, and Evan lunged away from the driver's door when the man swung the bat at the window. Evan braced for it to break, and when it didn't, he gaped in amazement. The unbroken window seemed to enrage the man even more, and he climbed onto the hood of the truck and whacked the bat against the windshield.

Evan and Jenna both screamed. Miraculously the window didn't break. The man reared his good arm up again and struck the glass. Again it didn't break.

"Let's try it," Michelle said.

"Okay." Evan nodded. He flinched every time the bat struck one of the windows. After several minutes, the man stood back, his breath heaving in his chest. A look of confusion replaced his rage.

"Jenna," Evan asked quickly, "change places with me?"

"What?" she said. "What for?"

"I think I know how to start the engine, and like I said, I can't drive."

"Start it how?"

"Just watch. Okay? I promise I won't hurt you." Evan tried to reassure her. "I know I must sound crazy. But please, just trust me. What do you have to lose?"

"Okay," she nodded, rolling her eyes.

They crawled over the seats, switching places as quickly as possible. Jenna put her hands on the steering wheel at ten and two.

"Once it starts, you need to give it the gas, I think. That's what my mom does. But move fast when I give you the signal."

Jenna nodded and placed her foot on the pedal. Evan leaned in and held his hand over the ignition switch, focusing all his energy.

"On the count of three, Michelle."

"All right. I'll count," Michelle said. "One, two, three."

Evan made the motion of turning the key and held his breath. *Please*, he pleaded desperately to the goddess. Like a miracle, the engine turned over.

"Now, Jenna!" he shouted.

Jenna pressed the gas pedal just enough and the

engine revved. She laughed, elation on her face. "Oh, my god. You did it."

The man had caught his breath, and now he picked up a rock and appeared to throw it as hard as he could. The driver's window shattered. He charged at the truck again. This time, he reached in and grabbed Jenna by the arm. She put the truck in gear and pressed the gas. The truck leaped forward, dragging him along the gravel driveway.

At that moment, the deputy cruiser pulled in, lights flashing, blocking Jenna's exit. She abruptly jammed on the brakes, throwing her and Evan into the dashboard. The man lost his footing and fell to the ground.

"Stay down!" a well-muscled sheriff's deputy yelled at the man.

The man stumbled to his feet. "These two kids were trying to steal my truck!" he whined.

"Put your hands up where I can see them!" the deputy ordered, "and back away from the truck."

The second deputy came around to the passenger's side door. Evan undid the locks, his body trembling. The deputy pulled the door open.

"Are you Evan Carver?"

Evan nodded. "Yes, sir."

"A lot of people have been looking for you," the deputy said. He looked past Evan to the girl.

"This is Jenna," Evan said.

"And for you too, miss," said the deputy with a kind smile.

Another sheriff's cruiser pulled into the driveway and parked. Two deputies jumped out with their guns drawn.

Evan glanced over his shoulder. Through the back window, he watched the deputies force the man to the ground and handcuff him.

"They got him, Jenna," he said. "You're safe."

Jenna slowly turned her head, her gaunt face unreadable. Her slim shoulders shook, and she burst into tears.

CHAPTER 41

"Mom!" Evan threw off the blanket the sheriff's deputy had put around his shoulders and raced into his mother's arms. He hugged her tight, and his father threw his arms around them both.

His mother kept whispering into his hair, "Oh, my goddess, oh, my goddess," and just held onto him. He felt her kiss him on the side of his head. "I'm so glad to see you."

"Not half as glad as I am to see you," he said.

"Sounds like you had quite an adventure," his dad said.

"Yeah, I guess you could call it that," Evan said, pulling out of his parents' group embrace. "I saw a bear. It was actually kinda cool. Scary but cool."

"I cannot wait to hear about all of it," his mom said. She threw her arm around his shoulder and pulled him close again.

"I need to get my backpack," Evan said. "I hid it behind the barn. Do you think that's okay?"

"Let me check with the deputies, okay," Charlie said. "I'm sure it'll be fine. And they're going to want you to give a statement. But you don't have to do that right this minute," she reassured him.

"Okay." Evan spotted the EMTs putting Jenna on a gurney. "Can I have a minute? I just want to check on her."

His parents exchanged a glance. "Absolutely," his mom said.

Evan ambled up to the EMTs.

"Can you wait?" he asked. "I'd like to talk to her for a minute if that's okay."

"Sure, kid," the EMT said. "We'll give you a couple of minutes. Then we've got to go."

"Sure." Evan nodded his head.

"You saved my life," Jenna said. "I don't know how you did it. I don't know how you did any of it."

"Can I tell you a secret?" Evan leaned close.

"Sure," she said.

He shrugged. "I had some help. I'm kind of a witch."

"I didn't know boys could be witches," Jenna said.

"Oh yeah, my mom would say witch is a gender-neutral term. And some of the most badass guys I know are witches."

"Is your dad a witch?" Jenna glanced at Evan's parents looking on with curiosity.

"Nah, he's still pretty badass, though. He's a doctor."

"They're going to take me to the hospital. That deputy said he already called my mom, and she's coming."

"Hey, that's great," Evan said. "I'm sure she's been worried sick about you."

"Hey, kid, we have to get rolling," the EMT said.

Evan nodded and patted the gurney. "You take care of yourself, okay?"

"I will, Evan the witch. Maybe sometime you'll tell me about Michelle." Jenna tried for a smile but her eyes closed as the ambulance driver asked Evan to stand aside.

Michelle materialized next to him. The two of them watched the EMTs load the gurney into the back of the ambulance.

"We made a good team," she said.

"We did up until you left me again," he complained.

"You can't blame me for that one. Your mom summoned me. I had no idea witches could do that. You should've told me."

"I'd had no idea that was her plan. Because you didn't let me text her," he quipped.

Near the edge of the property, a reaper appeared. Michelle flickered for a moment.

"That's your ride," he said.

"I know," she said. "I'm scared. What's on the other side?"

"My mom died. I mean not for a long-time, just for a little bit, but they resuscitated her, and she remembered."

"She remembered? What? Did she tell you what it was like?"

"She did. She said it was beautiful. She said it's different for everybody, though, like they go to their happy place, you know? So, whatever that place is, that's where you're going. And as far as the reaper goes, she won't hurt you. She's just there to guide you."

"How do you know so much?"

"My mom's boyfriend is a reaper. He's actually kind of cool."

"You know, Evan, you're really brave," she said.

"So are you." It surprised him when she wrapped her ghostly arms around him, and he felt her arms and her emotions—a mix of gratitude, relief, tinged with fear. "Don't be scared," he whispered.

The reaper flashed and appeared directly in front of them. Evan's heartbeat quickened, and he couldn't bring himself to look the reaper in the face. The reaper outstretched her bony hand. Michelle took a step back.

"I almost forgot," she said. "Tell the sheriff he'll find several graves inside the barn. There are other girls there." She stepped forward and looked into the black void of the reaper's hood. "I'm ready now." Michelle took the reaper's hand, and the two of them disappeared.

His parents approached him from behind and stood on either side of him.

"You okay, honey?" his mom said.

"I'm tired," he said. His stomach grumbled. "And I'm really hungry. But, yeah, I'm okay. What do you think will happen to her?" he asked and pointed to the ambulance as it pulled away.

"She will have a long road to recovery ahead of her," his mother said. "And really, that will be up to her how she does it."

His father put his hand on Evan's shoulder and gave it a gentle squeeze. "And she gets to recover because of you."

"I had some help," Evan said. "Do you think we could get some breakfast? I'd really love a huge stack of pancakes or maybe waffles."

"Absolutely," Charlie said. "I'll let the sheriff know that we'll be in later this afternoon for you to give your statement."

His dad put his arm around Evan's shoulder. "I'm really proud of you," he said. "I just wanted you to know that."

"Thanks," Evan said. "Maybe before we go camping again, you can show me how to use the compass."

"I think that's a great idea," his dad said. "So, you saw a bear?"

"I did. She stole my food." Evan laughed. "It turns out you can't really reason with a bear when they're hungry."

"Good to know," his father said. "Your mom told me you can sense animals' thoughts."

"Yeah. Her only thought was about the banana in my pack."

His dad chuckled. "Noted. Next time we won't bring anything quite so pungent."

CHAPTER 42

"Does everyone understand the plan?" Ben asked.

Jen stood beside him, their arms touching. It felt good to be part of his team again. She scanned the faces in the circle, grateful that Lisa and Daphne were part of it. Jen had never met the other three witches before, but she supposed that's the way Ben wanted it when he assigned them as security for Ruby and her father, Jack. They were masters of glamour and blending in.

Devon stood on the other side of Ben. Jen still sensed something demon-like about him, but it occurred to her, that in a way, he had pledged allegiance to Ruby before she was born. Had protected Jen and the child from Mark over the last eight and a half years. Or at least that's what she wanted to believe. If she let herself think it was pure revenge against his brother, she didn't know if she could carry on with any of this.

Devon gestured quietly to Jen. "I've set up spells so that any charms he has to sense magic—other than on Jen, of course—will go undetected." As he spoke, she felt all eyes on her. "Now, all you have to do is catch him." A devilish grin spread across Devon's face as he finished up.

"Okay, let's get into place," Ben said. He placed his hand between Jen's shoulder blades and stroked the center of her back in a circle. He leaned in close and whispered, "You sure you're okay doing this?"

Jen looked up into his large blue eyes. "I'm fine. Better because you're here." He leaned over and kissed her on the forehead. A feeling of security and warmth spread through her chest.

"I am always here, and I always will be," he whispered against her skin. In response, she wrapped her arms around his waist. "When we're done with all this, I'm going to take you away someplace warm, and you and I are just going to talk through everything until it's resolved. This has been the worst week of my life."

"Mine, too," she said. She tilted her head, and he leaned in and kissed her.

"Okay, okay, okay," Devon said, breaking into their moment. "You two will have to wait to get a room until after my brother's in custody."

Jen chuckled against Ben's mouth. "He's right."

Ben leaned in one more time and pecked her on the lips. "This is your show from here on out," he said.

Jen nodded and headed into the empty ruins of the restaurant's dining room. Ben and Devon ducked into the kitchen, along with Lisa and Daphne. The three security witches took their positions, leaving Jen all alone. She took a seat at the clean booth near the back wall and dialed Mark's number.

"Hey," he said when he answered. "I was just thinking about you."

"Yeah? I was just thinking about you too," she said. "I'm at the restaurant. Just thought I would do some cleanup. There are some bags of flour and rice damaged by the leak in the roof."

"Is it safe for you to be there?" Mark asked.

"Oh, yeah, I'm fine. Daddy put a tarp over the roof to keep any more water from getting in. The building is structurally sound, and Daddy removed most of the hanging debris yesterday. The lights are back on. Why don't you come by? Maybe you could lend a hand?"

"Sure. I'd be happy to," Mark said, sounding overly enthusiastic. "Have you eaten? I could stop and get us some breakfast or lunch if you'd prefer. It is almost eleven."

"That's sweet," she said, swallowing back the sour taste in her mouth. "I already had breakfast this morning. But I'd love a latte."

"Sure thing. Vanilla with 2% milk, right?" he asked.

"Yep. You remember," she said.

"I do." His breathy chuckle made her skin crawl.

"Great, I'll see you in a bit." She ended the call and carefully placed the phone on the table as if her deliberate move might erase the memory of Mark's voice from the speaker. The desire to scrub her skin raw while sitting in a hot shower nearly overcame her.

She removed the two photos that Devon had given her from her apron pocket and laid them on the table in front of her. How he'd broken through all her protection rings she could only guess. Bridges must have dug up her jars, broken them, and covered them back up. He'd probably broken the sigils on her house, too. She couldn't see Mark doing such dirty work.

Somehow, Bridges had gotten into her house without being seen and planted two cameras. Her stomach roiled with an emotion she didn't let herself indulge in often because she understood its destructive power. But hate fueled these feelings of disgust and rage boiling beneath her skin. Purging Mark Stonehill from her and Ruby's life seemed the only way forward. They all had their part to play, and she had to stay strong and let the DOL do what they did best. She replaced the photos in her pocket and waited.

Nearly half an hour later, Mark knocked on the door to the café with two large coffees in hand and a self-righteous smile on his face.

Jen unlocked the door and opened it for him, then

locked it behind him. She knew it wouldn't hold him if he wanted to get away quickly, but it might slow him down a few seconds.

"There's a clean booth on the back wall," she said. "Follow me." They stepped around Jen's unfinished work, the stacks of cans waiting to be returned to the shelves needing to be nailed back onto the walls. "I've cleared all the debris so we can sit there."

"Great," he said. He glanced around at the half-lit florescent lights. "You really took on a lot of damage, didn't you?"

She grimaced at him. "Yes, I did. As did many people on the street. And it's going to take time for them to rebuild their lives and their livelihoods."

Mark shook his head with a look of commiseration. "Sure. That must be so hard. But it could also be an opportunity," he said.

"So," Jen said, ignoring that opening and taking a seat across from him in the booth. "Where is Bridges today? He must not be having much fun."

Mark set a cup in front of Jen and took one for himself. "Bridges has been fine. He entertains himself. In fact, he's checking out one of the local herbal shops today before he leaves."

"He's leaving?"

"Yes, I had him on loan from a friend of my family."

"On loan? That sounds strange."

"Oh no, it's not at all. He's well compensated. But it's

time for him to report back to his Gerent and return to his usual duties."

"His what?" Jen cocked her head and gave him a puzzled look.

"His Gerent. There's a hierarchy within the world of sorcerers. The Gerent is just someone who runs the organization. And for protection, opportunity, other sorcerers pledge their loyalty to that Gerent.

"How very Mafiaesque," Jen said warily.

"I hadn't really thought of it that way," Mark said thoughtfully. "But I guess, in some ways, it's similar in structure."

"Are you saying you're like some Mafia Don?" Jen asked, not hiding her appall.

"No, it's really nothing like that."

"Right," Jen said. "But are you one of these... Gerents?"

"I am now. I broke away from my mother's organization a few years ago, and I'm building my own. In fact," Mark reached across the table and took her hand in his. She fought to let him hold on to her, not to jerk her hand away. "I hoped you might come back with me to San Francisco. And help me build that organization. Your skills are unique and would make an excellent addition."

"I'm sure," Jen mumbled.

Mark leaned in. "It would be a fresh start. You really have nothing else to tie you here now that your restaurant is gone," he said earnestly.

Mark's hand felt clammy in hers. "My family's here,"

she said, her lips curled with revulsion. "I could never just leave them."

"I understand. I really do but think about it. You could have your own five-star restaurant. Hell, you could have your own chain of five-star restaurants. That was your dream, remember?"

He paused as if giving her time to call up the memory.

"I can make that happen for you, Jen. I mean, look around you, this place is in ruins. It will take months to rebuild, plus, a lot of money. Ruby would get an excellent magical education in San Francisco. This could be our chance to try again. This time, I wouldn't hide anything from you. I'd be completely transparent."

Jen swallowed back the bile in her throat and gently slipped her hand out of Mark's. "It sounds almost like the tornado and my restaurant being destroyed is something you wanted to happen. Just another opportunity." She narrowed her eyes and reached into her apron pocket and gripped the photos Devon had given her. She held onto them as if they might give her strength.

"Did you do this?" she nodded at the ruined floor and boarded up windows.

"Do what?" Mark stared at her blankly. Jen couldn't be sure, but it seemed as if his charms had frayed around the edges, and the real Mark was emerging.

"Did you cause the tornado?" Jen asked.

"Jen, I told you I can't really affect the weather." Mark chuckled.

"It's interesting that you say that because that would mean storm witches are more powerful than you. And I don't know if your ego could allow that."

"Jen." He shook his head. "I...I..."

"Did you really think I would fall for your nonsense twice?"

Mark bristled, and his face hardened. He folded his hands together on the table. "I don't know what you mean."

"I think you do," she said. She slid the photos out of her pocket and laid them on the table in front of him.

Mark gritted his teeth, and his nostrils flared as he blew out a heavy breath.

"Dammit," he muttered. "I should've known he was making a copy when he tore them up."

"My father found the cameras, and he's disposed of them with a little help from the DOL." She grimaced. "I can't believe you spied on me and broke the protections around my house. Around our daughter's house. Do you know how dangerous that was? How exposed you left us? Spirits and many other entities try to break the protections all the time because of Ruby and because of my cousin, Charlie."

Mark's face hardened. "I would never let anything happen to you," he said. "That's one reason I had the cameras installed, so I could make sure..."

"Stop talking." She held up her palm in his face. "Nothing you say would ever make me believe that. Did you come here to take her? To make her pledge some sick allegiance to you?"

Mark shook his head. "I see my brother's been filling your head with lies." He sneered, but Jen deflected his victim vibes. "I can't believe you're listening to him. You hated him once, Jen."

"I never hated him," she said. "He was a creep sometimes because of the way he stares at people, but I never hated him. In fact, I owe him because he got me out of your life. He also protected me and Ruby for as long as he could."

"Don't give him credit where none is due. Devon does nothing unless it benefits him in some way."

"Right, and I'm sure you worming your way into your daughter's heart with stuffed dogs that come to life doesn't benefit you at all. My father found the camera inside the dog's nose."

Mark leaned back against the booth. "Listen, if I don't win Ruby, my mother will come after her and try to recruit her."

"I'd really like to see her try," Jen said.

"Jen, you don't want to mess with my mother. Trust me. She's dangerous. And she practically has an army at her fingertips."

Jen shrugged and cast a glance toward the darkened passage where Ben, Devon, Lisa, and Daphne stood watching. "What makes you think I don't have one at my disposal?" Jen shook her head. "No one is going to make my daughter pledge her life or her power to them. She belongs only to herself."

Mark sneered at Jen, then said, "Someday soon, she'll be too much for you. She's much more skilled than I first thought. You'll need me to handle her."

"I don't think so. She can be a handful sometimes, but at heart, she's kind, and sweet, and compassionate. But you're right. She is skilled. She saw right through you from the beginning."

"What do you mean?"

"She told me you make her uncomfortable, that you were weird. She also compared you to the wolf in *Little Red Riding Hood*."

"Well, weird is not very kind," Mark said indignantly.

Jen rolled her eyes at the fact he'd missed the worst trait Ruby had seen in him. "It's a seven-year-old's vocabulary for someone whose energy she finds threatening. And you are never going to see her again, because she's right. You are a threat. And I hope you get back everything you've put into the world."

"I can still take you to court," he said.

"I don't think so," Jen pursed her lips. "That would be really difficult where you're going."

Mark stared at her for a moment and turned his gaze to the darkened pass through. "Devon, you son of a bitch."

"That makes you one, too," Devon said.

Ben pushed past him and held a wand in his hand. "Mark Stonehill, you're under arrest."

"Seriously?" Mark sneered at Jen. "You could've had everything you ever wanted."

"I already have everything I want," Jen said.

Two of the security witches seemed to appear out of thin air when they dropped the glamour that made them part of the background. They moved in close with their wands drawn, aimed at his head.

"You're going to regret this," Mark said, his voice icy. "Ruby will have to pledge her allegiance to someone when she turns sixteen. And trust me, my mother won't let it drop."

"I think that's going to be hard for her to do when she's in prison too," Devon said.

The two security witches got Mark to his feet and bound his arms behind his back.

"Make sure to reinforce that binding with the spell I gave you, ladies," Devon said.

Jen's phone rang, a jazzy ringtone she'd assigned to her father. "She picked up the phone and answered it. "Hey, Daddy."

"Jen, Ruby's gone," her father croaked. "He took her."

"What are you talking about?" Jen turned around and stared at Mark.

"That man that was with your friend, Mark. The little guy. He knocked on the back door. I answered it, and then I don't know what happened. I woke up on the floor, and Ruby was just gone."

"Okay," Jen said. Her voice trembled. "Okay, I just have to think for a second."

"Jen, what's happened?" Ben and Mark asked in a chorus. They exchanged a look of disgust between them.

"Bridges took Ruby," Jen said. She marched over to Mark and slapped him as hard as she could. "You did this. And you're going to get my daughter back."

"Jen, I swear. I had no idea he was going to do that."

"I don't believe you," she said.

"I know where he's going," Mark said.

"Where?" Jen asked. Lisa and Daphne moved in close behind her, and their energy wrapped around her, calming her.

"Home to his Gerent in San Francisco."

"Why? Bartholomew Randall wouldn't have any use for a little girl." Devon sneered.

"Mother would," Mark said.

"Mother," Devon muttered. "Could he have been a double agent?"

"Possibly," A pained expression molded Mark's handsome features. "We should get to the airport."

"Why?"

"He's leaving today. This has probably been his plan all along. He's probably concocting a sleeping potion to make her easy to transport," Mark said. "That is if he were telling the truth about stopping at the herbal store. You have to let me out of my bindings. I'm the only one who can stop them."

"Geez, you and your fucking self-importance. You're not the only one here with power," Devon rolled his eyes.

"We all need to get to the airport," Ben said.

"Agreed," Jen said.

"Lead the way," Devon said.

CHAPTER 43

"Why are we bringing him, again?" Devon asked from the back seat.

Jen threw a quick glance over her shoulder. Devon and Mark sat across from each other in the jump seats of Ben's Toyota. The two security witches, Wren and Helene, sat next to the brothers; their wands trained on Mark.

"Don't worry," Ben said. "He's bound. And there's no way he can get away from us."

"I hope you're right," Devon said. He regarded his brother with caution.

"Why are you parking?" Mark asked.

"Well, because we can't drive into the airport," Ben said.

"You could've just parked in front."

"No. They'd have us towed," Jen said.

"No, they wouldn't. Not if you let me help you." Mark blew out of frustrated sigh.

"It's fine. I'm going to park as close as I can to the crosswalks." Ben took the ramp to the Day Parking garage and found a spot near the elevator.

"Can you at least free one of my hands?" Mark asked.

"That's a negative," Ben said.

"Fine, Devon, then you'll have to do the freezing," Mark said sounding irritated.

"No problem," Devon said.

"What are you talking about?" Jen asked.

Mark opened his mouth, closed it as if he were considering his words and then opened it again. "I have no doubt he's already passed through security. He has almost an hour jump on us," Mark said.

"Yeah, he's right we won't get past security. We have to call Jason and see what he can do," Ben said.

"No, no, no, you don't need to do any of that," Mark said. "If you would free my hands, then I can freeze the airport."

"What do you mean you can freeze the airport?" Jen said.

"I can stop people from moving. So, they're frozen in whatever position they're in for that moment," Mark said.

"And you can do this too, Devon?" Jen asked.

"Sure. It's very handy in my line of work. But it has repercussions, and I'm not sure how prudent it is to freeze an entire airport brother," Devon said.

"I don't care. It will delay the planes a bit, and the ones in the sky can just keep circling. We won't affect air traffic control."

"How are we going to explain that to people who just keep walking in?" Ben asked.

"They won't get in once we're inside the building. Essentially, it will trap Bridges inside," Mark explained.

"I don't know. This sounds dangerous. Not just for Ruby but for all the other people in the airport and passengers on planes in the air," Jen said.

"Do you want Ruby back or not?" Mark said. "Because once Bridges gets on a plane it will be nearly impossible to catch him."

"I'm afraid he's right," Ben said. "He could hide her with any of the sorcerer families."

"All right, fine," Jen said. "But let's get in and get out as quickly as we can."

"That is the plan," Mark said.

Lisa and Daphne and the third security witch, Anika, pulled into a parking space close to Ben's. Once he briefed them, the group of witches and the two sorcerers headed into the Charleston airport.

Jen walked into the main entrance of the Charleston airport with her wand drawn and her cousin and sister on her heels. The sight made people stop and stare at the three witches, but she kept moving. Devon caught up with her.

"You're a fast little thing, aren't you? Let's slow things down a bit, shall we?" He said and lifted his hand, while opening his fingers. Jen glanced around, dumbfounded. Every person in the airport froze in place as if time had stopped. But only the people no longer moved. The conveyor belts at the ticketing counters kept moving, carrying luggage around and around. The digital clock hanging near the entrance to the atrium moved a minute ahead.

"So time hasn't stopped," Jen remarked.

"Nope, just the people," Devon said. "Which is why we need to work fast. There are always repercussions to this sort of magic, and they can be far reaching if we're not careful."

"It sounds like you don't use this spell often," Jen said.

"Not if I can help it," Devon said. "I don't like to leave a mess behind."

"Wow," Daphne said. "This is crazy."

"You're not kidding," Lisa chimed in.

Jen shook her head. She couldn't wrap her mind around such an ability. And that much power frightened her. Devon waved his hand behind them and all the automatic doors shut, and their locks clicked into place.

"Does this mean Bridges and Ruby are frozen too?" Ben asked.

"Ruby may be, but Bridges probably won't be," Mark

said. "I made the mistake of freezing him the other night and I'm sure he'll have remedied that with protections or a counter-spell."

They kept moving through the terminal until they came to the place where the airport split into two concourses, A and B.

"We need to split up," Ben said. "Wren, Helene, Jen and Mark, you're with me. We'll take concourse A. Anika —your group will take concourse B. The first to find him, signal the other group and wait until there are enough of us to surround him. We don't want to hurt any bystanders or Ruby. Everyone clear on that?"

"Yes sir," the security witches answered.

"Absolutely," Jen agreed.

"Great, everybody be careful out there," Ben said.

JEN LED THE WAY PAST SECURITY. SHE IGNORED THE FROZEN TSA's and passengers standing in line or passing through metal detectors or body scanners. She couldn't think about them. The only thing she could think about was Ruby and getting her daughter back.

Once they passed security and reached the concourse, they stopped and scanned the five gates. She had not expected it to be so busy on a Saturday afternoon. But almost every gate had people sitting in the chairs nearby, and that didn't even count the people that had been frozen as they walked across the concourse.

"Please unbind me," Mark whispered. "I swear to you I will find him much easier."

"No," Ben said. "Just look for any movement."

Jen carefully surveyed the space. "I think I see him. He sat near that farthest Delta gate. The one in the right-hand corner."

"Yeah," Ben said. "I think I see him too." He held his wand up in the air and circled the tip until a bright red spark shot out of the end of it and traveled to the other concourse. "Okay, that should signal the others to come here. Once they are, we'll fan out and surround him."

"We don't need to do any of that. I could take him right this minute if you would let me," Mark whined.

"No," Ben said emphatically.

"We're here," Lisa whispered and crept up next to Jen. "Is he here?"

Jen nodded. "He's in the corner. Near the Delta gate."

"Let's do this in pairs," Ben said.

"What about me?" Mark said.

"You stay here. Anika stay with him."

"Yes sir," she said. She pointed her wand at him. "Move back over there," she said, directing him toward the wall.

"You are going to need me," Mark insisted.

"Just shut up," Ben snapped. "Wren, Lisa, why don't you pair up. Helene and Daphne, you're together. Devon, you're with Jen. And I'll bring up the rear," Ben said. "Let's fan out. He seems to be impervious to any kind of freezing spell."

"Only the kind that turns you into a statue," Devon said.

"Come on Devon, let's go this way," Jen said. The concourse was basically a box with three gates on one side and two gates on the other. Windows stretched on three sides of the box. Rows of chairs bolted together made of metal and a plastic covering that mimicked leather had been placed in groups around each gate.

Jen zigged right and Devon followed her through a break in the chairs. She traveled up along the window stretching to the gate where Bridges stood.

Jen's heart pounded when she saw Ruby hanging lifelessly in his arms. "Oh, my goddess."

She stepped up her pace. Bridges spotted her and Devon, a panicked look on his face. They had backed him into a corner and he really had nowhere to run, especially carrying a 53 pound girl in his arms.

"Bridges, stop!" Ben ordered as he approached from the middle of the concourse. Bridges bolted across the concourse but couldn't seem to keep hold of Ruby in his arms. He dropped the girl to the floor with a thud. Bridges turned on the witches and held his hands out with his thumbs interlocked. Then he pushed his hands away from his chest. A ripple of energy spread out across the entire concourse, knocking over anything in its way.

"Duck," Devon yanked Jen to the floor. Jen watched helplessly as Ben, Lisa, Daphne, and the other witches were thrown backward, landing against people, and knocking them over. Wren landed hard against the metal chairs.

"All right, that's it," Devon said and got to his feet. He made an intricate hand sign and then chopped across his body. Bridges stumbled and fell, but it didn't take long for him to get back up, heading for the other concourse.

"Ben, you need to untie Mark," Devon said. He made another hand sign and knocked the man down again.

Ben rubbed the back of his head where he had hit the floor hard. "Fine. Anika, release Mark!"

Anika raised her wand and let Mark out of his bindings. He moved quickly in front of Bridges, blocking him. Bridges spun on his feet, running the way he came. Devon charged at Bridges, throwing him to the ground. Devon got one good punch in before Mark pulled him off Bridges and bound the man's arms and feet.

* * *

"Not bad brother," Devon said and clapped Mark on the back.

"Not bad at all," Mark agreed. He eyed the three security witches and Ben as they approached him with caution.

"Sorry Mark, I appreciate what you did, but it's time for us to take you in too," Ben said.

"I know," Mark said. "Unfortunately, I can't do that. Not until I talk to my daughter."

"Mark," Devon warned. "Don't."

Mark joined his hands together and formed a steeple with his forefingers. He brought his palms together with a loud clap and Jen, Ben and all the other witches fell to their knees first before falling to the ground writhing in pain. Devon was the only one left standing. Mark rolled his eyes.

"Sorry," Devon said. "I've been impervious to your stupid spells since we were kids."

"Great. You want to do something right for a change? Help me get Ruby out of here."

"No," Devon grabbed his brother by the wrist. "No way. I am not going to let you ruin her life."

"Why do you even care?" Mark shook him off. "You've never cared about anything."

"That's not true. I cared about you once upon a time. Before you became the king of the dicks."

"You're just sour because Mother likes me better."

"That's my beef with her, not you. But you're turning into her. And you will scar that little girl for life, and I can't let you do that."

"It's not up to you."

"You're right. It's up to her. Unless you're too chicken-shit to ask her. Ultimately, it still her choice who she pledges allegiance to. And I hear you're weird so—"

"Shut up," Mark snapped. He rushed to where Bridges had dropped the girl. She lay on her back, her dark hair and pale white skin and rose-colored lips made her look like she belonged in a fairytale.

Mark gently stroked her hair. "Ruby? Come on, Ruby, wake up."

"What did Bridges give her, do you know?" Devon asked.

"No, I don't but it doesn't matter. I should be able to draw it out with just the right number of strokes over her forehead." Mark smiled. "See, she's opening her eyes."

Ruby's eyes fluttered. She blinked a few times and made a whining noise. "Where's my mom?"

"Hey, it's okay, it's okay, really. She's fine." Mark flicked his wrist toward all the witches lying prone in the middle of the concourse. "She'll come see you in a minute."

Ruby sat up and looked around. Panic shadowed her face when she saw her mother moaning fifty feet away. "What did you do to my mom?"

"She'll be fine. I promise. Listen to me Ruby, you and I need to have a talk."

"No. Not till I talk to my mom."

Mark grabbed the girl by her shoulders and gave her one hard shake. "Stop it. Listen to me now."

Ruby's eyes widened in horror.

"Hey, don't do that," Devon said.

"Shut up and stay out of this."

Ruby's bottom lip quivered, and her blue eyes became watery.

"No. No. Please don't cry. I'm sorry. I didn't mean to lose my temper." Mark stroked her cheek with the back of his hand.

"I want to go home," Ruby whined.

"See, that's what I wanted to talk to you about. I want you and your mom to come live with me in San Francisco. We will be a family with a mommy and a daddy and maybe even a sister or brother for you. And I will give you anything you want, sweetie."

"That sounds fishy." Ruby gave him a skeptical glare.

Mark jutted his chin back a little stunned at the reaction. "Wouldn't you love to have a pony or a real dog to go with your chickens?" He said.

"No," she said. "The only thing I want is my mom. I wish you'd just go away and leave us alone forever."

"Okay, that's enough," Devon said. He held his two fists in front of his chest, lifted them apart an inch and then opened his hands wide. The witches stopped writhing and slowly got to their feet.

"What did you do?" Mark asked.

"What does it look like I did? I broke your spell. I'm not sure exactly why you don't seem to get that I'm better at this than you," Devon complained.

"Why did you do that?"

"Because I will not let you torture her, the way Mother tortured us."

"Step away from the girl," Ben warned, his wand drawn. The other witches surrounded him; their wands pointed at him too. "Put your hands in the air."

Once Ben had bound Mark's arms to his side again, Jen scooped Ruby onto her lap and hugged her tight.

"She's still going to have to make a choice, you know. You're really putting her at a disadvantage." Mark struggled against his bindings.

"Not as long as her Uncle Devon's around," Devon said.

"Come on, let's get him and Bridges out of here. Devon, can you take care of unfreezing everyone?" Ben took Mark by the elbow.

"Sure thing." Devon gave Ben a brief salute. Jen got to her feet. Ruby clung to her mother's waist.

"One day, she's going to be too much for you to deal with," Mark said over his shoulder as the security witches pulled him away. "And you're going to beg me to handle it."

"Not likely," Jen called after him.

CHAPTER 44

"Fill me in," Jen said. She only had a minute before she had to put the finishing touches on Ruby's party. She counted out plates and placed them on the kitchen counter.

"Well," Ben said, "as you know, the DOL arrested Mark and Bridges, and my security team escorted them to Charlotte. They've got a long list of charges to face according to Devon. We've already dispatched a team to arrest their mother too."

"Thank the Goddesses," Jen said. "Mark is out of my life. At least for now."

"Well, I still have to deal with Devon."

Jen stroked Ben's hair and hurriedly kissed him on the cheek. "Don't give me that look. I asked him to stay for Ruby's birthday because I think he deserved it."

"I know," Ben said, "but just so you remember, I still have things to settle with his immunity agreement."

Jen gathered up the utensils onto the tray and said, "I won't forget. I have it on my calendar. You're heading to Charlotte Monday morning to take care of all that. Now go join the party while I take care of feeding these people."

Devon stood near the grill with Evangeline, Lisa, Charlie, and Daphne, everyone chatting and drinking beers. Evangeline opened the grill and flipped the burgers and hotdogs. The smell of grilled meat wafted across the yard, making Jen's stomach growl. She laid out the plates, napkins, and silverware and added condiments, a huge bowl of green salad, Evangeline's potato salad, and a large basket of hamburger and hotdog rolls to the table. When she had everything organized, she spotted Ben sitting in one of the lounge chairs around the fire pit. He wore a peaceful smile she couldn't remember ever seeing before while he gazed at Ruby running around with Evan and her friend Bella, a short blonde child with big brown eyes, playing frisbee.

Jen headed over to him and said, "I'm done with my chores for a few minutes. Want some company?" she asked.

"I'd love some," he said. She sat down on his lap and put her arms around his shoulders. Her stomach fluttered when he tilted his head and pressed his warm lips against hers. When the kiss ended, he looked her in the eye.

"You know, I'm really sorry that I didn't tell you about

running the background check on Mark. I honestly didn't see it as an invasion of your privacy, and that was my mistake. I should've at least told you," he said.

"Apology accepted," Jen said. "I'm sorry I got so mad. One of the things I hated when I was with Mark was that he seemed to infiltrate every little thing in my life. He wanted to control it all. But you are not Mark, and I know that. I know you only did it because you love me, and you wanted to see who hurt me so badly that I ran."

Jen looked away wistfully and said, "I probably should've told you more about him, so I own that part of the fight. If I'd been more open, maybe none of this would've even happened."

Ben stroked her knee and said, "I know you're scared of marriage. Hell, I'm scared of marriage, too. But I love you, and I'm committed to you and to Ruby. I love you both very much. You're my world. You're my home." He hugged her and kissed her shoulder. "And I've never really had that before. I'd love to promise I'll never do anything that will piss you off again but that would be pointless."

Jen laughed. "Yes, it would be. The important thing is that we talk to each other."

"Yes, I think we can do that. We can promise that." Ben grinned at her. "So, now what?"

"Well, now I rebuild my business. And you and I rebuild our trust."

They both looked up as a loud clatter in the driveway interrupted the lively chatter of the party, her father driving up in his pickup truck. Jack Holloway parked, wearing a mischievous grin on his grizzled face when he got out.

"Well, that looks like trouble walking," Jen said and rose to her feet. "Hey, Daddy, why do you look like the Cheshire cat?"

"Well, I've been thinking," Jack Holloway said walking toward her. "You were about eight years old when you got your first pet. Remember? That old hound dog that wandered up half-starved. If I'd had any sense, I would've put the poor old thing out of its misery, but you fell in love with it."

"Wags," Jen said. "His name was Wags. Oh, my stars, what have you done?"

"Hey, Ruby, come on," Jack called and waved at his granddaughter. She and Bella came running over, Evan not far behind. "Come see what I've got for you."

Jack walked back to his truck and opened the door. He reached inside and retrieved a small liver-colored puppy with golden brown eyes and a wagging tail.

"Happy birthday, Punkin," he said.

Ruby squealed, "Oh, my stars, Granddaddy, he's perfect." She took the puppy from her grandfather and hugged it close.

"He's actually a she," Jack said.

"My word, that is a beautiful dog," Evangeline said, joining the crowd. Lisa and Charlie came up behind her.

"Is that a Boykin spaniel?" Lisa asked and squatted down to pet the puppy.

"Yeah. I figure they've got such a sweet temperament, they're easy to train, and they make great bird dogs," Jack said.

"I see. So, this isn't just for Ruby then," Jen teased.

"I think she'll enjoy training her. She keeps talking about it. And even if that dog ends up not being a good hunting dog, she will at least bring many years of joy to this family."

Ruby was sitting on the ground holding the puppy while it licked her face.

"So, Rubes, what are you gonna call it?" Her grandfather asked.

"Her name is Clementine," Ruby said resolutely.

"Are you sure?" her mother asked. "That was a very fast decision."

"Oh, yes. Just look at her face," Ruby said, kissing the dog's head. "How could she not be a Clementine?"

Jen laughed. "How could she not, indeed."

✳ ✳ ✳

THANK YOU FOR READING *THE KITCHEN WITCH*. I'LL BE honest with everything going on in the world right now this was the hardest book I've ever written. I've struggled a lot the last six months with depression and had to force myself to write this, hopefully it doesn't disappoint.

In the next book, *The Green Witch*, Charlie takes a back seat and Lisa moves to the forefront. There will still be lots of mystery, intrigue, ghostly encounters and family time to keep you entertained, but the focus will be on Lisa, her engagement and a bit of a surprise when she invests in a florist business.

Get your paperback copy of The Green Witch on Amazon.com.

Printed in Great Britain
by Amazon